# The Widow's Lie

## Melanie Price

# Books by Melanie Price

*The Mother-in-Law's Secret*

*My Perfect Family*

*The Widow's Lie*

For my mother, Jessica.

Thank you for always loving me fiercely.

Published by Wendlebury Ltd in 2024

20-22 Wenlock Road
London N1 7GU



ISBN: 978-1-7384652-5-5
eBook ISBN: 978-1-7384652-4-8

# PROLOGUE

By the end of tonight, I'm either going to be dead or behind bars.

Slumping back on the plush grey armchair, I run trembling fingers through my long, silky hair. I'd spent an hour straightening it in preparation for the party this afternoon, wanting to make sure that I looked my best. But now, none of that matters. Not when my little girl has been taken. And I know it's all my fault.

I cover my face with my hands as utter panic grips me. I'm trying to retrace all the missteps that have led me to this moment. I thought I'd hidden my tracks so well, and yet I couldn't have been more wrong.

This wasn't supposed to happen. Today was supposed to be the day that I forced *her* to tell me the truth at long last. Today was going to be the day that I caught her out. Not this. Anything but this.

A firm hand rests on my shoulder, and someone calls my name, trying to coax me back into the present. But I can't return yet. All I keep hearing is that voice, and the phone call that destroyed my life in a matter of moments plays in my mind like a nightmare on repeat.

I thought that the threat was in this house, that it was this person in front of me. But I'd got the warning signs completely wrong. And now, I've played right into their plan.

The voice on the phone says that they'll hurt my little girl and reveal all my carefully curated lies if I don't do *exactly* what they ask.

But the thing is, I don't care about any of my secrets anymore, not now my baby girl is at risk. The lies were always supposed to protect her, but I realize now how they've utterly failed—because it's brought me to this moment anyway.

I swipe away the sweat dotted across my forehead, a cool determination replacing the crushing panic that had gripped me a moment ago. Finally, I look up. I stare deep into the eyes of the person I didn't think I could ever trust. And who now might be my only savior.

Their pupils are dilated with fear, but as they lock eyes with mine, their expression shifts to one of suppressed fury. It's like staring into a mirror. They look exactly how I feel.

My breath catches in my throat.

After what I've just heard, there's only one choice left for me: to trust them.

But if I do, am I about to save my child, or have all my lies led me to the biggest trap of all?

# Part One

# CHAPTER ONE

## JACQUELINE - TWO MONTHS EARLIER

I wrap my favorite blue cardigan tighter around my shoulders as I pad out of our airy kitchen and toward the front dining room, steaming cup of coffee in hand. Usually, this room doesn't get much footfall, except for the occasional dinner party, but it's the best spot in the house to see across the street. And I'm determined to watch the new family move in at last.

There have been what feels like years of renovations going on at the large period house over the road. I should know—I was the one who sold it to the third-party agent last November in the first place. Ever since the sale went through, I've been obsessed with discovering who our new neighbors will be. But even though I'm at the top real estate agency in the south west of England, no matter what I did, I couldn't find out who the buyers were. I suppose there is a first time for everything.

For ages, all I knew was the brief I sold: a *rare opportunity for a spacious 19th-century family home in one of Bristol's most sought-after locations.* In reality, that translates to a detached Victorian house that is very similar to ours, just bigger. It has an extra floor on our regular two-story home and beautiful double bay windows wrapping around the outside fringes. The back garden is triple our size, too, with a pretty little Juliet balcony delicately covered in ivy overlooking the manicured lawn.

I'm not jealous, though. I've just been taking a professional and personal interest in what's been going on. I'm hoping we'll be able to make some renovations to our house this year, so it's perfectly reasonable of me to have had one or two little "visits" over the road in the name of "research". It's not trespassing if no one was living there at the time, right?

By now, I've seen plenty to stoke my curiosity about who this new family will be. A few months ago, I had a quick look through the window at the brand-new marble kitchen and snuck around the back to see the bright and airy conservatory they'd added. They all seemed like luxurious but also quite reasonable renovations. Until the large, black—rather ugly if you ask me—iron gate went up across the drive.

Unfortunately, it put a stop to my visits as it stretches across the entire width of the property and is so high that I had to crane my neck up to see the points jutting out the top. It's a bit over the top for our notoriously safe neighborhood, and I hate how much it destroys the pretty aesthetic of our little cul-de-sac. But each to their own, I suppose.

In any case, after all this build-up, is it any wonder I've been desperate to know who this new family is? Wouldn't anyone in their right mind be dying to know, too?

Finally, last week, just as the snow started to fall, a moving van almost as big as the house arrived in our quiet cul-de-sac. I managed to sweet-talk the fancy movers into telling me when they thought the family was arriving—they said this week, and I've tried to keep an eye out when I'm not working. So far—nothing. But today is Saturday... and I have high hopes.

Because yesterday, I received a sign from the universe: a package came for Number Four Sneyd Grove. Of course, no one was there to receive it, and I happily accepted on my future neighbor's behalf. It would be the perfect excuse to drop over as soon as they arrived. And this package was the chance I'd been waiting for—I would finally get a glimpse of their name. But in my wildest dreams, I never expected that I would actually *recognize* it.

Yet, as I shut the door on the postman, I glanced down at the bulky package, and my mouth dropped open in shock as I read two little words: *Anastasia Drummond.*

Now, as I continue to walk carefully down the hall, my eyes are unable to help their curiosity as they catch on the neat package lying across the entry sideboard once more. They roam over it, trying to guess what's inside for the thousandth time. The address is handwritten, and the package is bulky but feather-light. The words "fragile" are written on the outside in a looping script. I trace my left fingertips along the top, tapping them across every word. What could it be?

I haven't been able to stop thinking about it. My husband, Charles, told me to relax and said that my "obsessive curiosity" was going to be the death of me one day. But I think there's nothing wrong with taking an interest in our new neighbors—especially someone who is so *notorious.* I live by the mantra, "knowledge is power". I swear it's the only way to survive in this world.

And everyone had heard the name Anastasia Drummond in the last year—it had been all over the news a year ago after her fabulously wealthy husband, Sir David Drummond, had died suddenly in the middle of a charity event he'd been hosting. It had caused quite a stir at the time, the newspapers reporting that he died of a severe nut allergy from food made in his own kitchen. Apparently, his EpiPens were nowhere to be found in the entire home.

After the package arrived yesterday, I spent all afternoon googling *"Anastasia Drummond"* trying to discover more. But there wasn't a lot about her to find online other than the same stories and rumors surrounding her husband's death. The newspapers seemed obsessed with Sir David's beautiful, elusive younger widow. There had been an almost thirty-year age gap between them, and the tabloids were not subtle about their theories that she had married the rich hotel mogul purely for his money or their thinly veiled suspicions that she could have planned his death somehow. Little seemed to be known about her, though, other than that she was only thirty-four with a twelve-year-old daughter—the exact same age as my Matilda. But considering that Anastasia and Sir David Drummond only married four years ago, I don't think that he was the father.

Other online forums I found dove into elaborate theories about how exactly this stunning woman might have planned the perfect murder so she could lay claim to the Drummond family fortune, with extensive charts and diagrams of Anastasia's potential "step-by-step" plan. I'd rolled my eyes at that. Everyone is a true-crime detective these days. Though then again, maybe I'm no exception. I have so many burning questions about what this woman is really like and her reasons for moving here that I can hardly contain myself.

I know I should feel sorry for her, and I definitely shouldn't judge her before I meet her, but the articles have made me question her motives for marrying Sir David. Did she really love him, or had she only been with him for the money? And was there anything to the rumors about her involvement in his death?

So, I've decided that I need to get to know her. The very first thing I want to assess, fortune-hunting and possibly doing in her husband aside, is whether that one blurry image of her I've seen in the newspapers really lives up to reality.

Because ever since I saw that photo, a niggle of worry has formed at the back of my mind. I can't quite put my finger on why exactly. But there's just something about her that has me on edge.

I've put it down to paranoia. It must be because even though it's taken from quite a distance, she is clearly stunning. So now, all I can wonder is whether the beautiful, rich widow in the market for a new husband? And if she is, I don't want her anywhere near mine. Charles and I have been a little rocky over the last year, and I desperately don't want anything, or anyone, to get in the way of our rekindling romance. I'm ashamed of the thought, but I still can't quite silence it. I think any wife would feel the same if they'd seen this photo, though.

In it, Anastasia looks wistfully out through the windowpane of what must have been their South Kensington mansion. It's like she's a princess stuck in the middle of a fairytale, waiting for her knight in shining armor to appear. Her shimmering, raven black hair tumbles down her shoulder, contrasting with the pale beauty of her heart-shaped face and rosy lips. Even in apparent grief, with no makeup on, she is one of the most stunning people I've ever seen. And that's only from a grainy photo at a distance. I am praying that it's been airbrushed. No one can be that naturally beautiful. It would be unfair to nature.

Strangely, I hadn't found another photo to compare it to. I guess she must have hidden inside the house with the curtains closed until everything had blown over and the newspapers had moved on. But even from their few years of marriage, I couldn't find a proper photograph of her and Sir David together. There were lots of photos of Sir David and his grown-up son and heir Jasper online, but nothing of Anastasia or her daughter Matilda. I guess she avoided public photographs whilst her husband was alive for some reason.

All this research has made my head spin, giving rise to even more questions. And the fundamental one is why would Anastasia Drummond, a glamorous young widow with so much money that she could move literally *anywhere* in the world, want to move to Bristol—a quiet city in England's South West?

Deep down, I think I know the answer. It could only be because of the exact same reason I did.

It's the perfect place if you have something to hide.

# Chapter Two

I drag my eyes away from the package. It's time for me to get a move on. As I push the heavy wooden door open, I sigh as I survey the large, ornately old-fashioned space that is our dining room. I've wanted to renovate the floor plan of our detached period house since we moved to Bristol from London four years ago. Given my profession, it's already embarrassing that it hasn't happened yet, but after seeing everything going on at the house across the street, I'm determined to get a move on. I refuse to be second best on *my* cul-de-sac.

My dream has always been to knock through the connecting wall to have a beautiful open-plan kitchen and dining room. It was something Charles was supposed to talk to his architect friend about to "keep the costs down". But now, we're long overdue with the renovations. Like with many things that Charles promises will get done quickly, it hasn't happened yet. It won't ever happen without me pushing for it, but the problem is that Charles and I haven't been in the best place lately. So, I'll have to approach it delicately. And then I'm sure I can get it done within the year. I'm very good at always getting what I want.

As I sit in the chair facing the window to drink my coffee, the perfect spot to see across the street, I spot a small but glaring smudge mark on the pane of glass. My skin starts to crawl at the urge to immediately clean it off. I must have missed a spot earlier. *How disappointing—you can't even clean properly.* My mother's voice flies into my head unbidden. I push it away, telling myself that it's okay. No one else will notice. But her words knock at me once more: *Do it again. It's not perfect. Excuses are for losers.*

I try to breathe deeply, forcing my mind to be still. I can't help glancing over my shoulder to check she's not here. But the room is museum-like in its emptiness, aside from the dark mahogany table, duck egg blue fleur-de-lis patterned wallpaper, and sparkling crystal chandelier glinting back at me in the weak morning sun. I take comfort in everything being as it should and push away her lingering presence. I hate it when this happens. Because whenever I let my mother in, her echoing words wrap around me so tight, suffocating the air out of my lungs. But I can't help how ingrained these little sayings from my childhood are. All I can do is try and replace them with my own.

I close my eyes, pushing away the echoes of my mother's memory. *She isn't here. I'm fine.* I clutch onto the words as I turn back once more to my peaceful vigil. On the outside of the double-fronted windows, the melting snow glistens, and I reframe my thoughts into a more positive bent. Spring is just around the corner. Today is the day I will hopefully meet this elusive widow at last. And if she and her daughter arrive, I already have the perfect plan: Matilda and I will casually drop over with the mysterious package, as well as my famous casserole, to welcome them to the neighborhood. I've already told Matilda to be ready at a moment's notice – she's currently hidden away in her bedroom, lost in one of her many books. It's always a battle to drag her away, but no need to worry about that now.

I lean back and settle into my comfortable chair, sipping the dark, rich blend. My shoulders relax at the familiar taste on my tongue. That is something I miss so much about the States: a real cup of coffee the way I like it. At least when I'm home on mornings like this, I can make it almost right. Even though I've lived in England for almost twelve years now, I will never understand the appeal of tea. I need a high dose of caffeinated zing to put some pep in my step. Otherwise, I could never put on the energetic show that I know everyone expects to see from Jacqueline Banks.

As I take another mouthful, I repeat to myself: *I am Jacqueline Banks, the top estate agent in England's south west, happily married to successful barrister Charles Banks and mother of Matilda. I am a far cry from the little girl of my childhood. This Jacqueline is beloved by all, full of energy and determination. No one can get in the way of what I want.* I shut my eyes as I finish my daily mantra. It always pushes away any lingering dregs of my mother's ghost. I feel a buzzing confirmation as the coffee floods my veins. There, better already.

When I blink my eyes open, I lean forward and peer outside through the frosty window. As usual, the view makes me smile: our tree-lined cul-de-sac is even prettier than normal, with snow sprinkled across the fringes of the uppermost branches. I watch Charles shovel the last of the powder out of our driveway. I asked him to tidy up ahead of the new neighbors moving in. It's important we look presentable, after all.

He'd grumbled about going out in the "unseasonably freezing weather". It's mid-March, and this latest surprising fall of snow has given Bristol a bit of a shock. All this week, I've received constant news alerts about canceled trains because of frozen tracks and other unforeseen weather problems. I still don't understand how this country can fall apart whenever there's any "extreme" weather situation—be that "too hot" or "too cold". But then again, perhaps I'm hardier than most—having grown up in Ohio, where it can get far hotter and colder than here. But never mind, I shouldn't complain—it meant a fun family snow day earlier in the week with Matilda and Charles because he couldn't get up to London for work. It was a shame for his client, of course, to miss his barrister on a crucial day, but secretly, I was glad we had this time with him. In my opinion, he spends far too much time worrying about his criminal clients, who are invariably guilty, and not quite enough time at home with his family.

I chide my harsh thoughts as I take another sip of the hot coffee. It burns my tongue a little. We'd made the choice together to move to Bristol from London so Matilda would have a better quality of life. It meant we were able to afford both the detached house with the huge back garden in desirable Sneyd Park, just on the other side of the leafy Clifton Downs, and to send her to a beautiful old private school on the other side of the Clifton Suspension Bridge, right in the heart of the idyllic South West countryside.

As I watch Charles through the window, I tap on the glass with my free hand. He looks up at the sound, leaning back on the shovel. I can't quite read his expression as he pushes his floppy dark hair away from his face. He needs a haircut, but I also love how much more relaxed he appears when his hair is longer. It reminds me of the Charles from our earliest days of marriage—the smart, switched-on lawyer who could tell you the definition of every law article but often forgot to eat, let alone cut his hair when he was working on something. I wish we could go back to those days. He'd always been prone to periods of quiet withdrawal, but it's felt like these are happening more frequently at the moment. Honestly, it's been a bit exhausting, as it constantly feels like I'm walking on eggshells around him.

This happens, I remind myself. I just have to ride the wave. I think back to how instant our connection had been. He'd blushed the shade of a red rose when I asked for his number. Now, even wrapped up in his parka jacket and gloves, he cuts an impressive figure. Tall and broad-shouldered with his rower's build. He rowed competitively for his Oxford college and still spends hours at the rowing machine in the basement, "sweating through his cases." Between his athletic build and impressive crop of dark hair with only a smattering of silver, you would think that he was in his early thirties—not approaching mid-forties. If I were up close, I know I'd see the tell-tale little grey hairs starting to streak through, but from here, his hair looks as dark as the mahogany table behind me. I smile and give him a thumbs-up as he turns back to his work with a shrug. One that I hope doesn't mean he's still grumpy that I'd sent him out there.

The sudden sound of car tires over the tarmac pulls me out of my reverie. My head snaps so fast toward the entry to our road that I'm surprised I haven't given myself whiplash. A black Range Rover cruises into view, and its windows are so opaque I can't see in from this distance. I hastily discard my coffee on the dining table behind me, not even bothering with a coaster for once, and press my face as close to the window as I can to get a better look.

The car stops in front of our house, braking as though to double-check which house they're arriving at, and I watch as a window winds down. So slowly, two figures are revealed. I spy a small dark head peeking out of the passenger side and a woman with long, shining onyx hair and sunglasses in the driver's seat on the other side. My first glance of Anastasia Drummond.

Charles is only mere feet from the car, and he stops shoveling to put up his gloved hand in a friendly hello. I see the little girl raise her hand back, but then a hand lunges off the steering wheel, pulling her arm down with a sharp tug. The woman shakes her head at the child before replacing her hands on the wheel and making a sharp right-hand turn toward their gates. They swing open at their approach as though pulled by invisible hands. And then the car is gone, crunching down the drive and around the shade of the trees to where a garage lies.

It takes me a minute to process what I've seen. I stare at Charles, who has shrugged off this snub and returned to his shoveling. He doesn't seem to care, but I know that if I looked in a mirror right now, I'd be the shade of a tomato.

I cannot believe how rude that was. Well, I guess money can buy you many things, but it certainly can't buy you any manners! Charles was being a gentleman, welcoming his new neighbors, and that woman completely dismissed him, pulling away her child's hand as though Charles was a speck of dirt that she shouldn't acknowledge.

I've instilled in Matilda how important it is to be neighborly. But clearly, Anastasia Drummond is not teaching her daughter the same values. No, it almost seems like she's teaching her child to ignore or maybe even fear those around her. And why on earth would a mother want to do that?

# Chapter Three

The tall black gates remain open after the car disappears inside them. I sigh. I know I shouldn't judge Anastasia for being cautious. Really, I should know better than anyone how important it is to keep your secrets under lock and key.

Even though she has purposefully snubbed my husband, I still think that my family and I should put our best neighborly foot forward. I will try to give her the benefit of the doubt. So, regardless of that little blip, I will drop over her package and the casserole I made last night for them. As an Irish American, there are some welcoming traditions that I cannot ignore. It's just good manners.

I don't want to look desperate, so I spend a few hours trying to relax my nerves by cleaning before starting to get ready. Upstairs in our bedroom, I study myself in the floor-length mirror hanging inside our built-in closet for the thousandth time. I'm wearing black jeans and my favorite cream turtleneck wool sweater. I hope that I look chic but without trying too hard. Surely you can never go wrong with a pair of jeans and a nice top? I must admit that I try very hard with my fashion—I know how important appearances are. But it has never come easily to me. It's something I'm always working on.

All the same, I think this look strikes the right tone: the soft cream sweater brings out the hues of honeyed chestnut scattered throughout my hazelnut curls. I run a hand through my mane and sigh at the tangles that stop me from pulling my fingers all the way through. I envy women who have straight hair. If I don't stay on top of my thick locks, they turn into a bird's nest by the end of the day. I turn away from the mirror. An elegant bun it is.

I shut the wardrobe door behind me and walk toward my vanity table in the opposite corner of our bedroom, pausing to straighten the pale blue coverlet on my bed. I always need to make the bed perfectly. It helps keep my mother's voice out of my head.

Carrying on to the vanity, I lean across and open the top drawer on the left, which holds all my hair paraphernalia. I select a light pink silk scrunchie and sit on the little gray stool to look in the mirror as I carefully position my hair back into a bun. It takes me about five tries to get it right.

I study my face in annoyance, rubbing at the rogue smudge of mascara smeared onto the top of my eyelid. When it's gone, I practice my friendliest smile at my reflection. Crow's feet creep up the edges of my round, light brown eyes, and I quickly return to a neutral expression. I examine the few lines beginning to furrow across my forehead. I turned forty in January, and I definitely feel it. Growing old is so exhausting. But at least, even after the long winter months, my naturally olive complexion remains, and my skin is as clear as a blank canvas. I pick up my favorite lip oil and reapply it.

I cock my head to one side as I look into the mirror, assessing my overall appearance. My mother's voice whispers the refrain I know so well: *You'll never be as pretty as the other girls.* I shove it away—hard, and close my eyes as I counter with my mantra: *You are Jacqueline Banks—beloved by all.* When I open my eyes, I'm back in control and flash a smile back at the reflection I see. There—just right. At last.

I pull my shoulders back tight and march out of our open bedroom door.

"Matilda," I call as I stride down the stairs, "are you ready to g—?"

My words are interrupted by a squeak underfoot. I glance down to see that in my haste, I'd almost stepped on Matilda's hair. She'd been sitting at the foot of the stairs, her dark brown waves flowing out from a low ponytail at her back, while her face had been buried in a book, as per usual.

Now she's jumped up in anger and stands ramrod straight; her current read clutched tightly against her chest as though it is a precious piece of treasure I am about to steal. "You almost stepped on me!" she says, the sharp edge of accusation in her gray-green eyes.

Twelve going on teenager, that's for sure. Her judgment makes me bristle, reminding me of a similar look her father has given me one too many times before. "Oh, come on," I say as I finish stomping down the stairs. "You shouldn't sit in silly places."

But instead of fighting back, her shoulders slump at my dismissive tone. I am constantly forgetting how sensitive she is. So I hastily add a light tug on the crook of her elbow as I reach the bottom of the steps.

"Never mind, though," I say with a smile, "Let's go and meet these new neighbors. I spotted a girl who looks a similar age to you. Imagine how wonderful it could be to have a best friend across the street?"

Her hurt gaze softens at my words as she thinks about that exciting possibility. Isn't it every girl's dream scenario? And for Matilda, I desperately hope it will be so.

She's very shy, often preferring imaginary friends in her books to ones in real life. Charles says I worry too much about how quiet she is and how she doesn't seem to have as many friends as some of the other girls at school. "She's just more of an introvert," is his usual refrain. But I'm not so sure; at sports games and the school gates, I see her often hovering on the edges, looking for all the world as though she's wishing for a friendly face to turn and invite her into the group. I think that making a new friend will be exactly what she needs to help build her confidence.

"Right," I clap my hands, "let's go." Matilda nods solemnly in agreement before turning to place her book on the corner of the hall table. Her hand lingers over it for a moment as though she wishes she didn't have to let it go. I sigh. Maybe forcing her to make friends in the real world will be harder than I thought.

I grab the large Tupperware container and balance the parcel precariously on top as we step outside and walk along our drive. I glance down at Matilda beside me, her forest green bobble hat that she hastily shoved on flops right and left as she looks both ways before nodding that it's safe to cross the street. I smile.

Even though there is hardly a dribble of traffic down our isolated little road, it makes me proud that being safe and sensible is so ingrained in Matilda that she will still check. It was, of course, the safety of this cul-de-sac that made me choose our house. A quiet, forgotten little street that hopefully most people would overlook.

I'd assume that by now, the new neighbors would have closed the security gates, but Anastasia appears to have left them open. Maybe they're waiting for another arrival—who knows? But I don't mind. It makes it easier for me to slip in and observe any new changes to the house that I haven't seen properly since the gates went up a few months ago.

As we pass through the gates, the sleek iron shimmers in the weak afternoon light, ominous clouds blocking out the sun. My neck cranes as I look up. The pointy spikes on the tips seem almost to touch the sky. An involuntary shiver goes up my spine, which I ignore and instead continue toward the house. Close up, it's even more impressive than the last time I snuck over here. There had been scaffolding up for a while, and in that time, they had cleaned every inch of the façade. Now, I can see how bright the sandstone surrounding the bay windows has become, as what had been dark gray brick has now become a lovely light gray. A new buyer would snatch this off the market in a heartbeat and pay even more than Anastasia paid for it, too. I shake my head—I'm not here to assess its reselling potential, I remind myself.

Matilda and I follow the driveway's offshoot as it slims into a path toward the freshly lacquered front door, the centerpiece of the large house. As we take the few stairs up, I refuse to be intimidated by the gold doorknocker shining back at me.

"Here we go," I force my best smile down at Matilda. She refuses to look up at me and shuffles her feet, wrapping her arms tighter around her dark blue puffer jacket. I shrug, balance the package and container under my arm, and rap the door knocker.

Once. Twice.

I step back and don't realize I'm holding my breath until an exhale rattles out of me. We wait for what feels like hours, but no one appears at the door. I try one more time, and still nothing.

"Can we come back another time? I'm cold," Matilda says, her voice twanging up at the edges in a little whine.

It grates on me, and I snap back. "Nonsense. We have a gift and their parcel, so we *must* hand it over."

I turn on my heels and hear Matilda scramble to follow as I stomp down the steps. I'm cold, too. But I'll be damned if I don't meet this woman today. I've been patiently waiting for months, and I'm sick of it.

I step over the manicured grass, not caring if my sturdy knee-length boots make irritating imprints in the melting snow. I head straight to the first window that I can easily peer into.

"What are you doing?!" Matilda shrieks behind me. I turn to see that her face has gone bright red.

I refuse to be embarrassed by her judgment and return to peek through. "Trying to see if I can spot anyone."

"You can't do that!" she retorts.

"Oh, come on," I say. "Let's try the back door." I march past Matilda and don't miss the miserable expression on her face, her brows furrowing as deep as she can make them.

Leaving the grass, my purposeful stomp is even more noticeable on the pebbles as they crackle in my wake. Matilda trots beside me, trying to keep up. We stride down the narrow path along the extensive length of the house until we eventually reach the start of the back garden.

It brings me to a stop as I take a sharp intake of breath. A complete relandscape has happened since I last locked eyes on the garden when I snuck a look at the new kitchen conservatory added to the back. Before they put the large gates up, of course. The conservatory is here, but the rest of the garden has been altered unrecognizably. Before, it was a lovely, large expanse of green grass with sloping tangles of wild shrubbery and trees running amok along its edges. Now, most of the grass has gone, and it has turned into a large sandstone patio with a glass roof overhead. A small path wanders off the edge of the patio toward a beautiful circular wooden hot tub. Freshly cut grass spreads out across the rest of the remaining garden, the snow already melted from most of it, and the wild hedging that framed the garden before has been entirely replaced by perfect neat rows of matching cedar trees. The walls backing onto other neighboring properties peek out from behind them.

"Wow," Matilda says, mirroring my thoughts exactly. She tugs on my sleeve, and I look down at the bright excitement on her face. "Can *we* get a hot tub too?"

I stifle a groan. Our garden is a bit of a jungle—with Charles's various gardening projects taking up nearly every corner. Of course, twelve-year-old Matilda is much more impressed by a hot tub. I can't blame her.

"Well, there's no need; you can make friends and come over here."

Matilda chews on her lip doubtfully. The stakes of friendship have been raised a notch.

"Come on," I say, marching forward again and down the few steps onto the new patio. Glass sliding doors run along my left, and I see straight into the brand-new kitchen. I pull on the sliding door handle with all my might. There must have been a part of me that expected it to be locked, but to my surprise, it slides with ease. I stumble back but regain my balance before I drop the Tupperware and the parcel.

"See," I turn back to face Matilda, "they *are* in. Let's just announce ourselves." Her mouth drops open at my declaration. I shrug, and stepping inside, I ignore her mumbled protestations and start to call out, "Hello! Is anyone home?"

Silence greets me, so I walk a little further into the house. Matilda shuffles as quietly as a mouse behind me. I hover on the edge of the doorway connecting the kitchen to the rest of the home. I gulp. I'm starting to regret this decision, but I don't want to admit to its rashness in front of Matilda. At least not yet.

We pass behind the light walnut dining table and enter a white hallway. A few more steps take me to the beginning of the staircase. "Hello!" I call up into the tall expanse. No answer. I frown; even I would draw the line at stomping upstairs to drag the new neighbors down. Maybe we'll just have to go home then and try again later.

But as I turn around to start making my way out again, I blink in surprise.

Because where Matilda should have been right behind me is now just an empty corridor.

She's gone.

I frown in annoyance. This is just like Matilda to let her curiosity get the better of her. "Matilda!" I call out in as loud a whisper as I dare.

Silence greets me. I blink frantically around the freshly painted white walls. They're too blank. As the seconds tick by, my pulse starts to race. This was a bad idea. It would be beyond embarrassing to be caught sneaking around my new neighbor's house. I try to breathe. *Come on, Jacqueline*, I say to myself. *She can't have gone far.*

I retrace my steps, back the way we came, and notice that there is another offshoot of the corridor—a large window at the other end framing the trees beyond. And on either side of that window, two doors. One of them is ajar.

I start toward it but slip on the smooth surface, almost dropping the casserole all over the waxed wooden floorboards. I regain my balance, my heart in my throat, and look around to make sure no one has noticed. All is clear. Slowly, I peek my head into the room.

Bookshelves line every visible surface—floor to ceiling; they wrap around the whole perimeter to where the bay window juts out directly opposite me. It's beautiful, but I can't take it all in. I step inside as my eyes start to scan every corner, and then, as I turn to face the small section hidden from my immediate view, I see her. Matilda is staring up in awe at the ladder leaning against the bookshelves' back corner. Her hand hovers as though all she wants to do is touch it, but she knows she shouldn't.

I almost sink to my knees in relief at the sight of her, but it's only a moment before a hot temper replaces it. "Matilda!" I hiss. She jumps back in shock, her hand lashing back from the ladder and up to her mouth to stop the scream that would otherwise have escaped from her lips. Her eyes are wide and frightened. But then they relax at the sight of me.

"Matilda," I step toward her. "What on earth were you thinking, running away like that?" My words make her lip wobble.

"Sorry," she sniffs. "I was just trying to help with the search. I wanted to get out of here. But then I discovered this library." She pulls away, her eyes now bright with wonder. "Look at it—isn't it *incredible.*" She sounds breathless. "And this ladder..." She rushes back to it and, this time, touches it longingly, without hesitation. "It's *just* like Belle's in *Beauty and the Beast*! It's all I've ever wanted," she finishes with a dramatic sigh.

"Oh, sweetheart, yes," I say, turning back to face the rest of the room now, "it is very impressive." I take more than a second to observe my surroundings. It is stunning. The walls of the shelves are already stuffed with books. They run down both sides of the room to frame what isn't only a simple bay window but a perfect reading nook with a comfy chaise across it and cushions on either side to lounge on. An elegant bronze rug with light gold edging runs across the whole room, and two couches face each other in the center. This room didn't look like this when I sold the house. I must admit Anastasia's done an impressive job in here.

I turn back to face Matilda, who has started to study the volumes on the shelves intently, and that's when I notice what's behind her. Hollowed into the wall is a safe. And it's wide open.

It's narrow, but it looks like it runs very deep. I step closer and see another alcove right at the back with a separate handle. It must have been purpose-built. It certainly wasn't part of the house specs when I sold it.

I frown, trying to get a better look. Because instead of jewels or cash, it appears to be filled with stacks of... paper?

I take another step forward and realize it's filled with stacks of 6x4 size photographs. Why would you put a bunch of old photos in a brand new safe?

Before I can investigate further, I hear a muffled sob. It's enough to jolt me back to the present. But it's not Matilda, who is still totally engrossed in the shelves before her. It must be *them*.

I whirl around and start to move when I hear a soft voice say, "Sofia, come on, you *know* we can't have this old photo of us on display. I need to keep it safe and locked away for a reason because—ARGH!"

I never hear the end of that sentence. Instead, the tall woman who appears in the doorway almost jumps out of her skin. She clutches her throat, pale as a sheet flapping in the wind. Behind her, a girl with a raven black bob screams, and her emerald green eyes flash with fear.

I'm about to say sorry and explain who we are and what we're doing here, but the look on the woman's face makes the words die on my lips. Because it's no longer terror that I see there. No, it's undiluted hatred.

And there's something else.

Something that wasn't clear in that distant photograph I'd seen before. And it's a realization that sends a shiver down my spine.

I swear I've seen those icy-blue eyes before.

# Chapter Four

Before I can process anything, she speaks in a voice as hard as the ice emanating from her eyes.

"What are you doing in my home?"

For a minute, my mind goes blank, and my heart starts to race. It's all I can do to tell myself to calm down. *This beautiful, willowy woman is not going to hurt you.*

Her daughter watches us with her arms wrapped around herself tightly as though for protection. She is a lot shorter than Matilda, making her appear a lot younger. Her soft green eyes are puffy and full of tears. She doesn't look like a happy kid. But is it because of her mother or because of the shock of finding me, a stranger, roaming around her home?

I feel a surge of shame as I sense Matilda step behind me to hide herself, too.

That kicks me into gear and back into the present moment. I throw my shoulders back and try to explain.

"I'm so sorry to have scared you both. We appear to have got lost in your house trying to find you! We live across the road—and we received a parcel for you, so we thought we'd drop it off at the same time as introducing ourselves and welcoming you to the neighborhood with one of my world-famous beef casseroles." I try to chuckle, but it sounds forced. Anastasia's cold eyes continue to stare at me. It's like she can see straight through me.

"I'm Jacqueline," I go on, forcing my mind to stay in this moment. I have to get us out, and *then* I can think more about the strange familiarity in her gaze. "And this is my daughter, Matilda. It's great to meet you." I stick out my right hand, cradling the container and parcel in my left.

Anastasia stares at my outstretched hand with disgust written across every inch of her face. It almost makes her ugly. *Almost.* But as I wilt under her withering gaze, I realize that it would be impossible for this woman in front of me to look truly ugly. She is at least half a foot taller than me and stick thin under her navy silk blouse and matching skirt. But it's not only her height and slim frame that's so striking; it's her face.

Her skin is the color of snow, her lips the darkest shade of ruby I've ever seen. Her hair is raven black, and as she tosses it over her shoulder, it shimmers as it catches the light. It seems that she really does live up to the photo in the newspapers. If anything, she's even more striking. It makes me want to scream.

And all the while, those ice-blue eyes never waver—as seeing them close up locks onto something deep within me. But why? Whose eyes do they remind me of?

My hand has continued to hover in the air, and I'm sure my mouth has dropped open as I've been ogling. I snap both back under control. Anastasia stares at me, unimpressed, and I notice that she is holding an old Polaroid photograph. Before I can get a closer look, she crosses it around her back and out of sight.

"Have you been snooping around?" She tries to frown, but her tight forehead prevents it from being much more than a curious furrow. *Surely* Botox. Her brow cannot be that naturally tight. That would be far too unfair. I resist the urge to run a finger across the light grooves permanently embedded into my own forehead.

"No, no," I say too quickly. Come on—where is the confident, calm Jacqueline? I shake my head, trying to regain control of the situation. I *hate* being out of control. "No," I say again firmly. "I'm so sorry. I tried to call out hello, and we were about to leave when I realized that my daughter, Matilda'—I gesture behind me again as she tries to shrink even smaller—'wandered off into this room. You see, she's obsessed with books," I add in as apologetic a voice as I can muster. "I'd just found her and was making her leave when you arrived. I can't apologize enough for scaring you. But like I said... world-famous beef casserole..."

I swear I saw her expression soften for an instant when I mentioned Matilda's love of books, but as soon as my eyes greet hers again, the look of steel returns. "Please, get out of my home," she says, in a voice even colder than the look in her eyes. "You had no right to barge in here unannounced, and besides, we're vegetarian. So you can take *that* with you." She looks down at the container in my hand with disgust.

Shame and embarrassment flood every inch of my body. I feel like my mother's daughter again. And I hate it.

"Come on, Matilda, let's go," I manage to say, pushing down the tears that are threatening to erupt. *You're being ridiculous. Big girls don't cry.* My mother's voice rings in my ear again, and it's all I can do to keep my chin up high as Anastasia and her daughter step out of the doorframe to let us past.

Pulling myself together, I turn back and say, "I really am so sorry." This time, I see a small moment of hesitation flicker across her expression before she shrugs and turns away to check on her daughter, who has started to cry quietly once more. I hear the door slam shut behind us as we race back out the way we came. The phrase "tail between my legs" never felt more apt.

It's only when we get outside, and Matilda starts to shriek at me about that being *the most embarrassing moment of her life* and *wait until she tells Dad* that I let my mind float far away and follow the tiny niggle that has been nibbling on my thoughts ever since I saw Anastasia Drummond.

It isn't just the strange new safe full of photographs or the unhappy look in her daughter's eyes. Seeing Anastasia close-up for the first time, seeing her *eyes*, I am starting to realize that there is something familiar about her that isn't only because I've seen her photo in the newspaper.

No, I can feel it in my bones that there is something else.

I have always made it my business to know everything going on around me. My secrets haven't remained buried all these years just by chance. No, not at all. It's through assessing and dealing with any potential threat that comes my way quietly and efficiently.

So, as we trudge back to our house, I make a promise: I will discover the truth, no matter what. Because nothing and no one can come in the way of the life I have worked so hard to build.

And if I discover that this woman across the street has anything to do with my lies, then there's only one option: she'll have to go.

# Chapter Five

I hardly slept last night, tossing and turning as I thought about the events of the day. Had I jumped to conclusions about Anastasia's strange familiarity because I'm so paranoid about my own secrets coming out? Maybe so. All my fears about being found out have been amplified since my marriage started to become a little rocky last year.

When we got back, Matilda rushed straight up to her room. Charles called out, "Hey! No slamming doors!" from the direction of the study.

I'd taken a deep breath to try and stop myself from crying. Jacqueline Banks does *not* cry. Charles appeared at the entry to the study, and his brow furrowed as he saw me still clutching the Tupperware container. "The new neighbors not in, then?"

I felt myself go red at his words.

Charles's eyebrows flew up in surprise. "What happened?"

I placed the container on the side table and, as I unwrapped all my winter layers, carefully tried to explain to Charles what had happened, removing certain crucial details about a pair of familiar eyes, of course. I can't let him know about that. He has no idea about my secrets. And it has to stay that way. It's for his own good.

But as I started to explain the parts of the story that I could tell him, I became more annoyed with Anastasia's behavior. I was only trying to be neighborly. She was the one who had acted terribly. And the more I spoke, the angrier I became at the whole situation, finally finishing with, "She basically kicked us out of the house! How rude is that!"

Charles let out a long exhale, shrugging his shoulders in defeat. "Honestly, Jackie, I think you probably shouldn't have gone sneaking around her house. You're going to get yourself in trouble one of these days."

I was about to retort when he turned back into the study, shutting the door with a click. Probably wise—I didn't want us to start a fight about this. Not when we were trying so hard to stay on a good track.

So I massaged my temples, trying to push it out of my mind as I allowed my methodical mindset to take over: cleaning everything in sight and getting the dinner ready. Charles and I didn't speak about what had happened again, and Matilda, when she finally emerged from her room, didn't bring it up. Seemingly, she'd taken a vow of silence and barely spoke the rest of the night.

It wasn't until Charles was fast asleep beside me that my mind started whirring again, trying to place Anastasia. I kept coming up blank, and by the time I finally nodded off and woke up in the morning, I was starting to convince myself that I'd simply imagined it. Perhaps my deep embarrassment and feeling of being out of control had merely shaken up my worst fears that one day, someone dangerous would turn up in my carefully curated life.

I do *not* know Anastasia, I tell myself. Her sneering tone and dismissal reminded me too much of my childhood, that was all: of my mother always making me feel so small and insignificant. That was what it was. I'm almost certain of it.

And now, as I take myself on a Sunday morning run around the Downs, the large parkland just behind our house, I fully convince myself. Anastasia Drummond is no one to me other than the newest wife—or should I say, widow—on our street.

I need to stop being so easily distracted and focus on my husband and my marriage. By the time I pass the edge of the path that overlooks Bristol's famous suspension bridge and start the journey back down the hill to our quiet little cul-de-sac, I am almost feeling back to my usual self. Full of simmering strength and can-do energy. The run has helped put everything into perspective, and I'm much more positive about my situation. As I ran, I realized that even if Anastasia is drop-dead gorgeous, she's certainly not friendly. So I don't think I have to worry about the risk of her trying to catch Charles's eye—he abhors rudeness.

I'd even managed to push to one side the withdrawn mood Charles had been in this morning. I'd tried to corner him into agreeing to go to a last-minute drinks party tonight that my fellow PTA co-chair Lydia had texted me about. But he'd looked at me like I was asking him to sell his kidney before he'd thrown a mask over his expression. He'd massaged his temple as though he had a deep ache and said that he couldn't face seeing people today. He said he needed to work and was desperate for some peace and quiet. After that, he'd locked himself away in his study. I knew when he was in this headspace that he needed some time to come back to the real world. I blamed his criminal cases for weighing down on his shoulders. Charles cares too much. It's always been both his blessing and his curse.

My breathing is labored as I finally stop outside our house. I double over, trying to get it back under control. I look up at the gloomy, overcast sky; my breath comes out in small puffs, the color of pale clouds. It's still cold, but at least the snow is on the retreat. The grass on our front lawn is back to green, and if I look closely, the edges of the trees along the street are starting to show a few shoots of regrowth. Getting back into running will be so much easier when it becomes warmer. I hadn't realized how unfit I'd become over these winter months. But glancing down at my watch, I feel proud that I've completed a 10k. *Very* slowly, it had taken me over an hour. But I've done it. Jacqueline Banks is back. I will never give up. It's all about having the right mindset.

In control of my breathing once more, I make my way back down the path to our house. I'm not cold yet, but I know that if I don't get inside and stretch quickly, my muscles will get all stiff. Either way, I'm sure I'll feel this tomorrow. The joys of my forties.

I press on the buzzer and wait for the usual sounds of footsteps rushing to the front door. I always leave my keys at home when I go for a run when I know someone will be there to let me back in, as they are today. Except as I wait now, there is only silence.

I bang on our front door, and still, no one comes. There is only the sound of the wood reverberating back at me. Where could they be? Our house isn't so big that you can't hear when the door goes. Could they both be in the back garden? But it's freezing out here; normally, at ten o'clock in the morning on a Sunday, Charles and Matilda would be in the kitchen, rustling up breakfast. I try to look through the edge of one of the small panes of frosted glass—but all I can see is a scrap of our gray marbled flooring beyond.

Sighing, I try the handle. I don't have much hope, but it's worth a shot. I pull down on it and push hard through my mounting frustration—but predictably, nothing happens. Well, I'll just have to go around the back and hope I can see them through the kitchen window.

Starting to cool off, I wrap my arms around myself as I make my way down the side path that leads to the back garden. I swing the side gate open, which thankfully is unlocked, and step onto the patio.

And then stop dead in my tracks. There is Charles—crouched low over the vegetable patch, with his back to me. Gardening is one of his only hobbies—he says that losing himself in the outdoors helps to clear his mind after hours working on a long case. I personally don't understand the appeal of getting your hands covered in mud—but then again, he doesn't understand my obsession with reality television shows like *Selling Sunset*. They say it's good to have different interests in a marriage, after all. But considering the distance that was built between us last year, I'm not so sure about that. And I'm especially not sure at this current moment. Because he's not alone. There's a woman next to him.

They're so close that it looks like she's leaning her head on his shoulder, her long, shimmering dark tresses cascading down her shoulder like a waterfall. I watch as she leans her head back and laughs at something he must have whispered in her ear. She nods enthusiastically back while Charles turns his head and beams up at her.

To anyone else watching, they would look to all the world like a tableau of a happy couple tending to their garden. But to me, it feels like I've been punched in the stomach. I can't remember the last time my husband looked that happy. I don't know what it is, but they look so at ease; it's almost as though they've been in this exact situation before. I need to put a stop to this. Pronto.

I let go of the side gate, and it swings shut behind me with a loud bang. The noise is enough for the cozy pair in front of me to be disturbed. Charles jumps up in surprise, and the woman next to him whips her head around in shock. Of *course*, it's Anastasia. Just like I suspected. I throw my shoulders back, refusing to feel like a stranger in my own garden.

Charles pushes his glasses up his nose and squints, recognition at last dawning that it's me, *his wife,* standing in front of him.

But instead of going bright red like I'm expecting, he waves enthusiastically. He doesn't appear the least bit concerned.

I ball my hands into fists and chastise the voice in my head. I must have been projecting again. What is it about this woman that's putting me so on edge? It must be my own insecurities about my marriage playing on my mind.

"Oh Jackie, hi!" Charles says, walking toward me. "Sorry, I must have missed you at the front door—Anna dropped by to introduce herself properly while you were out. She says you caught her at a bad time yesterday. Then we got to talking and it turns out she loves gardening. I was showing her what I'm starting to plant for the spring..." He gestures behind him as he almost glows with happiness. I bite my tongue. Anna?! *Anna?!* When did Charles develop a nickname for our new neighbor? I want to check my watch to make sure that I've only been gone an hour. It seems I've missed a lot. But after our first encounter yesterday, I don't want to appear even more unhinged. I must regain control of the situation.

Digging my fingernails into my palms, I relax my shoulders and say, "Oh, how nice. And what a pleasant surprise to see you again... Anastasia. I wasn't sure if I would after yesterday..." I venture with a small smile.

To my astonishment, Anastasia lowers her eyes to the floor.

"Well," Charles hops in, sensing the awkward silence between us begin to form, "that's why Anna wanted to drop around..." He glances over at her with a secret smile as though he's already given her a little pep talk about how to approach this. I try not to frown.

"Yes, Jacqueline." She walks toward me, following behind Charles as she tosses her long locks over one shoulder with a wave. Her careful grace is like that of a ballerina dancing across the stage. "I wanted to come over and apologize for my rudeness yesterday. I was shocked to see you in my house, that's all. We'd had a long day. But I appreciate that you were only being neighborly. Can we start again on the right foot? I'm Anastasia—but please call me Anna." She sticks out a delicate white hand, mocking the one I extended yesterday.

For a second, I consider ignoring it, snubbing her like she did me. But then I see the flash of concern in Charles's eyes. I know I cannot, and besides, being the bigger person in public is always the winning option. So, I pull my lips back into what I hope is a relaxed smile and take her proffered hand. It's as soft as silk. Of course, it is.

"Absolutely—I'm sorry again about yesterday," I say, continuing my jolly appearance. "Shall we get inside before we freeze?"

"Yes," Charles pipes up. "The coffee I put on earlier should be ready now."

I try not to raise my eyebrows at this. I can't remember the last time Charles made coffee for me. He's clearly smitten. I guess it's hard for someone like Anna not to make an impression—her elegant beauty is like something out of classic old-world Hollywood. *You're nothing in comparison*—my mother's voice lashes into my head like a whip. *Shut up*, I tell it as I exhale a deep breath. Just because she's attractive doesn't mean Charles will desert me. Charles *loves* me. Or at least I hope he does.

"That would be wonderful if you're sure it's no trouble." Anna's soft voice interrupts my warring thoughts, tugging them in another direction. Her lilting tone is so delicate it's almost as if every time she speaks, she doesn't really want to be heard.

"Not at all," says Charles with a laugh. "I want to hear all about your plans for your new garden." She beams back at him.

I feel my insides heat up with rage at the look on my husband's face, but I manage to throw cold water over my insecurities once more. "Of course. No trouble. It will be nice to get to know you," I manage in a cordial tone.

Charles smiles broadly as he walks toward the kitchen door, opening it for the two of us. I really should be relieved that he's in a good mood now and seems happy to be back around people. This morning, before I left, all he wanted was to be left alone.

Biting my tongue, I try not to let it get to me that the only thing that seems to have perked him up is the arrival of this beautiful widow on his doorstep.

As I pass through the double glass doors behind Anna, I catch my reflection in the large mirror opposite. My face is beetroot red from the run. My hair is up in a high ponytail, but a few wisps have fallen out, sticking to my sweaty face. Well, this isn't going to help me compete.

I hastily tidy the wisps back off my face, heading behind the kitchen counter to pour the coffee.

"Where's Matilda?" I ask over my shoulder.

"Oh, she's gone upstairs with Anna's daughter, Sofia. It turns out they're both book mad," Charles supplies, pulling out the chair of the island bench for Anna to sit at. She gratefully smiles at him, flashing her perfectly straight white teeth. Charles grins back. As though on cue, my mother's voice pipes up. *Why would he want to be with someone like you when he could be with someone like her?* I shove it away angrily as I search for mugs.

"Oh, and isn't it great news, Jackie?" Charles jumps in. "Sofia is going to Briar Prep School as well—she will be in the same year as Matilda."

I turn back to them and smile as I fill three mugs with fresh coffee. I know this news should make me happy—isn't it exactly what I wished for yesterday morning? But there's something in Anna's mirrored grin that doesn't seem right. It almost looks *too* happy. I shake my head to knock the thoughts out.

"That *is* great news..." I start to say as I open the fridge to get some milk.

Charles cuts across me. "Anna, I know you were saying earlier that you were hoping to get involved in the school community—well, you've knocked on the right door. Jacqueline is the co-chair of the PTA. And you could really use some help right now, hey Jackie? With that venue for the summer fundraiser falling through? She's been so stressed about it." He adds conspiratorially.

Bringing the milk back over, I frown at Charles. I'd told him to keep that a secret. I was going to sort out this latest little problem before any of the other mothers caught wind. My co-chair Lydia would never let me live it down otherwise. She and all the rest of the committee are so judgy when something doesn't work out—and I have a reputation to keep up. None of them know about the insecurities that chase me daily, like a dog after a bone.

"Oh, no milk for me, thanks—I'm lactose intolerant," Anna says, curling her shiny hair around one finger. Charles looks down at her in sympathy as he grabs the milk and pours an excessive amount into his own mug. "And I don't think I'm ready to get involved in that lion's den quite yet," she continues with a smile. "I think I'll probably find my feet first."

Next to her, Charles guffaws as though she's made the funniest joke in the world. Her voice was perfectly pleasant as she spoke, but when our eyes lock, I don't miss the coldness laced through them. Like yesterday, the strange familiarity makes my heart start to race. I grab the milk and turn away to return it to the fridge as fast as I can.

When I turn back, my emotions are under control, and her expression is neutral once more. Had I just imagined it? I can't dwell on it now.

"Oh, don't worry about that," I say with a casual air. "I'm sure I'll get it sorted. I always do!" Deciding to change the subject, I add enthusiastically, "Briar Prep is a lovely school. Good choice!"

That is something I wholeheartedly believe. It's a wonderful school, set in the middle of the countryside with plenty of fields and playgrounds for the children to run around. Only a small intake is allowed in, and I'm impressed that Anastasia's managed to get Sofia in so quickly. But then again, I suppose anything is possible when you have millions in the bank.

"Yes, that's what I heard," Anna confirms, her dark lashes blinking up at me over the countertop. It doesn't look like she has a lick of makeup on—yet her skin is glowing, her eyelashes luscious as if she'd spent all morning applying mascara obsessively. She *must* have had her eyelashes tinted and extensions put in. There's no way they can be natural. I shake my head to focus on her words as she adds, "It seems so peaceful and safe around here, just what Sofia needs."

I don't have a chance to ask what she might mean by "safe" and why that's so important to her before I hear barreling footsteps down the stairs. Two faces appear breathlessly in the kitchen doorframe. The girls try to push past each other into the room and then descend into helpless giggles.

I can't help but laugh as I look at this absurd scene, their contrasting limbs tangling together, Matilda towering over little Sofia's diminutive figure. They tumble onto the floor, and Matilda lands on top of Sofia. They're both still laughing, but Anna lets out a screech of horror and rushes to grab her daughter.

"Sofia!" she cries in alarm as Matilda's gangly frame covers her body. Anna bends over her with urgency, as if she's about to rescue her daughter from a car wreckage, not from an innocent game.

"*Muuuuuum*, I'm fine!" Sofia pleads as Anna grabs her arm and pulls. "Ouch, you're hurting me!"

And sure enough, when Matilda finds her feet and hops up, there's a red mark and scratch on Sofia's arm where Anna has pulled hard.

Matilda, who had been so happy a moment before, now looks crestfallen and like she might cry. A sharp tug of anger pulls at my gut. I've rarely seen Matilda so at ease on a playdate with another girl—and now her mother has made my Matilda feel bad.

But before I have a chance to intervene, Charles swoops in. For a second, I think he's about to yell. This is just the sort of silly behavior he loathes when he's in a bad mood, and it can cause him to snap at us. But instead, he says with bravado, "Come on, you two—let's slow down and have a biscuit." God, Anna really *has* snapped him out of it. I know I should be thanking her, but...

"Yes, please," they both chorus and Charles hops up and goes to the cupboard.

"I—uh—actually," Anna pipes up. "I think we need to go now. I'm sorry—I didn't realize the time, and we have to prepare everything for Sofia's first day of school." She grabs Sofia's hand, pulling her up from the floor. "Thank you for having us," she says in a robotic voice before turning abruptly toward the door. I can't help but notice that she avoids my direct gaze. What was it about Sofia having a tiny accident that made her so jumpy?

"Oh Anna, I'll walk you out," Charles calls after her and follows—the biscuit jar he'd been retrieving long forgotten. Matilda hurries after the two of them, leaving me hovering by the kitchen island. All alone and extremely confused.

Have we offended her somehow? But as I hear laughter drifting through the house, I discount that. Anna and Sofia seem perfectly comfortable with Charles and Matilda. I start to tidy away the coffee cups, methodically wiping down every surface to clear my mind. I'm being silly; of course, Anna didn't just suddenly leave because of a silly little accident.

Lost in my cleaning haze, I hear the door slam dimly, and after a few moments, footsteps approach the kitchen door again.

I look up to see Charles. He leans casually against the inside panel. I try not to flinch—he knows how much that stresses me out, as it always leaves marks. Is he trying to rile me up on purpose?

But he seems oblivious as a lazy grin spreads across his face.

"Well, aren't they sweet?" he says conversationally. "Anna is nothing like I was expecting after you told me those terrible rumors." He shakes his head as he springs off the wall. I relax in relief. He walks around me to retrieve the biscuit he must have been craving after all. Then he turns to face me expectantly, as though waiting for my assessment, too.

"Yes," I manage to say. "She was much friendlier today than yesterday."

"Well, you did sneak into her house." I brace myself for the telling-off I might have received if he'd still been in the mood from this morning. But instead, his jovial side has taken over, and he taps my nose playfully. "My silly wife."

"You know that wasn't my intention," I begin as I furiously wipe the surfaces I've already cleaned.

Charles doesn't seem to notice that his words have irritated me as he goes on. "She really is something. She built herself up from nothing—joining as a maid at the Drummond Hotel Group before working her way to the top. That's how she met Sir Dave."

*How convenient—falling in love with your billionaire boss.* I can't help the uncharitable words as they pop into my mind. I push them away. Maybe it wasn't like that. I really have to stop being so judgmental all the time.

Charles continues, oblivious to the turn of my thoughts. "And all the while raising Sofia by herself. What an incredibly strong woman." He cocks his head to one side. "Did you know that she was married beforehand?"

I contain my flicker of jealousy at his slightly too-zealous admiration and shake my head as curiosity gets the better of me. I hadn't found anything specific about her first husband in my bits of research over the last few days. It seemed like the newspapers either didn't know or hadn't cared.

"It's so tragic; her first husband—Sofia's father—passed away too. I can't imagine how she's feeling, having to go through it all again." His eyes cloud over as unwelcome memories sweep over him. And then he coughs and says gruffly, "Well, I'd better get back to my case." Before I can say another word, he's out the kitchen door.

But that might be a good thing because at least he can't see the look of horror that I'm sure has crept onto my face. I slump back to rest against the cold island bench as I realize that it's not just me being paranoid after all. *At last* all the cogs are clicking into place about why there is something so familiar about Anna's eyes.

Because she might not know anything about my secrets. But she might be here for something else entirely.

Anna is so familiar because there's something in her eyes that resembles Charles's ex-wife.

The one that died. But whose body was never found.

# CHAPTER SIX

The rest of that day, I kept telling myself that I was being absurd to even think that Anna could be connected to Louisa. Charles didn't appear like he'd made the same leap, and surely, if there was something in Anna that resembled his missing ex-wife, he'd have been the first to say so.

It was purely something in those haunting blue eyes that had thrown me off—I bet millions of people have eyes like that. Though, I had to admit they also had perfect heart-shaped faces and rosebud lips in common. But from what I knew, Louisa had shoulder-length *blonde* hair, whereas Anna is the complete opposite with her long dark tresses.

The thoughts turned my stomach, but I reasoned with myself that I was being ridiculous. I'd just become too obsessed over the years with the idea of his ex-wife, studying the small photograph I knew Charles kept inside his bedside table again and again. It was his own little way of keeping her memory alive, and I'd never begrudged him that. He deserved to mourn in his own way.

I was simply jumping to wild conclusions. Yes, Louisa's body was never found. But the police had ruled her dead—an assumed drowning with no foul play. The last time she had been seen was on a wellness retreat in Lake Tahoe. The police had determined that she had likely got lost or fallen during a walk as she was last seen heading toward some dangerous rapids. Though, I've always wondered whether it could have, sadly, been on purpose. Charles had said that Louisa wasn't quite herself at the time. But I'd never wanted to pry too deep. Every time I even came close to the circumstances around her death, Charles shut down, falling into one of his silent, solitary moods. I've always secretly suspected that, in some way, he felt responsible that he hadn't been there to save her, carrying some guilt with him all these years.

I'd never wanted to push him to relive those awful days. When I met Charles back in San Francisco, he was trying to move on from the trauma of losing his wife. He'd said that being with me was the first time he'd felt happy in longer than he could care to remember. How could I ruin that by quizzing him intently? I maintain that I'd been a good person—letting him mourn his first wife in his own way, and I'd believed that he had told me all the important things anyway.

Our relationship had always been like we'd pressed play at the moment we'd met, keeping the past locked away where it belonged. It had suited me, too. *I* certainly hadn't wanted to answer many questions about my past.

So, everything about our unspoken agreement had worked well. Until now. Because with the appearance of this mysterious widow across the street, I was starting to wonder whether I'd been wrong to not ask more questions about Louisa.

I suppose I could have questioned Charles about it as soon as the thought entered my head—but with our marriage feeling like it was made from glass at the moment, I didn't want to risk it. Not with what happened last year. The year our relationship almost shattered into a thousand tiny pieces.

We'd struggled to make enough time for each other with our full-time jobs and childcare. Charles had to be up in London more than any other year before, and whenever he was home, he made an effort to be helpful around the house, but I still found myself nagging at him to do this or that. He'd always been prone to the occasional sullen mood swing where it felt like he was isolating himself from me, but they started to become more frequent. Soon, he began staying in London even longer. I was mad at first, but then it hit me that perhaps I was steadily driving him away. He probably thought that I didn't even want him around. I realized that if I didn't do something about it, my hard-won life could collapse. And no matter what, I needed Charles.

One day, I decided enough was enough—and that I'd go up to London for the night and surprise him. Maybe our relationship had become stale because we were stuck in a rut of routine. A few years ago, we had sprung ourselves out of a similar situation by marrying at last after almost a decade of being together. But now, I wasn't sure what the next big gesture could be?

I decided that if I did something spontaneous for once, that could jumpstart us back to our early days when we first met in San Francisco. Back then, our attraction was instant. So I arranged a babysitter for Matilda on a Thursday night and hopped on the train up to London straight after work.

It was early December, and rather than taking the Tube, I decided to take a classic black cab over to Temple. I wanted to see the Christmas lights sparkle through the center of town. Watching the throngs of people laughing in these familiar streets, I felt a pang of nostalgia. Remembering my first London Christmas when Charles had brought me to see the lights on Regent Street. I'd had so much darkness in my life and there was something about London at Christmas that had made me feel lighter than I had done in years. As the cab drove along the Strand, I hurriedly topped up my lipstick using the camera on my phone. Hopefully, tonight would be what we needed. When, at last, I hopped out of the cab, wrapping my black woolen coat and soft cream scarf tightly around myself, I veered off Fleet Street. I tottered down the uneven cobblestone steps of the pedestrianized street leading into Middle Temple—where I knew Charles's chambers were.

But as I arrived, I was told that he wasn't there—I'd just missed him going to the pub around the corner with some colleagues. Well, it would add to the surprise, I told myself. When I arrived outside the building, the first thing I saw was Charles in the window. He wasn't with multiple "colleagues," though, only one. One very pretty female colleague. My stomach twisted as I watched them laughing together, the soft lights from the Christmas decorations inside the pub casting them in an intimate glow. And suddenly, I felt my eyes filling with tears. How could I have been so naïve? Of course, he hadn't been busy only *working* up here all these months—he'd been having an affair. I was turning forty the next month. Of course Charles couldn't help being swayed by an attractive younger female associate. Especially when whenever he was home all his wife did was snap at him.

I shook my head to try and think more clearly. Maybe I was jumping to conclusions. So I texted him. I watched as he glanced at his phone when the message came through. He blinked once and then put it down again, more intent on his conversation with this woman in front of him. It felt like I was being stabbed in the chest. I called him—again, he looked at his phone and ignored it. Now, fiery anger pulsed through my veins. How *dare* he do this to me? I'd stuck by his side through thick and thin, supporting him through his toughest times. And now, he was throwing it all away.

Before I knew it, my legs were making a decision for me, and I marched toward the door. I pushed through the crowd until I was there, standing right above them. Charles jumped up in fright as he saw me hovering, his chair scraping across the floor like nails on a chalkboard.

"Jackie," he said, confusion flooding his features. "What are you doing here?"

"Oh, I don't know," I retorted, my hands on my hips. "Why don't you tell me why you were ignoring my calls? Was it because of *her*?" I glared down at the girl, her eyes wide like a deer caught in the headlights. I normally wasn't this aggressive, but between the effort I'd gone to tonight and all the guilt I'd felt over these last few months, something had flipped inside me. I'd convinced myself that the growing distance between us was *my* fault—when really Charles appeared guilty of so much more.

"What?" he replied, his face going bright red. "Jackie, this is Amelia—my new assistant."

I laughed bitterly. "Of course she is."

"Jackie," Charles grabbed my arm urgently, concern in his eyes, "are you drunk?"

For some reason, I felt tears pricking at my eyes again. God, what was wrong with me? I never cried. But I could hear her: my mother's voice cackling in my head. Telling me that, *of course, you aren't worthy of a man like Charles. Of course, he will leave you the first chance he gets.*

I shook my head and gulped, trying to keep the tears at bay. Charles tilted his head with concern and said something to Amelia that I couldn't hear. The next thing I knew, I was being steered out of the bustling pub and back out onto the street.

"Jackie," Charles said, his deep brown eyes full of genuine concern, "what's going on? Why are you here?"

I dabbed at the corners of my eye carefully with my scarf. Charles looked horrified. In over a decade of being together, I'm sure he'd never seen me so out of control. Normally, I kept all my emotions bottled deep inside. It was easier that way. Because when they came out—well, it was messy. Maybe that was yet another reason why our marriage had slowly been crumbling away: we never shared enough about our true feelings or the scars of our pasts.

"Are you okay?" he asked gently.

It was the kindness in his voice that made a sob escape, and all at once, it tumbled out. My attempt at a romantic, spontaneous evening, my belief that our marriage was falling apart and that now it looked like he was having an affair with his assistant. The happy Christmas music emanating from the pub felt like it was mocking my every word.

By the time I was finished, I looked up at my tall, strong husband and saw pain etched across his ruggedly handsome face.

"God, we're making a bit of a mess of things this year, aren't we?" he said, shaking his head. He explained that Amelia really was just his new assistant—he'd been taking her out for a drink to celebrate her passing probation. His eyes were wide with pleading honesty. As far as I knew, he'd never lied to me before—unlike my own little lies. It wasn't really fair of me to not trust him now.

He pulled me in for a big, enveloping hug, and I inhaled his comforting, woody scent. But... I sniffed again. It smelt wrong somehow. Like it was mixed with a lighter, more feminine scent. I tried to sniff once more, but before I had a chance, he brought me to arm's length and tipped my chin up like he'd done in our early days. He dipped his head down and planted a sweet, soft kiss on my lips. Instantly, I melted. Feeling like that lost twenty-eight-year-old girl again. The one in desperate need of someone like Charles to sweep her off her feet.

He drew back and looked deep into my eyes. "Let's start again next year, shall we?" he said. "No more paranoia, no more "work comes first" for either of us—let's make *each other* our top priorities."

I nodded. I needed this promise of a fresh start for our relationship. I couldn't let everything I'd worked for fall apart. So, for once, I clamped down on that desperate need to know everything. I locked it away tight—for the sake of saving my marriage. I said yes and told him that tonight was going to be the start of the new chapter we both needed.

And since that night, we've been making good progress. I've tried to forget about the perfume I'd smelt on his clothes. I've even forced myself not to sniff his clothes or go through his bag whenever he returns from a week of work in London. I've kept telling myself that I should trust him. We've both had our faults recently and we'd promised each other we would turn over new leaves.

Now, we were still a little delicate but back on track.

I just had to make sure it stayed like that.

So, instead of confronting him about the strange similarity, I tried to push it out of my mind. I told myself I was being paranoid to think there might be a connection between Anastasia and Charles's dead wife. Charles had told me that she didn't have any family. And I was even more silly for entertaining the thought, in my darkest moments, that she could actually *be* Louisa. Besides, Charles surely would have recognized her.

It was just because Anna was *so* beautiful, combined with this slight similarity to Charles's ex-wife, that had me panicking. It all came down to feeling insecure about my marriage. I knew I had to clamp down on my urge to pick at this well-healed scab. It wouldn't do my relationship with Charles any good to start down this path.

Because people don't just come back from the dead.

# CHAPTER SEVEN

Ignoring everything turned out to be easier than I expected—as work took off at breakneck speed for the final couple of weeks before the spring vacation, with non-stop viewings and auctions all around the South West to prepare for.

It was actually a bit of a relief to slip into my professional work mode. I could switch off my fears about Anna—and do what I did best. I was so busy that it was a godsend that Charles's upcoming trial was postponed, meaning he could stay at home in Bristol and help while my schedule was so jam-packed. It meant two things: his mood drastically improved as he had more time to prepare. So, he was back to his smiley, happier self, and he could take over the school runs and home duties. Before I knew it, it was the end of March. The "Easter holidays," as they call it in this country, were just days away, and I was in organizational mode trying to get all my loose work ends tied up.

That week, Charles's brother, Freddie, had called me about a potential new client—a friend of his from Vermont who was moving to Bristol with his family. As always happens whenever someone mentions an American friend, my stomach twisted with nerves. I never want to meet an American if I don't know exactly where they're from first. But

Vermont, I thought, should be fine. We'd arranged for him to come over for lunch with Freddie on Sunday, and I was looking forward to it. I've always enjoyed Freddie's company, and Matilda adores her uncle. Even if he sometimes puts Charles on edge.

So now, waking up on Saturday morning—the last before school breaks up—I am determined to see everything in a fresh light. Matilda has been telling me this last week how much fun she's been having at school with Sofia, and I will likely see Anna today as it's the final morning of Saturday sport at school before spring break. I tell myself that it will all be fine. As I snuggle under the covers, I remind myself: *Don't listen to that dark echo inside of you telling you you're not worthy. You've built this life for yourself. And you deserve it. Don't listen to the voice telling you to not trust anyone. Don't listen to her.* Once again, I have my mother to blame for all the damage she has wrought. I repeat my daily mantra and tell myself once more that my paranoia about this widow across the street is just that. Besides, worry causes wrinkles.

I hop out of bed, walk straight to the curtains, and pull them open to let the bright sunshine streak in. Charles groans as the light hits his face.

"Come on, sleepy head, rise and shine. It's going to be a great day!" I declare as I turn back to face the open window. The house across the street is just visible from this angle. I haven't seen Anna since she first dropped over two weeks ago. I didn't have a chance to go to the game last weekend as I was busy doing house viewings, and I haven't bumped into her otherwise. I must say I'm relieved. I'd gone from desperately wanting to know all about her to feeling a slight sense of trepidation at seeing her again.

The idea of a rich and notorious widow moving in across the street and discovering whether the rumors around her were true had been exciting when it was just that: an *idea*. But after meeting her, she appeared much more the damsel in distress type. I'm certain that there's no way she could have been capable of killing her husband. However, what I'm still not sure about is whether she's capable of stealing *my* husband. Her similarities to Charles's ex-wife aside, they seemed to have a strange connection when I'd caught them together, bonding over the vegetable patch. I'd rather not find out if they are more compatible together than we are.

So I've decided that the best course of action is to make sure that Charles doesn't spend too much time with Anna. At least, not until *I* get to know her better first. Over the last fortnight, I'm confident Charles hasn't had much of a chance to see her. He is hopeless at organizing social plans without me. In fact, Charles hasn't mentioned her once since that day, and he's been making more of an effort with me. He's had the dinner ready and waiting when I've gotten home each night from my busy day, and he even bought me a bouquet of roses to congratulate me on completing a big sale.

I smile at the memory. Things with my husband seem to be back on track at last. Watching the windows opposite, I tell myself that it's high time I stopped jumping to conclusions. I need to get to know this widow across the street properly first. If I become good friends with her, then that could be a perfect way to ensure she would think twice about trying anything with Charles. I could even bring her into my orbit. God knows how tough I found it trying to become friends with the other moms in this exclusive school. I'll show her the ropes. I'm sure we'll become good friends, and my worries will soon feel like distant memories. But first, before I can relax, I need to understand what type of woman she really is to relieve any of this lingering unease. And that will start today. With a renewed spring in my step, I pad across the cushioned carpet and straight into our bright bathroom to start getting ready.

Half an hour later, I bundle Matilda into the car after coordinating what I hope is the perfect school outfit: black knee-high boots, a matching oversized woolen coat, and my favorite checkered Burberry scarf. I'd bought it as a present to myself when I'd sold the house across the street. The irony isn't lost on me that Anna probably could afford thousands of these.

I push the jealous thoughts out of my mind as I drive a sour-faced Matilda to school in near-freezing conditions for the sake of forcing her to be more social and "active". She hates playing sports. Especially netball. As an American, I don't really understand the rules either. But I can't let her think that I'm not into it, or she'd refuse to go. All the same, I wish spring would hurry up and arrive already. Charles is going to join later, once he's made some progress on the new case that's come in at last. I don't mind—it's better for my plan to get to know Anna better.

As we make our way over Clifton Suspension Bridge, I keep my eyes glued to the road ahead. I avoid casting my eyes out toward the gigantic gaping space below us. Even though I've driven over this bridge more times than I can count, it always shocks me how high up we are above the rushing Avon Gorge.

My pulse starts to slow as we reach the other side and start driving through the leafy streets of Long Ashton. I console myself that at least it's the last game before school breaks up. Then there's three weeks of occupying Matilda amidst a busy work schedule... But that can be next week's concern.

When we turn onto the long driveway that marks the entrance to the school, I can't help but brighten a little. Towering trees run down the long gravel lane, the little glimpses of dappled light between them bringing flashes of flowing fields. The beauty and isolation of Briar Prep—a converted Edwardian country pile on the outskirts of Bristol—always reinforces that we were right to make the move down here. It never ceases to amaze me that this countryside setting is only a twenty-minute drive from our residential home in the center of Bristol. It's certainly a far cry from where I grew up.

At last, we pull up outside the front of the towering mansion, and Matilda jumps out to head straight to the netball courts. It took me so long to drag her out the door this morning that we're running late. I follow the snaking trail of cars to the woodland car park discreetly hidden behind the trees. They would *never* want something as ugly as a car park to be on open display. At Briar Prep, appearances are everything. It's something that I wholeheartedly agree with, as it's the exact same way I approach my life.

After parking the car, I glance at my watch and realize I better get a move on. The game is due to start in five minutes, and the netball courts are at least a five-minute walk from here. I race through the school, rushing along the back of the main building, past the heated outdoor swimming pool and new science block we fundraised for last year. I organized the most spectacular casino night. Everyone said so.

Finally, I make it around to the courts, nestled inside the old walled kitchen gardens. There are three courts so that each of the A, B, and C teams can play at the same time. Regardless of where our children are playing, it's an unwritten rule that all onlookers gather in the middle against the far wall. It's the most sheltered and closest to the door that will take the adults back through to the "post-match tea" in the grand hall of the main building. It's such a cute British tradition. Some say the tea is the primary reason why most of these parents show up each week. I couldn't possibly comment.

As I make my way around the edges of the wall, the whistle blows to signal the start of the game. I'm too preoccupied with the gaggle of women I'm steadily approaching to watch the start of play. As I get closer, I hear a loud screeching noise. No, wait, that's *laughter*. Very unusual. Usually, it's more whispered conversations, followed by a chorus of groans and the occasional cheer at the state of the games.

I bustle forward, saying a quick hello to some of the women on the outskirts of the circle. But my eyes are trained on my fellow PTA co-chair Lydia, who I desperately need to speak to about our fundraising plans. With how busy I've been at work the last couple of weeks, I haven't had a moment to find a new venue for the summer fundraiser, and I need to reassure her that everything is under control. I can't allow my carefully curated place at the head of the committee to begin to crumble. Even though we've become close "friends" over the years, I know that Lydia wouldn't hesitate to push me out if she had the chance. She has a penchant for control. Of course, I can understand; it's one of the reasons we bonded in the first place three years ago, at a similarly freezing netball match when we decided that the previous chair was dreadful. We'd both realized that we had an intimate understanding of the refrain, "If you want to get a job done, you have to do it yourself". We hatched our plan to overthrow the previous Chair—lovely but useless Gloria—and have since been running everything ourselves.

Having grown up in the countryside surrounding Bristol and being a former pupil of Briar Prep herself, Lydia had given us the necessary access to the crucial clique. And I, with my American charm, had won over any of the parents who occupied a place on the outer fringes like me. We'd known we had to run a joint campaign to get both groups on our side—and now here we are. But over the last year, Lydia has started to turn a little frosty toward me, and I think I know why. Through her endorsement, she's unwittingly let me into her exclusive group, and over the years, I've made sure to become close to every one of the parents inside it. Now, I am positive I could win the Chair position outright at the next vote if I want to. And I do. I want it so badly. I know some might see it as a frivolous use of my time, especially when I have a successful job in my own right. Charles certainly doesn't see why I do it. But I know why. It brings me into the folds of an Establishment system—one that I've never been a part of before. Not really. Not here, and definitely not where I grew up.

Some of these women are my friends. Some I don't trust, of course, but many of them are kind, and I know I'd be able to rely on them in a crisis. And crucially, by being an integral member of the PTA at one of the country's top private prep schools, I am afforded unbridled access into the homes of some of the wealthiest parents in the South West of

England, which helps with selling them beautiful new houses. I would never give up this role willingly.

So now, under no circumstances do I want Lydia to realize that I haven't been able to quite finalize the venue for the summer fundraiser yet. This would be the perfect proof for her argument that I can't handle another year in this position, let alone be the sole Chair. I know that she would use it against me without a backward glance.

I brace myself, tucking a stray strand of hair behind my ear, as I spy the back of Lydia's head over the crowd—I can never miss the always-perfect blonde curls that she must blow out every single morning—so I weave in and out, trying to make my way to her.

Just as I'm about to tap her on the shoulder, she throws her head back in a giant laugh, almost hitting me smack on the nose. I let out a gasp, and she turns around, her eyes wide.

"Oh, Jacqueline! *So* sorry!" she manages between giggles. She starts to say something, but I'm not paying attention to what, as my attention is now fixed on the person in the center of the group. The woman who is making everyone laugh so hard.

That familiar grace, those dark, flowing locks, the sparkling eyes. The last time I saw Anna in my house, she had all those things, but then she seemed nervous, more softly spoken. She certainly didn't seem like someone who would like being the center of attention. But here she is, my new neighbor. The life and soul of the group, making it look effortless to be in this collection of fierce mothers—something that has taken me years to perfect.

Anna tosses her silky hair over her red designer jacket and waves a delicate hand in greeting as though she's introducing *me* to *her* friendship group.

"Hello, neighbor," she says with a sleek smile, twirling a stray lock behind her ear. "I haven't seen you around lately."

I stand there, my mouth slightly ajar at this welcome.

"Of couuurse," Lydia says in her rich, plummy accent. "You two already know each other. Jacqueline darling, you are sooooo lucky to have dear Anna as a neighbor now. She's a hoot! And so incredibly talented when it comes to event organizing. When we met last week, she passed on that you'd told her about your little issue with the venue falling through but that she knew of the perfect alternative. What a lifesaver!" She beams at Anna. But I can't help it as it feels like a stone has dropped into the center of my stomach.

"Oh... oh, really?" I try to sound relaxed, but I know it comes out with more of an accusatory tone than I intended. *Stay calm, Jacqueline,* I tell myself.

"Yes!" Lydia exclaims. "And now I'm not even mad at you for keeping that little secret from me. But, were you ever going to tell me, co-chair? It's like you've disappeared into thin air the last two weeks. As I've said before, perhaps having a full-time job and the co-chair responsibility is a little too much for you to manage right now? Seriously, thank *God* for this one. I don't know what we would have done without her."

Lydia places one slender arm around Anna's tiny shoulders and squeezes tight. I can't believe Anna's done this—she heard me say that I was going to sort it out. Besides, she said emphatically that she wasn't interested in getting involved in this kind of thing when she was still settling in. Has she told Lydia on purpose, knowing that it would make me look bad? But no—surely not. She can't have known the full picture. That must be it.

All the same, I can't help but send an accusatory look straight at Anna. She beams broadly back at me in response, misreading my glare.

"Oh, you don't mind, do you, Jacqueline?" she asks. "Charles mentioned last week that you'd been flat out at work and still hadn't managed to sort another venue yet. So I thought I'd try and help."

Charles *told* her? Have they been meeting up without me realizing? A flash of annoyance races through me. I've been too busy to realize that this doe-eyed widow has been weaseling her way into my territory at home and school.

Beneath my coat, I clench my fists. Whatever my tumultuous feelings might be beneath the surface, I must stay in control. I can't give Lydia or Anna the satisfaction.

So I force myself to say back, "Of course not; thank you so much for your help."

"Yes, honestly, she is an absolute wizard," Lydia says. "She's even volunteered to join as a permanent member of the PTA."

I blink in surprise. That's not what she'd said two weeks ago in my kitchen.

"Oh, it was no trouble at all," Anna says with a laugh. "It's just so lovely to spend time with like-minded parents." Her phone starts to ring, and I'm watching her so closely that I don't miss the flicker of worry that momentarily blemishes her otherwise flawless forehead. But in less than a second, a sweet smile returns as she excuses herself from the circle and disappears around the back of the buildings to take the call.

My mind is whirling at Anna's change of tune. She seemed to have absolutely zero interest in getting involved in school activities the last time we met. What changed her mind? Or had she been lying then?

All I know is that this new peppy version of Anna is an entirely different one from both the nervous woman I found in my garden and the ferocious one I first met in her library. Who is the *real* Anna?

As I turn back to Lydia's continued blathering, all I can think about is that question.

That, and who was calling Anna just now? Because whoever it was managed to make her perfect mask slip. After all this, I want to know why.

# Chapter Eight

Anna never returns to the courts. But as we freeze to death on the sidelines, Lydia starts to catch me up on her version of everything that I've missed the last two weeks on the school gossip mill. Lydia knows everything about everyone. Except me, I always remind myself. I pretend to listen, but all I can think about is these three different faces of Anna, and what could have whisked her away from watching her precious daughter?

When the final whistle blows, all the moms and a few lone dads stampede through the back entrance to the grand hall for tea. I pause to give Matilda a little wave and a thumbs-up. She smiles shyly back at me before turning around to chatter animatedly to Sofia. At least that's a positive outcome from our new neighbors across the street. Matilda and Sofia do seem to be becoming close friends.

I'm near the back of the gaggle by the time I make it to the doors. The children will all go off and have their own tea in the school dining hall. Isn't it just so civil? I can't imagine anything like this happening back where I grew up. You were lucky if you made it through a basketball match without someone knocking you to the ground and screaming threats if you blocked them again. That is one of the many reasons why

I avoided team sports growing up—though I would never tell Matilda that, of course. I want her to have the perfect childhood that I never had.

"Yoohoo," a loud, high-pitched voice calls behind me, and I turn around to see Caroline and Claire, two other members of the PTA. I don't see them much outside of that; both of their daughters are on the A team, and Matilda doesn't seem to have become close with either of them. Perhaps growing close to Sofia will bring her out of her shell and help her make more friends.

Their blonde heads bounce in unison as they keep walking toward me, and Caroline twinkles a little hand. "Oh, Jacqueline," she calls in a sing-song voice.

"Didn't you hear us calling?" adds Claire as they reach my side. "Or are you trying to avoid us?"

She says it lightly, but I can see the steely expression in her grey eyes. These two come as a pair, and I often think of them as "double trouble". Both from established families in the Bristol region, they grew up together. They gossip like mad, and you can't trust them as far as you can throw them. But you would *never* want to get on their bad side. It will not end well for that person. I saw it happen to poor Andrea Sawyer when she decided not to invite them to her husband's birthday party. Andrea still refuses to do school pick-ups after the vicious rumor about her affair with her personal trainer spread. I would never want to give the two Cs a need to dig up a story about me. I have far too many real secrets that must remain buried.

So I give them my friendliest, most flashy American smile.

"Oh my god, I'm so sorry. I was in my own world, reminding myself to ask Miss Cooper whether there are any extra training sports camps we could send Matilda to during these school holidays. I'd love for her to move up to the B team next year."

A lie, but I know they'll buy it. In their world, sport is the number one priority.

"Oh, good idea, she needs it," Caroline says. I try not to bristle at the obvious insult as she exchanges glances with Claire. "We should ask her the same about Millie and Araminta. One can never do enough training."

Claire nods. "Absolutely! You're always full of good ideas, Jacqueline." Thankfully, we are nearly at the doors—when we're inside, I can get away from them. I'm not feeling up to my usual Jacqueline self. I don't want to accidentally snap at them and have that get spread around like wildfire. Besides, I'd really like to check on where Anna has gotten to.

"I'm glad you seem back to normal. We were really worried about you," Caroline says, holding open the door for Claire and me to walk through. "It sounds like you haven't been yourself lately."

"Yes, is everything okay?" Claire echoes as she steps through into the hallway before turning to face me.

Caroline continues to hold the door open, but my suede-booted feet refuse to budge. "Sorry," I say, shaking my head. "What do you mean?"

"Oh, nothing," Caroline says, trying to wave me in. "Just from what Anna said, it sounded like she's met quite a different Jacqueline than the one we know."

"What do you mean?" I shoot back at her without thinking twice that my quick line of questioning might come across as defensive.

"Only that we knew you were an estate agent, but we didn't think you'd let yourself into someone's house unannounced." Caroline laughs, but to my ears, it sounds more like a derisive shriek. I feel myself blushing red. Oh my god—Anna must have told them all how we first met. How embarrassing. Why would she do that? Surely only if she wanted to make me look bad? Anyone in their right mind would know it would fuel this gossip-hungry mill.

Claire grins with mischief in her eyes. "Oh, don't be embarrassed. It's *such* a funny story."

"A little odd, too, though," Caroline adds with a giggle. "What came over you?"

I feel like a mouse cornered into a trap by two Cheshire cats. I have to get out of this.

So I force a laugh of my own and sweep my curls over my shoulder in an attempt to appear breezy. "Oh, ladies, what a strange story. But I don't know what you're talking about. Can I pass?"

In any situation where it's your word against theirs—denial is always the best policy. And especially here, in *my* school. What game is Anna trying to play with me, spreading this story while my back was turned? I had come here today with a view to trying to become friends. And yet, she seems to be already stabbing me in the back.

Caroline and Claire move in unison, stepping aside as their eyebrows shoot up in surprise at my words.

"Oh, sorry," Claire says uncertainly as I walk past. "Just, Anna told such a tale. We must have got the wrong end of the stick."

"Yes," Caroline adds with a little nervous laugh. "We didn't mean to offend."

Inwardly, I smile. Because yes, you don't want to get on the bad side of these two. But any of these moms also wouldn't want to get on the bad side of me: their powerful co-chair. I could bite back at them, but instead, I want to get out of this situation.

"Not at all," I say with a winning smile. "How strange! Well, I better go and find my husband. Shall we go and enjoy the match tea?" I latch onto both their arms and pull them through the plush corridor, lined with school photograph after school photograph. "And you *must* tell me all about your plans for the house renovation, Claire."

It's a switch in subject that I know Claire could never resist, and she happily begins to chatter away. But all I can think as I make my way down the seemingly never-ending corridor is one thing: what is Anna up to?

# CHAPTER NINE

I'm hit by the noise first. Before I even step into the ornate grand hall of the school where tea is served, the cackle of laughter and gasps of delighted surprise greet me. It's always the same when the parents get together. It's honestly the only reason why half of them come to watch the matches—to enjoy a good gossip and cheeky slice of the head cook's delicious Victoria Sponge cake. But I'm not in the mood today.

After what Claire and Caroline have said, all I really want to do is find Charles and get out of here. He should be here somewhere, as he texted me at the end of the match to say that he'd arrived.

Anna's behavior has thrown me for a loop, and I want to carefully quiz him on how much he's seen of her these last two weeks without me realizing it. Her clear undermining of me in the school community with the other moms has brought all my initial fears back up. And now I can't stop picturing her ice-blue eyes, so like Charles's first wife's, staring up at *my* husband in our back garden. I'm back at square one again, and I don't feel like I can't trust Anna's intentions at all.

But as I squeeze my way past a group of tittering parents, I can't see Charles's usually obvious tall frame anywhere. My eyes sweep over the high ceilings, carved woodwork running along its edges. Through the crowd, I can just about make out the huge roaring fire in the center of the room, the carved lion at the head of the mantelpiece roaring in despair at the scene. I can relate. It feels like there are thousands of people pressing into this room. But I can't see Charles anywhere... Or Anna.

I push through the crowd, continuing my search. Every time I spot someone who I know will want to chat, I quickly duck and weave into another corner. I can't bring myself to be the Jacqueline that everyone expects today. My mind is too frazzled.

Eventually, I slide into the first door off the grand hall—which I know leads to the library. I'm desperate for a moment of peace, and I'll just get out my phone and call Charles. For goodness sake, he said he was here.

I breathe a small sigh of relief as I close the door with a quiet click. At last, I can hear myself think. But that's not the only thing I hear. A low murmuring is coming from somewhere in the room. I take a step further away from the door and into the swell of shelves. The library isn't very big, perhaps only twenty bookshelves between the doorway and the opposite wall, but as I enter the central walkway that leads through the shelves, I still can't see the source of those voices. The long table running through the center is also empty. Where could they be?

As I move through the library, I'm quiet as a mouse. It's not that I'm trying to spy, but it's always better to be on the front foot. I'd rather find out who is whispering before I announce myself loudly. And that's when I hear a delicate sob alongside an all-too-familiar voice.

"Oh, please don't worry; Jacqueline will take care of it."

The surprise of hearing Charles's voice makes me stumble. I knock into a chair, banging my shin and crying out in pain.

I look down and rub a hand on my leg to soften the blow. By the time I glance back up, shuffling footsteps emerge, and there's my husband. An arm around Anna's shoulder as she delicately dabs at her eyes with a striped handkerchief. *Charles's handkerchief.* He's the only person I know who insists on carrying one around. Just for this kind of scenario, I suppose—when he has to save a "damsel in distress." How convenient.

"Jacqueline!" Charles exclaims. "Perfect timing."

He doesn't appear concerned at all that his wife just found him in a corner of a room comforting another woman. A woman who, after this situation, seems to definitely be trying to get close to my husband.

"I was telling dear Anna," Charles goes on, "that she shouldn't worry about having to leave Sofia tonight—we can look after her. You're always saying that Matilda should have more sleepover nights with friends."

"Oh, Charles, are you sure? You'd be a lifesaver," Anna says, looking up at him with glistening eyes, a portrait of helplessness. I try not to roll my eyes.

He gives her shoulders a reassuring squeeze. "Absolutely. Right, Jacqueline?" His gaze bores into mine expectantly.

I feel like I've fallen through the cracks and into a conversation I only know half the story of. It seems like Charles is genuinely trying to help Anna out from some sudden situation she's gotten herself into, so I can't say no without a good reason. But aren't the stories she's been spreading about me—and how she's looking at my husband—reason enough to say no?

I can't call her out right now, though. I'll talk to Charles later. Alone. Because I'm sure Anna is up to something, but what? How could having to suddenly leave Sofia have anything to do with it? Whatever else she might be up to, she seems obsessed with her daughter's welfare. She wouldn't leave her unless she had to.

I know I only really have one answer, the answer that the usual Jacqueline would give to any other parent stuck in a tricky place. So I say, in as bright a voice as I can manage, "Of course, that's what neighbors are for."

Charles beams, opening his arms wide in triumph. "See, I told you so. Jacqueline to the rescue." I don't know if it's a trick of the light or if a flicker of a frown passes over Anna's perfect face.

It's gone before I can catch it, though, and she says with a sniff in my direction, "Thank you so much. I have to leave immediately. Unfortunately, there's a complication with my late husband's family that I need to deal with in person tonight."

I pause over her strange turn of phrase. I'm about to ask a question when Charles answers with a shake of his head. "That's the last thing you need on your plate." He says it with such familiarity I can't help but wonder at what, or how many, conversations have taken place between them.

Anna shrugs as though accepting her fate. "Can you give Sofia a big hug from me?" she says. "I must dash to make the meeting in time. I've texted her so she'll understand. I know she'll have a wonderful time with you all, and I'll be back to pick her up first thing in the morning."

"Absolutely," I manage to say, but she's already passed me on quick feet, stepping with that deliberate grace toward the entrance.

Anna waves before closing the door behind her. I was watching her so intently that the touch of an arm around my shoulder makes me jolt.

"God, Jacqueline, you're very jumpy at the moment," my husband whispers into my ear. It's meant to sound teasing, but it comes across as a little scornful.

I whirl around at him, folding my arms across my chest. "Well, how am I supposed to be when I catch you hiding away with our pretty new neighbor in the school library and apparently having secret conversations with her while your wife's been busy?"

"Whoa," he puts his hands up and steps back. But his nostrils flare in a tell-tale way. I know I've hit a nerve. "What on earth are you trying to say?"

"I think you know," I hiss back at him. "Why are you talking about me behind my back with Anna? Why is Anna trying to tear apart my position with the other moms on the PTA? And why am I walking in on you comforting our beautiful neighbor—who you apparently know everything about—in a deserted library?"

A flash of anger rushes across his features. "I think you're imagining things again, sweetheart," he says in an icy voice. "I thought we'd made a pact to start again this year."

My heartbeat quickens at that. I know I'm treading dangerously here. I don't want us to have a fight right now. The rational Jacqueline takes over. *Remember: we're in the school library. There's probably a reasonable explanation for all this. You just have to give him a chance...*

I take a deep breath and force a breezy laugh. "You're probably right…" I take a step toward him, but his bulky frame remains rigid, his nostrils flaring as though he's ready to pounce into an argument.

Tentatively, I take his hand in mine and give it a light tug, "Charles, I know I'm being silly; come back to me." He shakes his head, and then his frozen expression lifts. The Charles I know is back, and I can see the relief on his face. It's as though he knows how close he'd come to losing it himself.

"Oh, you are," he says, wrestling me into a tight hug. I'm sure it's supposed to be sweet, but he presses in a bit too forcefully, and for a moment, I struggle to breathe. But the next second he lets me go with a bright smile. "Look, there's really nothing for you to jump to conclusions about. Those mums are simply awful gossips. Poor Anna's had such a lot to deal with, and I was going to tell you all about it tonight when we had the chance to have a bit of time for the two of us. I've barely had a moment with you these last couple of weeks," he adds quietly.

I'm just relieved we've managed to avoid a public fight. Appearances are everything in this school. So, I give him a small smile. "You might be right there. Well, let's get out of here then and set the girls up for a fun sleepover. Then we can catch up properly over a glass of wine."

At that his eyes regain their usual sparkle. "Do you promise?"

I tug on his hand in answer, leading him from the quiet library and back out into the now much less busy grand hall.

After all these years, it's a relief to know that I can still read my husband so well and that I know how to keep him under control. Generally.

I'm sure I'll get the full story out of him tonight.

When we collect the girls, Sofia doesn't seem too concerned that her mom has left her behind due to a sudden family emergency. So far, she seems like a very polite kid, but far too quiet for my liking, with her deep, thoughtful eyes. It's so hard to tell what she's thinking. Like mother, like daughter, I suppose.

Sofia only really seems to come alive when she's chattering with Matilda, and as we all pile into the car, they are full of excited discussions about what movies they'll watch tonight at their very first sleepover. Even Charles chimes in every so often with a silly suggestion or two, and they kindly indulge him with his *Star Wars* idea.

As we drive over the suspension bridge once more and enter Clifton Village, I watch the rain start to fall outside the window, pattering across the pavements and onto the flowers starting to grow along the front gardens of the towering Georgian houses. They remind me of Anna—a lovely façade, but how many secrets might they be hiding on the inside? Because if this day has taught me anything, it's that what Anna appears to be on the surface, might not really be who she is underneath.

We sweep around the edges of Clifton and take the Circular Road up through the Downs. I stare out my window and peer at the thick trees that hide Avon Gorge from view before they open up to reveal a glimpse or two of the muddy river. A few minutes later, we slip down the quiet, picturesque roads of our neighborhood.

As we approach our house, my thoughts turn back to my neighbor. What could have been so urgent that Anna had to leave her precious daughter behind with people who are practically strangers?

It's only about four o'clock in the afternoon now, but the moody sky has made everything grey. And it's dark enough out for lights to be flickering on in homes along the street. I search the house opposite ours through the thick raindrops as we begin to turn into our driveway. For a second, I notice a singular quivering light in the topmost room. Then it winks out.

Is it my imagination, or is Anna actually still there? I'm sure she wouldn't have made it all up to get Sofia out of the house... would she?

But then I turn to look behind my shoulder at the little girl giggling next to Matilda. Their almost matching shades of night-dark hair are bent closer together as Sofia whispers something in her ear.

My eyebrows furrow as the car comes to a stop, and Charles declares, "We're home!"

A strange thought passes my mind as I watch the two of them exchanging secret whispers. This sudden sleepover could have been caused by Anna wanting a mole. A chance to get Sofia *inside* our house and report back. But that would be crazy. Wouldn't it?

# CHAPTER TEN

I try to keep a close eye on Sofia as she and Matilda paint their nails and finally choose which movie to watch. I stay busy cleaning so I can pop in and out of the living room where they've based themselves, but so far, I haven't been able to spot any tell-tale signs that Sofia might be somehow here at her mother's request. Maybe I was jumping to conclusions again—but when the girls sit down to share a pizza together and watch *The Princess Diaries*, I give it one last chance. I hang back outside the doorway, polishing the brass handle on the white door. I hate it when they start to look brown. I always need them to be shiny gold.

As the movie starts, I hear Sofia talking in an excited voice. "Oh hey, this is set in San Francisco. My mum says that you were born there?"

My ears prick up. Why would Anna know that? Charles must have told her. But we moved over to the UK when Matilda was only one, so it doesn't come up often. Either way, it's interesting that Anna told her daughter. And it's even *more* interesting for Sofia to be asking Matilda about it now.

"Yeah," Matilda says. I can tell she's chewing as her voice is a little muffled. "I don't remember it though. We moved when I was a baby."

"But technically, you're still American, right?" Sofia asks.

"I guess so?" Matilda responds. "I've never really thought about it or where I was officially born."

"I bet you could check on your birth certificate," Sofia says in a low voice. So low that I almost don't hear it. Is she trying to whisper on purpose, knowing that I'm only on the other side of the door?

It's enough of a strange suggestion from a twelve-year-old girl that the rag stills in my hand.

"What do you mean?" Matilda asks. I can tell by her tone that she's puzzled.

"Well..." Sofia starts. I don't want to miss what she is going to say next, so I peek around the door a little. But at that same moment, Sofia takes a little look over her shoulder. Our eyes lock, and she twists away too quickly. "I'll tell you later," she mutters. Then the volume on the TV gets a lot louder—she must have turned the sound up.

I want to storm in there and demand answers—but then I'd have to admit to eavesdropping on their conversation. Matilda would die of embarrassment, and I don't want to do that to her. Besides, I've heard enough to decipher what Sofia is interested in. Matilda's birth certificate. It makes my heart hammer hard in my chest. Sofia can't know what that birth certificate would tell Matilda—can she?

She *must* be asking these questions on her mom's orders. What twelve-year-old would think to ask about someone else's birth certificate? I remember when I was twelve—I don't even think I knew what one was really, let alone how much it could tell you.

The girls are lost to giggles and *The Princess Diaries,* and Charles is locked in his study preparing for an upcoming case, so I go back to cleaning the house, trying to calm my frazzled nerves. After all the strange little things that have happened today with Anna, and now Sofia asking about Matilda's birth certificate, I am starting to think that maybe my wild jump from Anna to Charles's first wife isn't so crazy after all. Louisa's body *hadn't* been found, after all…

As I start to prepare dinner for Charles and me, I decide that once the girls go to bed, I need to speak to Charles. It's high time I knew more about his first wife. Besides, if he isn't hiding anything, then he shouldn't get mad about me asking—right?

All I know is that in all our twelve years together, not one person has ever asked to see Matilda's birth certificate. Charles and I promised each other it would stay that way.

Because Matilda isn't my biological daughter.

She's Louisa's.

# Chapter Eleven

We never intended for it to become such a big secret. But we left it too late, and there's no way I want it getting out now.

As I stir the bolognese sauce simmering on the stove, I try to think back to those early days. It feels like I'm opening the pages of a long-forgotten book, searching out the fragments of what Charles told me about his life before me.

My memories of the day we met feel like a mirage shimmering on the horizon. I zoom in on the scene, finding my way to the person I was twelve years ago, back in San Francisco. The nervous young woman waiting outside the cream Victorian building at the top of Pacific Heights, just around the corner from Alta Plaza Park, for her first ever solo viewing. The sun had been shining on that late June day, and the gloom of the morning fog chased far away. I'd tidied my black pencil skirt and re-straightened my designer blouse as I hovered on the sidewalk. I'd been so happy about that shirt—having picked it up at a little thrift shop the previous week. It had been around three months since I'd moved from the East Coast to San Francisco after landing my first proper job in real estate. I'd learned the ropes quickly, and this listing meant a lot to me: my boss giving me a chance to handle this on my own. I'd reached out to people specifically for this viewing. Trying to find just the right person to take the lovely, airy apartment. I really didn't want to mess it up.

But as I glanced down at my faux leather wristwatch, a few butterflies fluttered in my stomach. The potential client was fifteen minutes late. Doubt began to claw away at my thoughts. Had I given him the wrong time? Or the wrong address? Now, the sun suddenly felt too oppressive. I covered my eyes as I pulled out my BlackBerry. I'd have to double-check.

As I started searching for the email chain, I heard a polite cough. I looked up to see a dark-haired man standing in front of me. He was handsome, even if his grey suit hung a little loose around his tall frame. His eyes were shaded from view by dark sunglasses.

"Hello, are you Jacqueline Kelly?" he asked. I blushed when I heard his British accent. He reminded me of Jude Law in *The Holiday*—my forever crush

I nodded and quickly found my voice with a smile. "Yes, and you're Charles Banks."

It wasn't a question, but he responded as though it was. "Indeed, I am." His tone suggested he wasn't happy about it.

It wasn't my place to ask, so instead, I plastered on my own grin and gestured toward the front door. "Right, this way to your hopeful new home, then, Mr Banks."

"Call me Charles," he'd replied with a wry smile as I turned away to take us through to the large two-bedroom apartment in prime upper Pacific Heights.

It was the entire ground floor of the building, so as soon as I opened the front door, the next one along led us inside. As Charles stepped through, he took off his sunglasses, and I saw his chocolate-brown eyes for the first time. But instead of an interested expression, all I read was a hollow emptiness. I shrugged it off and started to show him around, emphasizing all the wonderful selling points of the property—from the natural light to the modern kitchen and even the unique fireplace feature. He nodded along, barely asking any questions. When we'd finished the tour, and I let him back out to the street, I felt for certain that he wasn't going to take it. Disappointment coiled in my stomach like a snake.

But as I locked up and joined him on the sidewalk, he surprised me. "Great," he said. "Where do I sign?"

"Oh!" My eyebrows shot up in surprise, and before I knew what I was saying, my true feelings tumbled out. "I didn't think you were very interested."

I clamped my mouth shut, cursing my thoughtlessness. But Charles laughed. The sound seemed to have surprised him as he shook his head, and the somber expression I'd noticed earlier returned. He sighed.

"Sorry, I..." he started, as though about to explain. But then he shook his head. "Look, I definitely am. Let me know the next steps."

I was curious, but I pushed it to one side to explain what he'd need to do next: place a formal offer, send through his work credentials, and inform us of any other people who would be living with him.

When I finished my list, a small crease of worry appeared on his forehead. "Do you know if the landlord would be fine with a baby?"

"Oh yes, that would be fine." I couldn't resist asking, "Would your wife like to book a time to see the property herself?"

At my words, his face fell, and I knew I'd made a major misstep. "Oh, there's no wife," he said, looking away from me. "Just me and little Matilda." And on the last word, his voice cracked at the edges. I watched as he blinked furiously to stop... tears?

I wanted to put everything right again as quickly as possible. "I'm so sorry," I said, "I didn't mean..."

"No," he said, shaking his head and turning back to face me. The sad look in his eyes was more pronounced than ever. "It's just... my wife recently... died," he managed to say through gritted teeth.

"Oh my god," I gasped, unable to help myself as I stretched out a hand to comfort him. Immediately, I pulled it back, but I felt drawn to him. I pretended to smooth down my skirt as I said, "I'm so sorry for your loss. I'm a total idiot..."

"No," he said emphatically, "you didn't know. It was, well, a shock. This whole year has been an awful shock, really. And I never expected to find myself here. I..." He trailed off, realizing he'd been starting to go on a tangent. "Oh God, what am I doing? You're just trying to rent me an apartment—you don't want to know my whole sorry story..."

As he babbled, I took an involuntary step forward. There was something in his desperate sadness that called out to me. It was like finding a lost puppy on the street. "I do," I said quietly. "I'm a very good listener."

His eyes flashed in surprise. Then he looked down at me with something I hadn't seen before: hope. I didn't know I was capable of giving people hope—all I'd ever felt like I'd done in my life was give people pain. Or perhaps that was my mother talking.

All the same, a seed of an idea popped into my head: maybe I could turn over a new leaf and give this poor, lost man the one thing he desperately needed? A new friend.

Charles took the apartment, and I asked for his number. He blushed and asked, "Are you sure you want to get to know a hopeless guy like me?"

I nodded, telling him that I needed a new friend too.

When we met up for a drink a week later, Charles began to tell me some of his crazy tale. How he'd moved to San Francisco for work two years before that to help his tech-whizz younger brother on the lucrative deal he'd scored for his company in Silicon Valley. Charles had explained to me that he was a barrister by training, but his brother, Freddie, had begged him. Freddie had said he needed an English lawyer by his side, and Charles was the only one he could trust. Charles had felt that it was his duty to help his little brother out at the time. He'd told himself it wouldn't be forever, but long enough to get Freddie on his feet. Their mother had died from cancer when they were little, and their father, unable to cope, had become a distant parent, shipping them off to boarding school at the earliest opportunity. Their father had married their own "wicked stepmother" as soon as he could. They'd only really ever had each other.

And then Charles had met Louisa. She was quiet, mysterious, and a little bit fragile. He and Freddie met her when she was working at a bar one night, and Charles couldn't help but be attracted to her. She was so different from anyone he'd ever known back home—and they started dating. I couldn't help but feel a flicker of jealousy as he told me. But I nodded in understanding and sipped my martini.

He said he hadn't been sure whether it was going to be forever—but that had all changed last summer when they had found out Louisa was pregnant, due that September. They must have only been dating for a few weeks at the time she'd gotten pregnant, and for all those months, Louisa hadn't realized she was pregnant at all. She hadn't ever had a very regular period, and she only found out when she'd gone to the doctor for a routine blood test.

"Even though it was a total shock, she didn't want to give the baby up for adoption. And nor did I. So I wanted to do the right thing by her," he said, as he ran a finger around his glass. "I'd been raised with very traditional values. And Louisa was scared. She'd cut ties with her family years ago, and she didn't know how she was going to support this child on her own. I promised her that I wouldn't leave her, and to prove it, I asked her to marry me. She said yes."

So they'd had a shotgun wedding of sorts at the end of February, five months after Matilda was born. The only person who knew about their wedding was Charles's brother, Freddie. They had wanted some time to get settled on their own before telling any other friends.

He paused then, suddenly unsure. "Sorry, I don't know why I'm telling you all this. You must be wanting to run a mile."

I carefully smiled. "Not at all; I can't believe you've been through so much. It just makes me want to help you. And sometimes it's easier to tell a stranger what's happened and how you're feeling than anyone that's close to you."

Charles nodded his agreement. "I think that's exactly what it is. Thank you," he said with a small smile of his own, and this time, it even seemed to reach his eyes. Then came the hardest part of the story. What had happened to Louisa.

He took a gulp of his drink as he tried to find the right words to explain. "It had been hard," he said, "but we'd been adapting. I'd been living with Freddie before, but then I moved into Louisa's cramped apartment, and our lives revolved around little Matilda... It's true that we maybe didn't speak enough about how we were coping personally. We were so focused on trying to keep her alive. But I really didn't think Louisa was so unhappy. Just exhausted. We both were," he said sadly.

"She'd never had a huge group of friends, but the few she had, she lost touch with after Matilda's birth. I didn't notice at first; I was so sleep-deprived and consumed with trying to look after her and Matilda. But when I organized our quick courthouse ceremony, just the three of us, I asked if she wanted me to invite Freddie or any other friends. But she insisted that she didn't want anyone else there. I half-heartedly tried to change her mind, but she grew frantic and said she only wanted our new little family. Since the birth, her emotions had been all over the place—I thought it was probably a normal reaction to the sudden surprise. I was struggling, too, and I didn't want to add to her anxiety. So, I put her distancing herself from her old life just down to the fact that she didn't know how to marry these two new sides of her life together. I didn't have the time or capacity to be in touch with anyone else in my life, either. Our whole lives in those first few months simply revolved around keeping Matilda—and ourselves—alive.

"Like me, I thought she would reconnect with them in her own time; she just needed to figure out her life first. So when she said she wanted to go on a solo wellness retreat in early March, I thought it sounded like a brilliant opportunity for her to clear her mind. I told her I could manage Matilda on my own—of course, she should have some time to herself after everything she'd been through. But I... oh god," he put his head in his hands as he tried to find the words. "I didn't think that by the end of the trip, Matilda would have lost her mother."

He explained that Louisa had last been seen heading toward the edge of a precipice of dangerous rapids. Her body was never found. The police had ruled her dead—whether it was an accident or a suicide, the police didn't say either way. "It was an accident," Charles said emphatically, almost knocking over his drink. "There's no way that she..." He struggled for words. "It was a shock, but she loved Matilda—I know she did. She wouldn't have chosen to leave her."

Then silence fell as he took one more long drink.

"I'm so sorry for your loss," I said, and I meant it. "I can't imagine what you're going through. And now you have a baby to look after..."

"Yes," he said with a long exhale. "This is the first time I've left her with a babysitter since everything happened. It's been pretty tough trying to make it all work on my own. And my brother and I," he sighed. "Well, we haven't really spoken much since Louisa died. He keeps avoiding all my calls. We'd had a big fight right before she died. I told him that I wasn't sure I wanted to keep working with him in San Francisco anymore and that I was thinking of moving back to the UK with Louisa and Matilda later in the year. So, I guess he could still be mad at me about that. He and Louisa were close, too, though, so maybe he's just dealing with grief in his own way. I don't know... but it feels a bit like he's abandoned me when I've needed him most."

I cautiously placed my hand over his in sympathy. His shoulders relaxed at the touch. "She's a beautiful baby." And as he thought of his daughter, he brightened, the corner of his mouth twitching upwards. "I wish she had a mother." The corners of his lips slammed down into a frown just as quickly.

My heart broke at the expression on his face. I wanted to help him in some small way. "I love children," I said softly. "I'd be happy to help out if you ever needed someone."

"Really?" he said, his eyes bright with hope once more.

"Of course." The poor man was clearly on his own in all this. And I'd walked into his world like a lifesaver into a stormy sea. Because I wanted a family.

I wanted him.

After that, our instant friendship blossomed into a steady romance. And over that summer, Charles, Matilda, and I somehow turned into a family. I slotted into their world, feeling like I was always meant to belong. Charles must have felt that too because a few months later, he asked me to move to the UK with them. He said he couldn't imagine a world without me. I'd transformed all the pain in his life and made him whole again. How could I refuse an offer like that?

There was nothing holding me to San Francisco really, other than them. And if they were moving to the UK, then so was I.

It was his idea to keep the truth about Matilda's birth mother a secret when we first moved to London. Well, not a secret, he had said—but why correct anyone if they assumed she was mine? And why give Matilda that pain when she was too young to properly understand? We were moving to a new country, and I would become Matilda's mother—after all, her biological one wasn't ever coming back.

Louisa had told him she didn't have any close family. But now, after everything, I have to wonder. Why on earth would Sofia bring up Matilda's birth certificate if not for Matilda to find out that it isn't *my* name written there—but Louisa's?

Charles and I had always planned on telling her one day, but we hadn't discussed in a long time when that might be. For so long, I've told myself that she would be too young to understand, so I've kept putting off even bringing it up with Charles. But now, I don't really have that excuse anymore. At twelve, she is old enough to understand.

The problem is, and it might make me incredibly selfish to admit it, I'm not sure if I want to tell her anymore. Matilda is *my* daughter now. I'm the only mother that she has ever known; Louisa disappeared from her life when she was only six months old. I am terrified that if she knew the truth, she would see me differently.

I have no idea what to do. But what I do know is that I need to tell Charles what I overheard. I have to demand more answers about his first wife and her family. I have to know if there is anything I'm missing. Come what may.

# Chapter Twelve

Sofia and Matilda are onto popcorn by the time Charles and I are ready to sit down and eat. I should probably be encouraging them to develop more healthy habits, but my mind is full of ideas on how to approach this conversation with Charles.

He emerged bleary-eyed from his study about fifteen minutes ago and helped by selecting one of his favorite Tuscan wines to go with the meal. We'll eat atop our island bench in the kitchen—there's no need to set the large table in the dining room when it's just us eating. He pours us two large glasses, passing one to me before he slides onto a bar stool and takes a long sip.

As I serve up the spaghetti bolognese, I look back over my shoulder to see him run a hand through his hair. "Everything okay?" I ask between scooping spoonfuls into our bowls.

"Just a difficult case," he exhales heavily. "We need more evidence, or we're screwed."

I nod sympathetically as Charles starts to explain some of the intricacies of his latest case. Sometimes, I find it fascinating, but tonight, I don't want his mind lost to his latest criminals. I need it to be laser-focused on me. But, no matter what I try, I can't seem to stop his long explanation.

"Sorry," he says between mouthfuls. "I've been banging on. I know you're having a crazy time at work, too. But I'm just feeling a bit stressed about the whole thing. I can't have another case collapse." He finishes the last bite and washes everything down with another gulp of wine.

I bite my lip. Is this the best time to bring it up if he's already feeling stressed? I don't want to cause a fight. But maybe if I approach it delicately, it will be okay.

Just as I'm about to open my mouth to say something, two faces appear at the doorway, their little eyes pleading.

Sofia elbows Matilda in the ribs, and then she pipes up in her most polite voice, "May we please have some more popcorn?"

I'm about to say an automatic no—they've already had pizza and a serving of popcorn tonight—when Charles looks up and smiles indulgently.

"Why don't we all have some?" He glances at me. We've finished our meal now, so there's no real reason for me to say no. And I don't want to look like the Grinch. Especially not with Sofia watching with those hawk eyes.

"Sure," I respond. "Just this once."

Matilda beams at Sofia. Charles hops up and starts searching for a new microwaveable bag. I look down at our empty bowls and try not to sigh. Well, I'll have to try again when they've gone to bed. It's probably better that way, anyway. No listening ears.

I wash up as Charles plays host to the girls, serving up some more popcorn as they go back into the living room to finish the movie. When it's over, I decide it's time to usher the girls upstairs and shut the door on copious amounts of giggles. I'm not sure how much they will actually sleep. But there is no point in me worrying about that. It's time for Charles and me to spend some proper time together. And for him to answer my questions.

But now, by the time we finally sit down together on the sofa, I see smudges of blue under his eyes. He sips his ruby red wine and sighs in contentment. He's already finished one bottle over dinner with little help from me and is onto his second. I know he drinks to help wash away his anxieties, but sometimes I worry that he has a bit too much.

"So, shall we watch something?" He looks up at me, hopefully, the remote in his hand.

"Well, actually," I say, placing the rest of the bottle on the coffee table in front of him, "I was hoping we could catch up a bit on our new neighbor. Like you said earlier in the library."

His eyes widen as though remembering. He'd clearly forgotten that entire conversation.

"Of course," he says, and I know he's trying to keep the exhaustion out of his voice. "Come and sit with me, and I'll tell you anything you want to know." He pats the spot next to him.

My mouth twitches in a small smile as I sit down. "Thank you. Then I promise we can watch something."

His weary eyes brighten at the thought. "I'll hold you to that. So what do you want to know?"

"Well," I start carefully. I don't want to come across as accusatory when he seems to be in a talkative mood right now. I know how quickly he can shut down when a conversation starts to get difficult. "Why don't you tell me about how exactly you've gotten to know our new neighbor so well these last couple of weeks? I didn't realize you were spending so much time together."

He bristles at my last sentence. I probably went too far too soon, but I can't take it back now.

"Look," he says, leaning over to top up his glass. "I haven't spent *that* much time with her—but you were so busy. So yeah, I guess our paths have crossed a fair bit on the school run, and then Sofia came over for a last minute playdate last Saturday when you were out at work. We've chatted now and then. She doesn't know anyone else in Bristol."

I raise my eyebrows at this. I hadn't realized Sofia came over for a playdate. Have I really been that oblivious the last couple of weeks, lost in my work bubble?

"So I guess I've asked the right questions, and she's opened up to me a bit. She says she's moved here for a fresh start. She's had such a tough year with her name being plastered all over the news with those terrible rumors about how her husband died. Do you know they painted her as an upstart 'gold-digger'?" He shudders at the words. I top up my own glass to avoid his eyes. Of course, I knew about that.

"But you know she was devastated after Sir David's death," Charles continues. "She's a very private person and wanted to mourn in peace. I think she's still not over what happened. I mean, how could you be? And she couldn't even mention anything about her first husband, Sofia's father." He shakes his head in sadness. "It also sounds like there are still problems going on between her and David's son—who isn't very happy that his dad left everything to thirty-four-year-old Anna. The son is a few years older than her, closer to our age. Anyway, he's still contesting everything—that's what the problem today was. Her lawyer called about some urgent problem that he had to talk to her about immediately, and when she texted me to meet her in the library, she was beyond frantic..."

I interrupt him. "Sorry, what? She texted you to come and comfort her?"

"Jackie," he frowns. "Come on, that's the one thing you're picking up here? I'm the only person around here that she feels comfortable enough to speak to. I'm being a good neighbor and friend. She's trying to start again and look after her daughter. What's got into you? You never used to be the jealous type. I thought we'd moved on from that blip last year."

The accusation yawns between us. I bite my lip. I know, of course, why I'm being more suspicious than normal. And I think it's time for me to tell Charles why.

I cough and decide to try a different approach, "Look, it's just... Don't you think that Anna looks a little... familiar?"

"Familiar how? Because she's been in the newspapers?"

I shake my head and fiddle with my wedding ring. I glance down to watch the diamond sparkle.

"No... Now, don't get upset," I say pre-emptively, and then the rest rushes out, "but don't you think, in person, there's something about her that resembles Louisa?"

Silence greets me, so I drag my eyes up toward his. A strange look flashes across his face, but the next second, it's gone. Replaced by a deep frown.

"What are you trying to say?"

"Well, from pictures I've seen of Louisa, and now seeing Anna in real life... There's something similar about them. Like they could be related..." I stall again, searching for the right words. "I guess it made me realize that we never really talked much about Louisa's family back then. You said that she wasn't in contact with her parents, and she didn't have any other close family. But do you think there's any chance that maybe she did? That there were other relatives that you didn't know about?"

Charles shakes his head in dismay. I plow on—it's too late to go back now. "And, well, I wouldn't have mentioned it at all. But I'm really bringing it up because, well, I overheard Sofia asking Matilda about being born in San Francisco, and Sofia mentioned that they should look at her birth certificate. And why would Sofia ask Matilda about that?" I lower my voice. "Because it's the only way Matilda would find out who her mother really is. I can't help but think that Sofia's mother might have put her up to it somehow... Don't you think?"

I look up hopefully, half expecting his eyes to be full of concerned agreement.

But instead, he lunges forward. For a second, I think he's about to slap me, but then he throws his arms around my neck and pulls me into a tight hug.

"Oh, Jackie... Jackie, Jackie, Jackie," he murmurs into my ear. It tickles and sends a shiver down my spine. Then he pulls back and holds me at arm's length. "You do have a wild imagination. I promise you, you know as much as I do. Louisa didn't have any close family. Besides, you know that she was American, like you. Anna is British. So I don't know what part of the story you think you're missing, but I really did tell you as much as I knew back then."

Then his expression turns stony. "And I don't know why you're accusing poor Anna of putting her daughter up to something? The woman has already gone through so much. Why on earth would she care about Matilda's birth certificate? So please, let's drop that thought right now and not mention it again. It's beneath you to accuse a twelve-year-old girl of something like that. And besides all that, I don't think there is anything similar between Anna and Louisa, okay? You know how much it hurts me to think about... *her*."

His shoulders tremble. I know that he's doing everything possible to stay in control of his emotions. Then he adds in a cold voice, "I thought we were trying to turn over a new leaf this year? What's the point if you're only trying to see the worst of things? It's like you don't trust me at all."

My shoulders slump as he turns away from me and grabs the remote control with a sigh. He flicks on the TV, shutting this conversation down and me out.

Sirens start to wail on the screen as some action show begins.

I want to protest, but I don't know how. Because he's right—all my suspicions link back to just that: a lack of trust.

I stand to leave the room. I don't want to watch this, and I don't know what else I can say. I need some time by myself to think everything through.

Because perhaps he's right. Maybe I am jumping to conclusions. But then again, I've made it my life's study to know my husband's every tell.

And I know when he's trying to hide something.

# Chapter Thirteen

Charles came to bed late last night. I know because I'd lain awake for ages, staring at the ceiling and counting down the hours. My mother's voice whispered to me in the darkness, telling me this was what I deserved. I wasn't honest with him—so why should I expect him to be honest with me?

I'd turned away from him, a single tear slipping down my cheek at my feeling of hopelessness. It felt like my carefully planned life was starting to spiral out of my control.

But somehow, I'd fallen asleep, and now, it's Charles waking me up by pulling the heavy curtains open.

"Look, Jackie," he says brightly, "it's sunny at last."

I groan, blinking blearily up at him. He moves over to my side of the bed and sits down on the edge, holding a tray in his hand.

"I got up early and prepared my only breakfast special: coffee and a croissant. Just the way you like it." He tousles my hair at the surprise written on my face. "Look, I know I was a bit defensive and unresponsive last night. I'm sorry. Just what you said about Anna and Louisa..." he shrugs. "It shocked me, that's all. And you know how talking about Lou can be painful for me."

"It's okay," I say, reaching out a hand to grab the still-warm pastry and my chance at getting us back on track. I take a bite, the rich chocolate trickling down my throat. "Mmm, my favorite. You know they're my weakness!"

He chuckles. "I know… I must know all your weaknesses by now. And I suppose you know mine," he adds with a wink. I pause mid-chew. I know it was supposed to be a joke, but there's something forced in his delivery.

Before I have a chance to ponder anymore, Charles declares, "Right, I'd better get to the crew downstairs. Sofia and Matilda are attempting to make pancakes."

"Oh dear," I say, my nostrils flaring in alarm at the thought of the mess happening in my kitchen. I try to hop out of bed, but he pushes me back. I blink up in surprise at the force.

"No," he says firmly but adds a last-minute smile. "Let me sort it out. You relax and enjoy your breakfast in peace. Come down when you're ready."

I sigh, resigned, and make a show of settling back in. He hops up and treads out of the room with a wave. As the door shuts behind him, I take a sip of the hot coffee. Not bad, not bad. But it doesn't have the usual soothing effect of my first ritualistic morning coffee when I make it perfectly. All the same, what Charles has done is sweet—though there was something a little erratic in it. Like he was trying to make up for yesterday a bit *too* much. And his reference to knowing all my weaknesses?

I shake my head. Honestly, since Anna's arrival, I've been unable to think straight. My husband has brought me breakfast in bed, for goodness sake. My wonderful life isn't spiraling out of control.

*Look at me now, Mother!* I want to cry out. But obviously, my mother is long gone. Thank God.

I take my time enjoying my breakfast before an alert goes off on my phone. I glance down and blanch at the calendar reminder. Oh no, I'd completely forgotten. Charles's brother Freddie is coming for Sunday lunch today with his American friend, who is on the hunt for a suitable new family home in Bristol. I'd booked it in a few days ago when I'd been racing around at work and then forgot to tell Charles.

He generally likes to have some advance warning when his brother comes to visit, but he'll have to get over it. Let's just say that Charles and his brother Freddie have a bit of a love-hate relationship now. Over the years, they've slowly rebuilt the relationship they seemed to have lost around Louisa's death.

A few months after we moved to London, Freddie eventually reached out to Charles, trying to repair their damaged relationship. He said he was sorry about everything, that he'd just really struggled with the shock of Louisa's death and didn't know how to speak to Charles. He knew he'd been selfish, but he was desperate to make up for it and get to know his niece.

I was a bit nervous about the whole thing; it suited me that they were estranged in some ways—he was one of the few people who knew the truth about Matilda's birth mother. I didn't want him to jeopardize my new, happy family by spreading the real story around. But Charles reassured me; he said that he'd told Freddie that one of the conditions for coming back into his life had to be respecting his choice not to tell Matilda about Louisa yet. At least, not until she was old enough, like Charles and I had always agreed. Apparently, Freddie agreed, too, so the date was set.

When we first met, I was still prepared to dislike him on principle. But once we started talking, it seemed like we had a lot in common. And much to my surprise, over the years, we've become better friends than he often is with Charles.

He's the only one of Charles's family that we still see fairly frequently. Charles's distant father and evil stepmother had been just as described. Thankfully, we rarely see them. So even though I'd been worried about Freddie initially, over time, I came to realize that it is important for us to still have *some* family. I know what growing up without any was like, and I didn't want Matilda to have that. I want her to know her uncle, and he dotes on her, not having any children of his own.

I leap out of bed and race to the shower to start getting ready, telling myself that I'm sure both Charles and Matilda will be pleased at the surprise visit.

***

It has been quite a rush to get everything in order. Sofia was picked up by Anna while I was out at the shops. I haven't even had time to quiz Charles on how Anna seemed after her emergency lawyer appointment, nor a chance to discuss with him how sullen Sofia had seemed at breakfast when I'd momentarily rushed in to tell everyone that Uncle Freddie was coming over for Sunday lunch.

Predictably, Matilda had smiled and Charles had frowned, saying, "I wish you'd told me before."

Matilda had started animatedly telling Sofia all about her brilliant uncle, Freddie, but Sofia appeared to withdraw. It was another thing to add to the list of questions for later, though. I didn't have any time to ponder as I raced around getting everything ready.

I'm putting the finishing touches on my apple crumble when the doorbell rings. I take a second to check on the roast chicken, and the heavenly aroma hits me as I open the warm oven door. The rich bronze color glistens in the light. Perfection. As per usual.

Excited cries from Matilda greet me, and the heavy tread of large footsteps start to make their way down the hall.

I turn around just as the looming figure appears in the doorway. Freddie is so tall that he has to duck through to enter the kitchen. The top of his fair hair brushes against the tip of the arch, and I notice, as I always do, how surprising it is that Freddie's hair is so light compared to Charles's night black. At the sight of me, Freddie breaks into one of his brightest smiles—one that I'm sure has broken many a heart. He's had a lot of girlfriends but never quite settled down. I suppose it's all the moving between the States and here that he's done over the years for work. He says he's back in the UK for good now. I'll believe it when I see it.

"Look who it is, my favorite American," he says happily, his arms outstretched as he closes the gap between us in two long strides.

"Hey, what about me?" says an American voice from behind him.

I don't see the man as Freddie laughs and pulls me into an affectionate hug, dwarfing me in his strong arms. When he lets go, I look up to dazzle my most welcoming smile at the visitor in the doorway. He's as tall as Freddie, but his opposite: with dark hair and glowing, sun-kissed skin. He sweeps a hand through his hair to tousle it before smiling a wide, toothy grin. I can't help but instantly like him.

Before I can say anything, Charles steps forward from where he's been hovering by the kitchen island and loops an arm around my shoulder, pulling me tight.

"Quite the welcome, Freds," he says sarcastically, his tone as dry as sandpaper. Ah, the usual brotherly tension begins. I see Freddie open his mouth as though he is about to retort, so I step away from Charles and welcome our guest.

"Thanks for coming over—I'm Jacqueline, and this is Charles," I gesture at Charles, though it's quite obvious.

"Oh well, thank *you* for inviting me! I'm Nathaniel," he says with an open smile and outstretched hand.

He takes Charles's hand in his solid grip and then steps forward to take mine. As he shakes, I feel the warmth flow through.

Nathaniel performatively sniffs the air. "And it smells absolutely delicious in here. Wow!"

I grin, and Charles laughs, moving closer to me and sweeping me into a hug. He's being awfully affectionate today. It's terrible that I can't help but wonder why.

"Right," Freddie says, changing the subject. "Well, where has that niece of mine got to?"

As though on cue, Matilda reappears at the door. "Uncle Freddie," Matilda demands, tossing her dark hair over her shoulder. "I have to show you my new books."

"There we go, I'm summoned!" Freddie calls back over his shoulder as he's pulled away. "But let me know if you need any help, Jax!" And then he's gone. I let a small smile creep across my face at the nickname that only he calls me. *So* British.

I whiz around to face Charles and Nathaniel with a smile. "Do take a seat at the island bench, Nathaniel; Charles will get you a drink."

Charles smiles. "Of course, what'll it be?"

"Oh, whatever you have going," Nathaniel says jovially. "But I did bring a bottle of my favorite Californian red." He leans over to pull it out of a bag and presents it to Charles. Charles's eyes widen in delight.

"Fabulous," he responds. "One of my favorites, too! Well, I'd better go and find something equally special for later. I keep my best stuff in the cellar."

And with that, he strides to the door. I sigh, knowing he will potentially be down there for years now, selecting the right wines. I always ask him to start earlier, but he's never *quite* ready—forever working on a case.

Instead, I must put on a happy face. Especially when I have a potential new client.

"So," I say, taking my apron off and walking around to sit next to Nathaniel. "I hear you're moving to Bristol from Vermont. That's quite a journey!"

Nathaniel laughs. "Oh, is that what Freds told you? Not quite. I'm originally from a sleepy little town in Vermont, but I've been living in the UK for a while. Up in Edinburgh with my wife and children."

"A lovely city," I respond with a nod. "Is your wife Scottish?"

"She... she..." Nathaniel hesitates, frowning as though trying to find the words. "Well, no, she's not Scottish... *wasn't* Scottish. She died last year."

"Oh," I place a hand on my chest as I curse Freddie. Why didn't he warn me? "I'm so sorry for your loss."

As though I summoned him with my thoughts, Freddie reappears at the door. I shoot daggers at him, but he ignores them. He does seem to have heard my last words, though, and he walks over and claps a hand on Nathaniel's shoulder.

"Yeah, how are you going?" Freddie asks, ignoring my direct stare. I think he's trying to sound sympathetic, but it comes out a little uncaring. Why is he asking so directly in front of me?

"Thank you," Nathaniel responds, looking at me. He looks up at Freddie. "Yeah... well. I've been better." He looks away from us to hide his emotion.

"Of course," I murmur uselessly. I'm not sure what else I can say to give this man comfort.

"But I still want them to be close to their grandparents—which is partially why I want to move to Bristol. We've been up in Scotland for a couple of years, but Julia's parents live in Devon—so Bristol is a bit closer. Plus, of course, I couldn't give up the chance to work with Freddie again."

Freddie smiles and puffs out his chest. I try not to cringe. This is not the moment for him to be gloating about his work.

"The girls are staying in Devon with them right now," Nathaniel continues. "Until I can secure us a nice place to rent, maybe just outside of Bristol. The girls love having space to run around in. Freddie says you'll be able to help us with that?"

"Of course," I say softly. "Bristol is a lovely place for families."

"I'm glad to hear it," he adds, but with a note of sadness as though remembering that his family is no longer complete. I've completely put my foot in it.

"Here," I say, trying to change the subject. "Why don't I give you my number, and then you can get in touch when you're ready? I can think of a few places already!"

"Thank you, Jacqueline." He turns back to me, and I swear there's a twinkle of a tear in his eyes. "That's very kind of you."

As he opens his phone to pass it over so I can add my number, I spy a picture of two girls and a young woman smiling at the camera. The poor man, I think to myself. Life can be so cruel. Don't I know it.

At that moment, Charles appears at the door, two bottles in hand. "I've found the perfect thing for later!" he declares, but then pauses to frown as he sees us all gathered together around Nathaniel's phone. "All okay?" he asks.

"Yes, of course," I say, jumping up in a distraction. I'll tell Charles later about Nathaniel's sad story. He doesn't have to go over it all again now. "We were just talking shop. But great—you have some bubbles to start now. Let's get our guest a glass, then."

At first, the lunch goes smoothly. Matilda, Freddie and I are all in good moods, and Nathaniel is warm and funny. He charms Matilda, in particular, with his stories about his grandfather's maple syrup farm. Her eyes bulge wide with excitement.

Matilda also chats merrily away to Uncle Freddie about *everything* that has happened since she'd last seen him. But Charles has inexplicably fallen into one of his more withdrawn moods and sits at the head of the table, barely saying a word to any of us or our guest. I wonder if it just has to do with work or something else? I frown at him, but he either doesn't notice or doesn't care.

I'm keen for the lunch to be over, and it's with relief that I scrape together the last remains of the apple crumble in the well-worn dish.

"Oh, Jax," Freddie declares, leaning back in his chair. "You've outdone yourself with this one—I honestly can't squeeze in another bite!"

Matilda and I laugh, but the scrape of chair legs at the head of the table has us all swiveling toward Charles. When I see the flush on his face, I think he's about to storm out. But instead, he chuckles.

"Oh well," he says. "All the more for me!" He swoops over to take the heavy dish out of my arms with a smile. I feel relieved; the flush must be from all the wine he's been drinking stealthily. But at least it appears to have put him in a better mood again. I wonder what had caused him to withdraw over lunch.

"Hey, what about our guest!" I say, swiping at him.

"Oh, I think I'm stuffed, too," Nathaniel says with a smile. "But it was incredible." I beam in response. I look across at Charles to see if he's caught the compliment. But he's put down the dish and is busy frowning at something on his phone.

"Thank you for lunch," Matilda adds in her most polite voice. "May I go over and see Sofia now? She promised she'd show me some books in their library today..."

Matilda's cheeks blossom into a shade of a red tomato at her words—as though remembering what happened the last time she ventured into that library. I refuse to let my own embarrassment at the memory show on my face—not with Freddie and Nathaniel around. I don't want them to know about the library episode.

"Matilda," I say, starting to stack the plates. "You saw Sofia this morning, and your Uncle Freddie is here with a guest. Perhaps you could go over later this week?"

I turn away from her to fetch the wine bottle to top up the glasses when Matilda blurts out in a whine, "But I *promised*! I have to go!"

My head whips back to her in surprise—Matilda never talks back.

Charles doesn't seem to notice, still lost to his phone, but next to me, Freddie also stiffens at Matilda's rebuttal. We both know how unlike her this is. Nathaniel politely looks away from our family discussion.

I slide back into my seat, thinking of a gentler way to rephrase my "no" when Freddie leans toward me.

"Honestly," he mutters. "Don't stop her for our sakes. It sounds like Matilda has made a wonderful new friend. And a promise is a promise, after all. Isn't it, Jax?"

I swallow, feeling my cheeks start to flush, and my heart begins to race. I can sense Freddie's sea-green eyes staring at me from my peripheral vision. I refuse to turn and face him. I can't believe he's just made such a blatant reference to *that promise—that stupid drunken promise*—in front of everyone at this table. But especially in front of Charles. I swore him to secrecy.

Taking a quick sip of water to buy myself some time, under the table, I pinch my thumb and forefinger into the nook of my left hand to try and calm my rising panic. *It's probably just a turn of phrase, Jacqueline. Pull yourself together—he was so drunk—he wouldn't even remember last Christmas, and what you said...*

I look back up at Matilda, pasting a frozen smile onto my face.

"Okay... Matilda, you can clear the plates from the table," I gesture around, "and then you can run over. But only if Anastasia doesn't mind. I don't want you showing up and making a nuisance of yourself."

Matilda beams as she bounces up from the table, grabbing her plate. "Thank you!"

At last, Charles looks up from his phone and registers the conversation. "I'll help you clear the plates," Charles declares, getting to his feet.

Matilda beams up at him with one of her prettiest smiles. Of course, he helps her once, and he's a superhero—I do the cooking, the laundry, the schoolwork, and even freeze my butt off watching her netball game, and I get barely an acknowledgment. They take the towering pile of plates out of the room and toward the kitchen, leaving me, Freddie, and Nathaniel alone.

The grandfather clock in the hall, a lumbering antique given to us by Charles's parents for our wedding, chimes three. I sigh and sink back into my chair at last to take a sip of my ruby red wine. I don't normally drink very much, as I hate feeling out of control, but right now, I need something to take the edge off.

Everyone is acting a little out of sorts today—from Charles being up and down, to Matilda answering back, to Freddie referencing *the promise* that we unofficially had sworn to never speak about again. Why can't we all just be a normal family in front of a guest?

It all might be nothing—but I can't help but think that the only thing that's changed since the last time we were all together is the arrival of a certain mother and daughter across the street. But of course, Freddie doesn't even know anything about them.

"So, Jax," he starts. While Matilda and Charles have been clearing the table, Freddie has vacated the seat next to me and moved to sit next to Nathaniel, who is opposite me. My eyes move away from the door and back over to Freddie's face. "You think you can help my buddy here find a place?" He loops an arm over Nathaniel's shoulder.

For a moment, I'm startled by the new direction of conversation; my thoughts had been so lost in my family and the woman across the street.

"Oh, of course," I say quickly as I notice a little drop of wine has escaped from the edge of the bottle and onto the mahogany table. I swipe at it with my napkin before it can stain. I cannot *stand* marks.

Freddie follows my movement but kindly doesn't comment. He's always appeared understanding of my compulsive cleaning. Much more so than Charles, who frequently complains about my obsessive need to vacuum the house every day. But he doesn't understand—when I know the house is clean, it means we have order. And then we are safe. And most of all, I am safe from my mother's taunting voice.

"Well, as well as Nate, do you have time to help out *another* friend of mine?" he casts a glance over at Nathaniel. "You know Aaron?"

"Yeah, of course," Nathaniel replies with a roll of his eyes.

"Ha! What do you mean by that?" Freddie asks with a laugh.

"Oh, I think you know…"

Just then, Charles walks back into the dining room and surveys the three of us. He registers my flushed face and Freddie's grin.

"Having fun without me?" Charles asks with a flick of his eyebrow.

"Just chatting about work," Freddie says, grabbing the bottle of wine and topping up all our glasses. I'm surprised that mine is already empty. I've had more than I should.

Charles rolls his eyes as he drops back into his seat at the head of the table. "Not sure I want to hear about your latest venture, Freds."

I fidget in my seat at the awkward declaration. Freddie's latest tech business venture is failing. One of the other reasons why he is back in the UK now is to gather more investment. But Charles shouldn't so completely dismiss Freddie's work in front of a potential new co-worker.

"Charles," I hiss at him.

Nathaniel politely smiles as Freddie laughs. But even to me, it sounds hollow.

"It's okay. I know you sailed out of this world a long time ago and back into the oh-so-virtuous world of criminal law. It must make you feel so warm and fuzzy when you represent all those lovely murderers."

I flinch. But to my amazement, Charles snickers. "Oh Freds, my work is something you'll never understand."

I'm sure Freddie is going to hit back even harder. But instead, he lifts his refilled glass in a toast. "Cheers to that," he says, and they clink their glasses together. The brothers both turn to me, their arms still outstretched. I mask my surprise—I will never understand their relationship—how they can go from being at each other's throats one moment to joking the next. I guess that's just siblings for you, I think to myself—not for the first time.

I hastily pick up my glass to cheers them both, as does Nathaniel. We exchange glances with a look of shared understanding. Freddie and Charles smile—their identical broad grins contrasting with the dark red wine in their glasses. In so many ways, they look so different, from their hair to their eyes, but when they smile, the similarity is stark.

"To family," Charles declares solemnly.

Freddie echoes his remark. I say nothing, unsure of what to make of this whole scene playing out in front of me. Instead, I take another long gulp of wine. A rich, woody scent hits my nose, and the taste of cherry flickers on my tongue—God, that tastes good. Why don't I drink much again?

I'm musing so much that I almost miss Freddie's question about our neighbors. "So I hear you have some infamous new neighbors?" I'd told Freddie by text as soon as I'd found out that Anastasia Drummond was moving in. He'd known I'd been obsessed with finding out since I'd sold the house. We had our curiosity in common.

"Yes, well, I wouldn't like to call them that." Charles steps in for us before I have a chance to speak. "We simply have some nice new neighbors across the street. Anna, and her daughter, Sofia. Poor Anna was recently widowed..." His sentence trails off as he stares past us, through the window, and across to the looming new gates in front of the house opposite, as though imagining "Poor Anna" inside right at this second.

At Charles's words, Nathaniel stiffens, and Freddie rolls his eyes.

"What's that look about?" Charles directs the question at his brother.

"Well, everyone knows *how* she became widowed, of course. And let's just say Nate, and I know a thing or two about Anastasia Drummond... and I think you should both be very careful."

"*What?*" I ask in surprise. Why hadn't Freddie said anything to me in a text? But Charles speaks over me.

"What on earth are you suggesting, Freddie? She's lovely; her name was dragged through the mud about something she didn't do, and she only wanted to grieve for her husband. It seems like she's *still* going through hell..."

I frown at Charles's defense of her, and Freddie and Nathaniel exchange a serious look. Nathaniel nods as though telling Freddie to be the spokesperson for them both.

"Well, I wanted to talk to you about this in person." Freddie looks at Charles and me in turn—as though trying to explain why he never told me by text. "Nate and I are both good friends with Jasper Drummond—David's son—and he has a bit of a different story, it seems. In fact, Anastasia seems like quite the gold-digger. Jasper was in my year at school, don't you remember, Charles?"

"Oh, I try my best not to remember the crowd you were mixed up with at school," Charles says, and Freddie looks genuinely surprised.

"Right..." Freddie responds with another eye roll. "Well, anyway, I met Anastasia a few times before everything happened. And let's say that *unpleasant* doesn't begin to describe how she was with me."

"Oh, spare me," Charles barks. "Just because she didn't fall at your feet like most women, you think she was 'unpleasant'—get over yourself. And as if she's a gold-digger. If she were, wouldn't she have moved somewhere a bit more glamorous than Bristol for her next target?" He scoffs.

I tap the edge of my glass in a staccato rhythm, trying to find something to defuse the situation like I usually do. But I come up blank. Charles has never had much of a filter when it comes to Freddie. But this, especially in front of a guest, is a bit much.

"Why are you defending her?" Freddie arches an eyebrow, "Haven't you known her for what... five minutes?"

Nathaniel swirls his wine carefully in his glass. I can practically feel the awkwardness rolling off him. He might also not be a big fan of Anna Drummond, but it doesn't seem like he wants to get involved in this spat, either.

Charles tuts back at Freddie, completely oblivious. "Like you would have spoken to her for much longer than that. She's been nothing but kind to us, hasn't she, Jacqueline?" He swivels his gaze toward me. I take a sip of my wine in answer—unable to respond one way or the other. I wish I was anywhere but here.

Charles's eyes continue to bore into mine when his phone rings. He glances down at the number. "It's my client... Sorry, this is urgent. I have to take this." He stands up from his chair. "Let's just leave Anna alone. She's an innocent woman trying to recover." He looks at me with disappointment, furrowing his brow as he walks away. He pulls the phone up to his ear and shuts the door behind him with a slam.

Immediately, I turn to face Nathaniel. "I am *so* sorry for my husband. I don't know what's gotten into him."

Nathaniel waves his hand and smiles with that friendly grin. "Honestly, no need to apologize. Freddie told me that he can be a little direct..."

"That's one way of putting it." I grimace at Freddie.

"I actually said that he can be a total dick," Freddie says, with a finger raised in the air as though he is a teacher correcting the class.

With that, I can't help but burst into laughter at the absurdity. When I finally get my giggles under control, I turn back to Nathaniel. "I'm still very sorry. I think he's been incredibly stressed at work lately and is letting off some steam."

"Seriously, don't worry," Nathaniel replies. "And I can understand where he's coming from. Anna appears to be a lovely woman at first. But as Freddie says, appearances can be deceiving. And when you talk to our friend Jasper, well, unfortunately, he has a very different story." He shrugs as though in apology for his thoughts. "I'm sorry, but would you mind directing me to the restroom?"

"Oh, of course," I say, standing up on reflex. He looks at me, puzzled. Oh god, I hope he didn't think I was about to follow him. "It's just down the corridor and on the left," I say, trying not to blush, though I can feel my cheeks redden.

He smiles and turns to leave, leaving Freddie and I on our own.

"I wish Charles wouldn't embarrass us in front of guests," I sigh, flopping back into my seat dramatically.

We exchange knowing glances, and Freddie shrugs. "Don't look so surprised, Jax. This is classic behavior from ole Chuck."

"What do you mean?" I'm reaching for my glass again when I realize it's empty. Freddie leans over the table to grab the bottle. He pours me a generous measure and then helps himself before leaning back into his chair, stretching his broad arms behind his back.

"Oh, you know, his usual martyr routine. He's the criminal law barrister, fighting any perceived injustices—even little ones like this. And he's always loved trying to 'save' women by showing them *his* way of seeing the world."

I bristle at his words, crossing my arms over my chest. He doesn't seem to notice as he slugs his wine, almost finishing the entire glass in one go.

He tops himself up before adding in a softer tone, "Look, I'm sorry, Jax, that was blunt. But you know it's true," he adds meaningfully.

I swirl my glass in silence. Reluctantly, I have to admit that I know exactly what he means. When Charles and I met, he seemed like an oasis to me in the middle of the desert that was my life. He'd been struggling after Louisa's death, and other than trying to start building my new career in real estate, I really had no one in San Francisco. I'd been running away from my past, and he'd come along just at the right time.

Charles provided a safe harbor, and he brought me back to shore. Other than his shock over Matilda's birth and his trauma surrounding Louisa's death, he was so sure of himself. I loved the way he was so confident in his beliefs. If he thought something was right, it was. If he didn't, it was wrong. It was refreshing to have such clarity after floating for so long.

But now, I am put back together. And because of that, what I once loved so much in Charles, I have begun to find grating. Being with someone who only wants to see the world their way is exhausting. But that isn't what Freddie meant. He wasn't talking about how *I* felt. He was talking about what his brother might be subconsciously feeling. And I could quite clearly see that, yes, there was another woman adrift on the other side of the street. I could see how tempting it must be for Charles to want to "help" her now, too.

"That doesn't mean that anything might happen between them, Freddie." I frown into my wine. I don't want to meet his gaze. I can't believe I even have to say these words out loud. "He's faithful to me. He's *always* been faithful to me." I can sense the fire blazing in my eyes as I look back at him defensively. Perhaps it will imprint my belief in Charles's fidelity into Freddie's mind.

"That's not what you said last Christmas." I flinch in shock. He *does* remember what I told him. About everything that happened that night in London. I'd sworn him to secrecy. I try to catch his eye, but he's not looking at me; he's gazing out the window. "So tell yourself whatever you want, Jax, but I can only say that I've known my brother for a long time. And I can see the signs clear as day..." he sweeps his arm out dramatically as he directs my gaze toward the window.

I gulp as I follow Freddie's hand. On the very edge of our front lawn stand two people. They're almost out of sight as they hover underneath the large blossoming tree that meets the start of our tree-lined street. It is undeniably Anna and Charles. He must have stepped outside to take his call, and somehow, Anna had come to meet him. Has she been watching from her window and lying in wait? Or was the call even from Anna herself?

Charles has his hands in his pockets, making a casual gesture as he shrugs. I know that shrug; it's his "it's nothing" expression. And I can see how Anna twirls one strand of her sleek hair in her finger and then behind her ear as she touches his arm. Her hand lingers there for a second or two longer than it ought.

I feel sick to my stomach, but I can't look away. But Freddie lets out a low whistle, and I whip my head back to face him. My heart is racing—Charles cannot fall for another woman. Especially not that woman, who is quite clearly up to... *something*. My perfect life cannot fall apart. I refuse to let it.

"What?" I snap at Freddie in my most practiced tone. *Do not let anyone see a weakness.* "She must have wanted to thank him for having Sofia over last night," I add.

"Tell yourself whateverrr you like," Freddie says after taking another long gulp of wine. "But she is quite the looker, don't you think? And I wonder if you thought the same thing as me the first time you saw her..."

I roll my eyes, bringing my own glass to my lips, "And what's that?"

"Well, I've never been able to quite put my finger on it, but there's something about her that reminds me of Louisa."

My hand freezes midway off the table. I quickly place the glass safely back down and tuck my hands out of sight. I don't want him to see them shaking. Perhaps I should be relieved that Freddie also thinks that there's something similar. It means I'm not just imagining things.

And in that case, why is Charles trying to make me dismiss the connection? It makes me think that he really is trying to hide something. But I don't want Freddie getting involved. This is my marriage and my puzzle to solve. Freddie has a habit of blowing everything out of proportion. I have to figure it out in my own quiet way.

"I don't know what you're talking about," I manage to say without stammering. My head is now starting to spin. Is it from the wine or these strange revelations? "Why are you being like this?"

Freddie scoffs. "Like what, Jax? I just want you to see the truth." A note of desperation enters his tone. "Charles has always been great at playing the good guy and getting people to think what he wants them to..." He looks back to the open window.

"Not as good as me," I can't help but mutter under my breath.

His head whips back around. "What was that?"

I can feel my cheeks start to flush. Oh god, this alcohol has dragged me well out of control. I shouldn't have said that out loud. "Nothing."

He stares at me meaningfully, and it takes everything in me not to break his stare.

Standing, he wobbles before sweeping around the table to the seat next to mine. He sits down and grabs my hand, forcing me to look him in the eyes.

"Come on, Jax. I'm here for you. You can be honest with me—about how things are with you two, what you're feeling, and everything. Don't you remember our promise at Christmas?"

That cursed promise—that stupid drunken promise. When I told him about that ill-fated early December trip to London and we swore we'd tell each other the truth. Most especially, that I would tell him if ever things were on the rocks with Charles. Freddie said that he'd be there for me no matter what.

But I know that if Charles ever knew we had such a pact, he would go ballistic. I know his relationship with his brother; he would see it as the worst betrayal if he knew that I saw Freddie as such a close friend and that I promised to share secrets with him.

"Stop, Freddie, I'm Charles's wife. And he has to be my first priority. I can't betray his trust by talking about him behind his back."

His green eyes look at me sadly, and he says in a voice as soft as silk, "But can you trust him? I don't want you to get hurt. I've stood by before..." He shakes his head to stop himself from saying anything more. Or as though the memory is too painful. I open my mouth to ask what he means when he goes on, "And I see you, Jax. I see the show you put on for the rest of the world. You know that you can trust me."

We're so close now I can feel the heat radiating off him in this cold room. He's looking at me with such care that I know even though his words were harsh before, he means the best. But then he leans toward me and brushes a stray curl away from my face, his fingers trailing slowly along the edge of my cheek. The gesture is too close, too intimate, and I spring back as though I've been electrocuted, the scrape of my chair screeching along the wooden floor.

I'm flustered. I know Freddie can be a touchy-feely person when he's drunk, so he probably doesn't mean anything by the gentle action. But I can't help it as I bite out, "Why on earth would I trust a man who can't even keep his hands to himself?"

A flush of red stains his cheeks as though I've slapped him. In some ways, I suppose I have. He jumps up, at a loss for words. The only thing he can do is stagger to the door. He knows he's been dismissed.

"Jax—I didn't mean anything by it. I'm sorry. I've had too much to drink."

At that moment, Nathaniel walks back into the room.

"Everything okay?" he asks with a question on his face.

"Yes, of course," Freddie says automatically, and I plaster a smile onto my own face, wishing I was anywhere but here. "But Nate, I think you might have to drive me home now as the designated driver. It seems I've had a little too much to drink."

Nathaniel looks confused, but Freddie walks through the door without a backward glance. Shame rushes through me. Even though I know I didn't cause the awkward scene. That was Freddie.

"Can I help you clean up?" Nathaniel asks gently. The kindness in his voice almost makes me want to cry.

"No, honestly, thank you, though. And apologies again for my family. We're not normally so... dysfunctional."

He laughs. "Not at all. You've never met mine!" I smile weakly in response. "And I'll text you to organize those viewings," he continues. "I'm looking forward to working with you, Jacqueline," he says with a wave, and then he turns to follow Freddie out toward the front door.

I slump back in my chair and bury my face in my hands, feeling like my ordered world is truly slipping out of my control, all because of Anna's arrival. Everything was as perfect as I could make it in our little family before she arrived, and now it's like she's sprinkled poison on us all.

I stare out of the window to where Charles is starting to walk back to the house. Anna has already disappeared back through her gates.

I stare daggers at her house, wishing I could evaporate her out of our lives. And that's when it dawns on me: what I have to do. If Anna weren't here, my husband wouldn't be chasing after her. If Anna weren't here, everything would go back to normal. If Anna weren't here, my life would be perfect again.

It's clear to me now that Anna has to go. All I need to do is figure out how.

# Chapter Fourteen

It's mid-April already, and it really is the cruelest month because, unfortunately, not much has changed in the two weeks since lunch with Freddie.

The only small positive is that spring has finally sprung. The bright yellow daffodils have shot up from the grass, proud and tall. I wish I was feeling as confident about my own life. Every day, I do my confidence mantra and promise that I will make everything go back to normal. But as I sweep open the curtains each morning, the first thing I see is Anna's front door mocking me.

I tried a deep dive of her on the internet, trying to dig up any extra dirt. But I couldn't find anything more than I'd found previously. Then again, I haven't had much time to search as work has been crazy. For the first few days after Freddie's abrupt departure, Charles was up in London for a trial. Even though his being away made things difficult with Matilda on school break, it also meant he had no time to see our dear neighbor. So I was feeling better about that.

But all last week, he's been at home. I should have been pleased. Except he's been hanging out with Matilda, Sofia, and, of course, Anastasia—while I've been stuck running around at work. He's even started to help Anna out with her garden. Surely she has enough money to afford a gardener? But yet again, she's making it clear that she likes having him around. *My* husband.

As I knead the dough for the fresh pasta I'm making for lunch today, I try to still my mind as the rhythm takes over. *Deep breaths, Jacqueline. Deep breaths.* I let the earthy scent and the thump, thump, thump of my hands against the wooden board be my anchor. I almost lose myself in the moment—letting everything slip away—when a loud beep and buzzing noise interrupts my meditation. I glance along our little island bench toward the corner where I left my phone, cursing myself for not putting it on silent. But the name that flashes up makes me pause, and all peace that I'd momentarily gained vanishes.

It's Freddie.

We haven't spoken since his final parting shot the other weekend. I told Charles that Freddie and Nathaniel had dashed off due to an urgent work problem. Charles had rolled his eyes and muttered that Freddie was trying to compete with him. Even though it irked me that Charles thought the world revolved around him—yet again—I was happy enough for him to come to that conclusion. I didn't want him to guess the real reason that Freddie had run.

I hurry to the sink to wash my hands, cringing at the screech of the hot tap. Charles promised he would be sorting the plumber this week—but yet again, it hasn't eventuated. Too busy playing helper to Anna, I think darkly. I will have to do it myself. Again.

But I push these thoughts out of my mind as I twirl around, grabbing at the tea towel knotted at my waist to dry my hands. I quickly scan Freddie's text:

> J, I'm sorry about what I said. You know I can be an idiot, and I didn't mean a word. Please forgive this drunken fool. I'm back from another week in NYC, and I have more presents for Matilda (and this time, one for you—something suitably caffeinated). So hopefully I can buy your forgiveness if not given willingly. Ha. F

I can't help but smile as I scan his message again. Oh, he knows how to snare me. And relief washes over me at his olive branch. We can move on and go back to normal—forget that the whole conversation even happened.

I start to type back, my fingers flying in my haste to reply:

> Ah, the way to my heart. You know I can forgive any manner of sin when coffee from back home is involved! Consider everything forgotten. When can I retrieve my prize?

I press send with a grin. But as I scan my message again, I start to chew on the bottom of my lip. Reading it back, I regret referencing anything to do with my "heart" after that weird moment between us. I was just so relieved to be moving on from it that I didn't think twice when I was typing. I wish I could hit "unsend," but now it's too late.

The clock in the kitchen ticks by in a steady beat, and I hate how long it's taking him to reply. But then my phone buzzes:

> Ha I knew it! How about next Saturday? I have another present for you… My friend Jasper, your esteemed neighbor's stepson, is host-

> ing an Easter BBQ. He'd love to host you, Charlie Boy and Matilda. Nate will be there, and the other friend I mentioned who needs help with finding a new home. It should be a fantastic day—they always go all out on the Easter egg hunt. What do you say? Go on… whatever C says. I dare you. ;)

I frown, reading Freddie's message again to digest it. It will be good to catch up with Nathaniel again. Since we last met, I've shown him a few homes, and he's signed the lease for one to start immediately. It would be nice to see how he's going. Plus, the chance of finding another potential client is too good to miss.

And, of course, the primary opportunity is laid out on a silver platter: the chance to learn more about Jasper. The way that Freddie has phrased it makes it seem as though Jasper is very keen to meet us, too. Interesting. I tap my finger on the edge of the countertop, thinking. I will have to convince Charles that this is a good idea… But he can never resist a party. Perhaps I won't tell him *whose* party it is until we arrive. Potentially risky—but this is a chance I can't miss. And Freddie knows it.

A screech out the kitchen window drags my eyes away from the phone. Two cats are fighting on the thick brick wall separating our yard from the one behind. One tortoiseshell, the other black as night. The tortoiseshell pounces, leaping hard at the black cat. It jumps away just in time, and I watch them both leap off the wall and back down into the leafy garden beyond.

I smile at the thought of the tortoiseshell hot on the heels of the black cat. That's exactly the sign I needed. And before I can overthink it, I type out a simple message:

Yes. It's a plan. Send me the details.

Replacing the phone on the countertop, I return to my fluffy white dough. I start to knead it out as I think through my plan of action, determined to be the one that comes out on top.

If Jasper can give me any insight into Anna's potential lies then it is definitely worth the trip.

***

The next week flies by, and suddenly, bursts of emerald green and flashes of sunflower yellow whiz past us as we zoom along the winding lanes and deep into the heart of the English countryside. But I don't have a chance to appreciate the glimpses of ancient woods or sweeping views, as I'm too preoccupied with moderating Charles's complaining.

"Why did you agree for us to drive all this way again, Jacqueline? Whose house is this anyway? I had no idea the roads would be so terrible. I hope this party is worth it..." Charles prattles on, only pausing for breath and to take another sudden sharp turn down a hidden lane.

"Slow down," whines Matilda. "I feel sick." I look back to see her staring out the window intently and clutching her stomach.

"We'll be there soon," I say over my shoulder, then turn to Charles. "I don't know who the hosts are, but Freddie begged for us to go. He said it would be an incredible party—and besides, like I said, I need to meet these potential buyers. It'll be an amazing chance to make some new connections."

Charles harrumphs in acknowledgment. "All I'm saying is this is going to be a nightmare to navigate back—especially after a couple of drinks!"

I sigh. Of course, it comes back to this. I want to snap at him to control himself, but I need him on my side. So I say in a soft voice, "*I'll be the designated driver. That way you don't have to worry and can just enjoy the party. How does that sound?*"

He harrumphs again but in a more agreeable tone. I've clearly overcome that latest barrier. Not drinking is fine by me, anyway. After overdoing it the other weekend when Freddie came over and feeling so horribly out of control, I've gone back to my strict limited drinking rule. Today, I need to be in complete control if I'm going to find out more about Anna from the rest of the Drummond family.

But as we get closer to our destination—the sat-nav declaring we are only five minutes out—my stomach starts to flutter. When Charles finds out whose house it is, I suspect he won't be happy. Though he had said he didn't even remember Jasper Drummond from school—so maybe it won't matter. Either way, I'm sure Charles won't go ballistic at the party, but there's a possibility that his displeasure will come through later when we leave. Hopefully, he will have a fantastic time, Matilda will make some new friends, and I'll be able to find out what I need to.

At last, a set of ornate iron gates the length of a double-decker bus come into view. The ironwork is intricately crisscrossed around a large crest. From behind the gates, a long drive beckons with swaying trees overhanging. If this is just the entrance, I can't even begin to think what the inside might look like.

Even Charles seems impressed, giving a low whistle as he comes to a stop outside the front. "Who are these friends?" he says, more to himself than anyone else.

But before I can give a vague reply, an intercom buzzes to life. Charles quickly opens the window. "Hello," the disembodied voice says. "Welcome to Edgecliff House. Your name?"

"Oh, umm…" Even Charles is flustered, but he eventually says, "Charles, Jacqueline, and Matilda Banks."

After a short pause and a crackle on the intercom, the heavy gates swing back open. Charles slowly puts his foot on the pedal to enter this incredible family estate. He runs one hand through his ruffled black hair. His tell that he's feeling a little bit nervous. I look down at my bright yellow dress, suddenly feeling like a beacon shouting, "We do not belong here". It's nice enough, with its capped sleeves and little belt that cinches in my waist—but I don't think that the other guests will be wearing something so simple. Glancing back, I thank God that I convinced Matilda to wear her purple dress with pink flowers. Charles is immaculately dressed as always; that man only ever leaves the house in a collared shirt unless he's working out or gardening.

At last, we emerge from under the shade of the trees, and the house appears in full view. It looks like something out of a fairytale—it's not a castle, but it's not *just* a house either. Smatterings of ivy curl along the edges and frame the pretty façade. It's two stories tall, with picturesque gables reaching up high to the sky above. And the breadth sweeps far across a huge expanse—with arched windows studded all along it.

All this I see from my window as the drive turns sharply away from the house. We pass by the large front lawn, which must be at least the size of two tennis courts. It's perfectly mown, and even from this distance, I can see a line of pretty hedgerows bordering the front of the house with pops of color. If this is only the front lawn, I can't wait to see the garden at the back. The drive takes us to what must be a purpose-built carpark. At least a dozen cars are already parked here, ranging from Land Rovers, Mini Coopers, and regular people movers like ours. I breathe a sigh of relief. We surely can't be that out of place, then. Perhaps it's just the Drummonds themselves that are this wealthy.

It makes me wonder again about Anna. I know that it hadn't been proved that she was involved in Sir David's death, but seeing the wealth of this family estate, I can imagine where the papers got the idea from. Especially if she'd really come from nowhere.

At last, Charles parks under the shade of a magnificent oak tree, and we all emerge from the car. Matilda shuffles her feet and looks down at the ground. I meet Charles at the boot, where he's retrieving the wine and chocolates we brought. Thank God I never go anywhere empty-handed. At least my mother taught me one useful thing.

As he stands up to his full height, the springtime sun makes flecks of silver glisten in his otherwise dark hair. I look up to meet his gaze, and he lifts his brows.

"Well, I think you'll be right. This will be some party." And with that, he turns on his heels and starts a brisk march toward the house. I glance back at Matilda, who is still hesitating.

"Come on then—I'm sure there will be a library in a place like this. Let's go see, shall we?" Normally, that's enough to bring a small smile to her face.

But she crosses her arms and looks me dead in the eye. A look passes over her face that I've never seen before as she delivers the only two words that could cause my curated calm to falter.

"You lied."

# CHAPTER FIFTEEN

I'm frozen. My palms are clammy, and my heart is starting to hammer in my chest. What does she know? What lies has my girl uncovered?

"I saw your messages to Uncle Freddie," she adds before I have formulated a response. "I know that he told you whose house this is. Why did you lie and say you didn't know? And why are we at Sofia's evil step-family's house? I know it's called Edgecliff House. She told me all about the family. How horrible they've been to her and her mum."

I step back in shock and panic. I do not want Matilda to read my messages.

"Matilda," I hiss, grabbing her arm. "I can't believe you looked through my phone. Why would you do that?"

All I can do is shake my head, lost for words at Matilda's transformation. I can only put it down to Sofia's influence. It *must* be that. I want to scream at her—but I know that if I come across as defensive, then she'll just think that she's right.

"Matilda," I say calmly. "Tell me why you did that."

"Whatever," she rolls her eyes and then tugs her arm sharply out of mine. She sweeps past me, her long hair flapping over one shoulder. By the time I regather my presence of mind, she has already caught up to Charles.

I rush down the path behind them, trying not to trip on the cobblestones in my wedge heels. This conversation isn't over. Matilda has never done anything like this before. It feels like Sofia is trying to put Matilda up to something. I need to know why.

By the time I finally catch up, Charles and Matilda are almost at the looming front door, framed by a large stone arch. The walls are sparkling clean sandstone, and a chorus of bright yellow, purple, and pink flowers dance along the front of the house in the slight breeze.

While Charles knocks loudly on the brass knocker, I lean down and whisper into Matilda's ear.

"Excuse me, you can't just walk off like that." It's dark under the arch, and I can't see her facial expression, but she turns her head away from me. Her only acknowledgment that she heard me.

I bristle and am about to speak again when I hear a yawning creak and turn to see the elegant green door opening wide.

"Fancy seeing you here..." a familiar voice drawls from the entry.

I look up as Charles says, "Hello, Freds, why are you answering the door? The company going that badly that you've turned into a butler for the day now?"

"Ha... Surprise," Freddie says theatrically with some jazz hands. Then he waves a beckoning hand toward Matilda and me. "Hello, ladies, come on then, let's join the party!" And without another word, he twirls, his tall frame disappearing back into the house.

Charles follows, but Matilda is quickest of all, darting after her uncle. No doubt eager to escape me. Well, she's unlikely to say anything to Charles—she won't want to admit to him about snooping on my phone. I'll have to talk to her later. Now, I have to focus on why I've really come here: to get answers about Anna from Sir David's family. I must put on my brightest smile and the dazzling Jacqueline show. It always works.

Pulling my shoulders back, I step out of the gloomy entry and into the house at last. As soon as I'm inside, I try to stop my jaw from dropping open. It's such a contrast from the antique elegance of outside—it's like I've walked into a house in Beverley Hills. I've seen a lot of homes in my time—and never anything quite like this.

It looks just like a hotel lobby. I guess Jasper Drummond wants to be reminded of the legacy his father set up every single day.

They must have knocked out a bunch of walls to create the space needed for this airy entryway and to make it perfectly cylindrical. Shiny white marble floors sweep across the entire breadth, and in the middle is the emblem of a large glinting crown. Perhaps it's the family crest? Directly above it hovers a sparkling chandelier.

Freddie walks across the crown without a backward glance and strides straight across to the open arch on the other side. Matilda scampers after him, but I pause to drink it all in. Two other doors lead directly from the right and left sides of the crest, which must open through to the other "wings" of the house. Then, I spot the line of portraits on the wall. Directly above me is one of Sir David, his dark eyes squinting down at me as though in judgment. Next to that, his son Jasper. I'd seen his photograph online when I'd been searching about Anna. His strawberry blonde hair is neatly arranged, and he wears an affable but slightly condescending tight-lipped smile.

I'm so lost in studying the portraits that when I feel someone grab me around the waist, I let out a small scream.

Thankfully, I recognize the deep chuckle in my ear. It's Charles. I spin around. "God, you scared me."

He laughs, but there's a hard, mirthless edge to it. "Did you really not know whose house this was?" I follow the train of his gaze all the way up to Sir David Drummond hanging on the wall. His plaque is as plain as the disapproval on Charles's face. He looks back down at me, his eyes demanding an answer.

"I..." I pause, trying to search for the best thing to say. It's clear he doesn't believe me that I didn't know. And with Matilda knowing about my deception, deep down, I know it's only a matter of time before she will mention it to him. She can be such a Daddy's girl. So, I opt for the truth. "I'm sorry. I just didn't think you'd like to come here, knowing that Anna is wrangled up in some tense conversations with the rest of Sir David's family. I didn't want to put you in a difficult position."

He raises his eyebrows. "You mean, you didn't want me to say no on principle?"

I bite my lip. I can't tell him the real reason why I wanted to come here. That I wanted to find out what I could about Anna and why this family hates her so much. So, instead, I use the same excuse I gave him originally. "I need these new clients, Charles. Freddie said he'd introduce me at the party today. I had to bring the whole family, or it would look strange. I'm sorry I didn't tell you everything."

He shakes his head sadly and then says in a low voice, "I wish I could believe you, Jacqueline. I really do. But it's hard when you create all these little white lies..."

Then without another word, he turns on his heels and walks to where Freddie and Matilda have disappeared. My stomach flips in panic. I stare up at the portrait of Jasper Drummond. I just need to get answers. Then, everything can go back to normal. Because right now, my carefully calibrated family seems to be slipping out of control. Matilda talking back and snooping through my phone, Charles thinking I'm lying. I clench my fists in determination. When Anna is gone, everything and everyone will go back to the way they were.

With that, I race toward the door after the rest of the family. I try not to slip on the shimmering floors as I emerge into a huge conservatory.

Bright, airy windows panel around the room, connecting into a gabled roof in terracotta hues. Running my eyes along the rich orange and red tones, I tilt my head back to find a centerpiece of peaked glass far above us. There, another chandelier hangs, but this one is woven so intricately it looks like the scene from a fairy's garden: silver brambles interweave in circular knots, leading out to delicate bulbs of peaceful yellow light.

A Persian rug splattered with an assortment of soft green, pale pink, and baby blue expands across the huge width of the room, and sofas the color of the softest butter are dotted on either side. But beyond the lovely sitting area is the all-important view.

The expansive glass windows stretch out to reveal an open lawn. Tulips of every color run down the edges, and beyond the long lawn is a never-ending view of the Somerset fields. Greens and gold flicker in the springtime sun.

In the middle of the lawn is what we came for: the party.

A group of around twenty adults mill around laughing in front of a brightly decorated drinks tent. It looks out of place on the immaculate lawn, and I assume it must have been brought in for the event. Children run around the rest of the grounds clutching Easter egg baskets and scraps of paper. A cluster of picnic tables with colorfully striped tablecloths decorates another corner, a sign of a lunch to come.

"There you are, Jax," Freddie says, a bemused look on his face as he lounges against the arm of one of the vast sofas. "Getting some work inspiration?"

"Ha... something like that," I manage. I don't want him to see my face. I know he can read my expressions too well.

It seems that Charles and Matilda have already sped through to the garden because they are nowhere to be seen. Freddie must have waited for me to catch up.

"Come on then," Freddie beckons with a wave as he moves toward the open glass doors.

As soon as we walk through, I notice Charles talking to a tall, willowy woman. She's wearing a dress the color of the pale blue sky above, and long blonde waves curl all the way down her back, stopping at her waist.

Matilda isn't with him. She must have already been directed to the group of children to join in the Easter egg hunt.

I can barely take my eyes off the woman with Charles. The silk of her dress shimmers like the surface of a pool. It leaves nothing to the imagination: there isn't a scrap of stray flesh on her. She's tiny, and in a dress like that, she must want everyone to know, I think bitterly. I suck my tummy in tighter on reflex. *Stop*, I tell myself. *Don't revert back to Mother's way of seeing the world.*

"That's Vix," Freddie hisses over his shoulder to me as we start walking. "The lady of the house. But let's leave them to it. I want to find Nathaniel and introduce you to Aaron."

"Okay," I shrug. It's probably better for me to give Charles a bit of space after our conversation in front of the portraits.

We pick up some lemonade from the bar, and then Freddie steers me toward a gurgling fountain, telling me to wait right there as he excitedly runs around the lawn to grab Aaron and Nathaniel.

After a few minutes, I watch as Freddie returns, flanked by two men on either side. One I recognize as Nathaniel. And the other could have been Freddie, but in miniature. Still of average height for a man, but just small in comparison to Freddie's height.

"Hey, Jax," Freddie calls out from a few meters away with a wave. "I want you to meet Aaron. He's the one I told you about that's also moving around here."

I smile my best professional smile and walk toward them across the spongy grass, meeting them halfway under the shade of a tall tree in the corner of the lawn.

Nathaniel gives me a warm grin. "Nice to see you again, Jacqueline."

I smile back as Freddie continues, "Aaron, meet my lovely sister-in-law and real estate agent extraordinaire, Jacqueline," announces Freddie. "Jacqueline—meet Aaron. You can bond over your shared fatherland." He grins broadly down at me as though he's done the best thing in the world by connecting me with them. Except my stomach flips over. Aaron is American, too? Why didn't Freddie tell me? I hate meeting other Americans without knowing where they might be from first. I don't want to risk any potential run-ins with someone who might have any connections with my past.

I know I can't get out of this situation, though. So I smile happily back and ask the question before Aaron has a chance to. "Great to meet you. Where are you from?"

"DC born and bred. My family has always been there," he adds, puffing out his chest.

Nathaniel chuckles. "Don't we know it!"

Freddie joins in the laughter, and Aaron frowns, not getting the joke.

"Where are you from, Jacqueline?" he asks.

"Oh, I grew up all over," I say, hoping he'll leave it at that, as I try to turn the conversation. "So, when did you move over here?"

"But whereabouts?" Aaron asks again with interest.

"Well, I moved around a lot growing up," I reply neutrally. "So a bit of everywhere—Virginia, Texas, California, Ohio—you name a state, and I've probably lived there for a bit."

"Why so much moving around?" he questions again, and this time, I can't help but raise my eyebrows. God, when will this guy get the picture that I don't want to tell him?

It's like Nathaniel can sense the awkwardness in my responses as he jumps in. "Oh, hey Aaron, I forgot to say that Jasper asked if we can help run the Easter egg race."

"What, now?" Aaron sighs.

"Yes," he says, glancing at his watch. "We better go."

"Alright then," he says as he turns to follow Nathaniel. "Guess we can't disappoint the host! I'll catch up with you all later."

I, however, can't help but breathe a sigh of relief as I watch them go. This man seems far too curious about my past for his own good. I will need to steer clear.

I turn back to face Freddie.

"Aaron can be a little intense," Freddie says with a grimace. "But that's what makes him such a good developer. He always needs to figure out a puzzle."

I can't help it as my heart beats a little faster at his words. The last thing I need right now is a nosy American in my life. Not when Freddie and Charles don't know the whole truth about me.

I glance over at Freddie, who's watching me intently. "You did seem a bit... jumpy. Everything okay?" He quirks his eyebrow up in a question.

"Oh, I just wasn't expecting the third degree," I say with a false laugh.

"He seemed to make you quite worried, actually," he continues, swirling the remaining ice around his glass as though to appear casual. "I swear you told me you were born in Ohio. Why didn't you say that?"

I try to stop myself from frowning. I'd told him and Charles the truth because they have no connection to the place, but I never take that risk with Americans if I don't have to. I don't want Freddie to start questioning me now, but it seems too late for that.

"Well, I just don't really think of myself as from there. Like I said, I moved around so much."

"Right..." Freddie says, frowning. I can see he's about to open his mouth to ask more, so I glance pointedly down at my now-empty lemonade.

"Ah," I say, grabbing his glass out of his hand. "Shall I get us another drink?"

Without another word, I stride away. Everyone needs to stop asking so many damn questions. It's getting hard to keep all my stories straight.

I try to loosen my shoulders as I walk to the drinks tent and refocus myself on the plan. It's high time I started to mingle properly. I need to introduce myself to Jasper Drummond. The very reason I'm here today.

Advancing across the lawn like a soldier heading into battle, I try to look over the heads of a group of women who are blocking the view to the bar. Charles is probably still there, being occupied by "Vix." But then I hear Charles's name. I look around, expecting to see him in conversation with someone behind me, but realize it's just a woman at the fringes of the group speaking very loudly.

I slow my pace to hear better as I slowly walk around them, keeping my head down to avoid being noticed.

"Oh my goodness, yes, you're right, it *is* Charles Banks," she is saying. "You know, I heard about him doing something a little bit cheeky last year." I glance at them out of my peripheral vision and see that two women have turned in from the rest of the group to speak to each other.

"Oooh!" says the other woman, who has soft auburn curls. "What was it?"

"Well, you know how he's married to a bit of a Plain Jane..." the mousy-haired woman says. I pull my hair around my face defensively as she goes on, "Let's just say I heard he was seen about town with a rather lovely woman for a while last year... and his little wife in Bristol had no idea."

My stomach turns over at their words, and it takes everything in me not to fall over as a wave of dizziness hits me. At the insult, yes, but mostly at what they've revealed.

I can't believe that after all this time, Charles has betrayed me.

He'd been having an affair, after all.

# Chapter Sixteen

I need to get myself under control. Spying what seems to be the entry to a secluded rose garden, I make a beeline straight for it. Stumbling under the small ivy-covered arch, I enter what I would normally think of as a paradise. The roses aren't in full bloom yet, as it's only the second half of April, but bright tulips zigzag along the garden beds, zipping under the many winding paths and arches. I spot a small iron seat to my right and fall on it quickly, taking deep breaths to calm my racing heart.

Even though we're in the middle of a big fancy party, this can't wait. I need to confront Charles. Now. He'd told me point blank that I had nothing to worry about last year. And yet, now I am at a party full of the London crowd, and rumors of his infidelity are going around like a dodgy canapé. Will he just deny it? Will I choose to believe him when he does? I'll have to see if I can decipher the real truth from his face.

Because *no one* cheats on me.

Standing up, I whirl back toward the exit. But in my rush, I don't see the person who has entered the secret garden. I bash straight into their chest and go flying to the ground, falling with a heavy thump. My tailbone screams in protest.

"Oh my goodness, I'm so terribly sorry," a gruff male voice says, and I look up to see a stocky man with strawberry blonde hair hovering above me. He looks just like the portrait of Jasper Drummond—only a little older, with faint lines streaked across his forehead.

"Are you hurt?" he asks, pushing tortoiseshell-framed glasses up his nose as he extends a hand down to me. He wasn't wearing those in the portrait. "Please forgive me. I'm such a klutz. I saw you stumble towards this garden, looking rather unwell, and I wanted to check that you were okay. And now I've done this... But are you alright?"

"I'm okay," I manage to say, my voice coming out a little shaky as I accept his hand. A flash of pain runs through me as I slowly stand up.

"Oh, are you American? You must be Freddie's sister-in-law, Jacqueline. I'm Jasper. It's lovely to finally meet you. I'm sorry it has to be under these circumstances."

I nod as I brush off a bit of dirt from my skirt and pull myself back together. I smile, trying to channel my best Jacqueline self. I hope it doesn't look too forced. It's getting harder and harder, the more out of control I feel, to put on the show I need to.

"Oh Jasper, it's great to meet you at last. Thank you so much for inviting us today. Your home is incredible."

Now that I'm steady once more, I quickly flash my eyes over him in a quick assessment. He's dressed immaculately in soft brown chinos, a white shirt, and a light Barbour jacket. I look up to meet his gaze and see his piercing gray eyes staring back at me. They remind me of a summer storm. His lips curl upwards. "Ah, the pleasure is all mine. Freddie is like a brother to me."

I try not to raise an eyebrow at this. It is strange that Charles doesn't remember Jasper at all, if he and Freddie have been so close since school. Could Charles have been lying about not remembering Jasper, too? I can't help but mistrust everything after what I've just heard from those women about Charles's infidelity.

"I'm so glad we've been able to meet," I respond, focusing on the present moment. "Freddie is very dear to me, too."

Jasper looks over his shoulder and edges closer to me. "And Jacqueline, because you're an American, I hope you'll excuse me if I speak frankly," he says in a low voice, even though we're the only ones in this hidden-away garden. "But dear Freds has told me about your new neighbor. My dear *stepmother*." He rolls his eyes at the ludicrous word. If Jasper and Freddie are the same age, then that means that Anna is around seven years younger than him. It is pretty ridiculous.

"I hope you don't mind, but Freddie said you might have some concerns about her too." He glances behind me and to the bench. "Would you mind if we sit together and speak for a few moments? There are some things that I think might be helpful for you to know."

Speaking with Charles can wait; at last, I have an opportunity to find out as much as I can about Anna straight from the source. I'm annoyed that Freddie has clearly told Jasper about what happened at our house the other week and what we witnessed through the window between Anna and Charles. But equally, I'm desperate to know whatever Jasper can tell me. Knowledge is power, as I always say, and right now, I need it more than ever.

I nod and, without another word, turn back toward the bench that I'd just vacated. It's small, and so as Jasper sits down next to me, we're squished enough that our knees and arms touch. For some reason, as soon as we touch, my body wishes it could move further away. But I force myself to turn and face him.

"Yes," I say in a low voice. "Please tell me what you can about her. You're right; I have a few concerns myself about her... behavior."

His eyes shine behind his glasses in what must be excitement. "Well done you for seeing through her. She's awfully good at wrapping people around her little finger."

"Yes, I've witnessed that firsthand."

He raises his eyebrows as though to say, "Go on," but he's the one who asked me to sit down with him. I don't want to reveal what I've observed until I know what he has to say.

It seems like he understands my thoughts, however, and after a deep sigh, he goes on. "Yes, she is very good at that. It's exactly what she did to my poor late father."

His face freezes into a mask of sadness as he continues. "He honestly did everything for her and that little girl of hers. It's like he was blind when it came to them—but *I* saw it. I didn't want to. I wanted him to be happy. But there was something about her that I didn't trust right from the start.

"But he married her in secret a few years ago. They *eloped*." He rolls his eyes, "I told myself it was sweet that he had finally found new love after losing my mother so young. And they seemed happy together. But really, I should have known that was the beginning of the end."

He runs a hand through his ruffled hair as though the next part of the story brings him the most pain. "I was there, I was *there* when it happened, and I couldn't do anything to stop it." Anguish contorts his features. "It was a formal dinner hosted at our house in Chelsea to celebrate everything my father had done for his children's charity. It was *our* food, so everything should have been fine.

"Pa has—*had*—a terrible allergy to all nuts. He had to carry an EpiPen at all times and always double-check his meals out anywhere. That's partly why he wanted to start his hotel and restaurant business—so he could be in control of all the ingredients and create a series of restaurants that would be safe for him and others like him to eat in. But that night, the worst happened. Right in his own home.

"Somehow, some nuts had got into his food, and he went into immediate anaphylaxis at the dinner table. Everyone was in a panic, but of course, I tried to stay as calm as I could and told Anna to get his EpiPen from his pocket. He *always* carried one on him. She tried to find it, but it wasn't there. And then I panicked. Racing around the house, trying to find another EpiPen in any of the usual spots. There wasn't one anywhere, and by the time I got back into the room, Anna was lying on top of his body, trying to resuscitate him—no EpiPens in sight. All the guests were standing there in shock. Someone sensible had called an ambulance. But it was far too late."

Tears glisten in his eyes, steaming up his glasses, and he looks away to collect himself.

"I'm so sorry," I murmur. "You don't have to tell me all this."

He turns back, showing me the silver that still lingers on the edges of his lashes. "No, I really do, Jacqueline. So you will understand. Because I *cannot* accept that his death was simply a terrible accident. I knew my father—better than anyone, I like to think. After my mother's death, he was both parents to me. And in all my life, he's never been without his

EpiPen in his pocket—even in his own home. So I can't believe Anna's jumbled excuses that the police seemed to buy. It is impossible for me to accept that somehow no one could find it in the approximately thirty minutes we all had to race around the house before he succumbed." He lowers his voice. "Afterwards, they found one inside his nightstand. But I'd looked there. And I swear, there wasn't one at the time. So how did it get there?"

I shake my head in disbelief at his story. Jasper is obviously still deep in grief about what happened to his father. Listening to him tell the story, it does seem pretty unlikely that David Drummond's death was an accident. But equally, I need to know more.

"You think she arranged it," I say flatly. It's not a question, just a confirmation. "And potentially even tried to frame *you.*"

He nods wordlessly. "I didn't want to think it. I didn't want to consider it. But who else would have had so much to gain from his death? Who else could have so carefully arranged for his food to be tampered with? Who else could have ensured that no EpiPens were around right at the crucial moment?"

He fiddles with the watchstrap on his wrist—an antique Rolex, from the looks of it, with a heavily worn leather strap. "I tried to ignore the rumors and the whispers," he says, staring down at his watch. "Even when they began to swirl around the press and those online forums. Of course, with so many people in the room when it happened, we couldn't control the fallout. I declined to comment at every turn. I told myself I'd let the police do their job. But after everything, they couldn't find anything to pin on her. The only person they could have potentially accused was me for ignoring the EpiPen in his drawer. But, like I said, it *was* not there when I searched…"

He sighs heavily and looks up again to face me. "All this is to say that the press died down, and the police closed up their books, ruling it a tragic accident. I tried to accept it, but it didn't sit right with me." His face suddenly hardens with anger. "And then I found out about the will. And that changed everything."

# Chapter Seventeen

Time seems to slow as Jasper recollects his thoughts. We sit huddled together, and in the distance, I hear the screeches of laughter from the children searching for eggs. They feel a million miles away from this moment.

Finally, Jasper clears his throat. "This"—he waves his hands around to gesture the estate—"is all very new. We came from nothing, really—just a tiny backwater town. But Pa spent all his time building his business, and it quickly became successful. He did anything to succeed. For me, that meant as soon as he could, he shipped me off to boarding school. That's where I met Freds and all my best friends, of course. I did love it. But my mother died when I was away, and I didn't get to say goodbye.

"At least I still had my father, though, and I vowed I would do everything to carry on the Drummond legacy that they had built together. And that's what I've done—look, I'm successful in my own right alongside our hotel business and other investments. Any additional wealth from my father didn't matter to me and Vix. But he always said that I was going to continue his legacy."

His brows knot together. "And then the will was read. And it seemed that everything he'd ever implied was tipped upside down because he'd left almost everything to Anna and her daughter Sofia. Everything—except this house." He lets silence fall as though to allow me a moment to process. And in my head, I'm starting to connect the dots.

"You think Anna knew about the will beforehand?"

He nods again. "She said she had no idea, absolutely no inkling. But I remember the moment like it was yesterday. The solicitor told us in this very house, and she sat there staring into space as though it was a complete shock to her. I almost believed it myself. But"—a bitter laugh escapes him—"then I found out how good an actress she really is."

"What do you mean?" I wrap my arms around myself as the sun disappears behind a cloud and the warmth leaches from the air.

"I couldn't leave it alone. After she left that day, I remained in the study until late into the night, deliberating. I realized that I truly didn't know very much at all about this woman, my *stepmother*. All I knew was what my father had told me: that she'd been raised by her grandparents in Ireland but was sent to a boarding school on the outskirts of London. Hence the standard British accent, apparently."

*Ireland?* My heart starts to skip a beat, but I ignore it. It's probably nothing that I'm Irish-American, and she's Irish. Jasper goes on without a pause, as though he needs to get everything off his chest in one go. "When she fell pregnant at twenty-one, though, they forced her to drop out of university. They'd been devout Irish Catholics, and they didn't approve at all. They forced her to marry Sofia's father. And so they lived in that small Irish town for a while—until he died. He'd apparently taken to drinking and killed himself drunk driving. It forced Anna to take a good, hard look at her life. She'd grown resentful of her grandparents and what they'd encouraged her to do. So she decided to escape with Sofia and start again in London. Or so the story goes. Because that's how she came to work at one of my father's hotels—where they first met." Jasper rolls his eyes.

"But I started to wonder," he goes on, "did I really believe her? If everything about her past was true, then perhaps it did mean that everything she was saying now, about my father's 'accident' and about how shocked she was about the will, was true too. But if she'd ever lied about her past... then maybe she was lying about everything else. I realized that I owed it to my father to do some digging. He obviously never had, taking his 'sweet Anna's' word for it. I owed it to him to discover if she was really worthy of the great love and riches he'd left to her. So the next day, I began my thorough 'background' search."

As though the memory of it makes him restless, he jumps up and starts pacing in front of me on the soft earth. "I enlisted the best private investigator I could find. And it's taken a while, and not everything is crystal clear, but"—he stops suddenly in front of me as he whispers down at me—"it turns out almost *everything* about who she says she is is a lie."

"What do you mean?" I breathe. I can't believe that all my suspicions might have been right after all...

"Well, she sure is of Irish descent... but she's not only Irish. She's also *American*," he declares.

I feel my palms start to sweat, and I clench them tight. How can she be Irish-American, too? Just like me...

But before I can process his words properly, Jasper goes on. "And that's not all... it seems she grew up in the US, in Ohio, Colorado, and Pennsylvania, and only moved to this country around twelve years ago."

My stomach drops at his words. At the familiarity of the situation. This isn't possible...

He doesn't seem to notice my terror as he continues his pacing. "And so," he continues, "this proves that everything she told my father was a lie. I don't know why she lied about her past. I mean, it's not illegal. But the fact that she did lie makes me think she was hiding something or someone... And now, how can I trust that she didn't know about the will before he died? How can I not think that she arranged my father's death so she could get everything? I *can't*." He comes to a halt once more.

"All I need to do is prove it. I can't let a woman like this continue to be a Drummond, to have my father's wealth, knowing that she killed him to get it. But that's the *one* thing that I don't have proof of." He stares down at me, desperation written across his face. "That's why I'm telling you all this, Jacqueline."

Dropping back down into the seat next to me, he turns and grabs my clammy palms tight. "You are in the unique position of being her closest neighbor and someone I can trust—because Freddie trusts you. And now I'm begging you to help me... Help me find any evidence against her of planning my father's death or of knowing about the will beforehand. Anything that will help me in the case I'm building against her."

I don't say anything, my mind whirling, and I can't trust myself to speak just yet. Jasper presses his hands even tighter around mine. "Please, Jacqueline—I can't let my father's murderer get away with it."

The shock of the harsh word jolts me back to my senses as fragments of thoughts click into place. I've made a decision. The only decision I can make.

"Of course," I say softly. "I will do anything to help you."

"Thank you, Jacqueline, thank you," he murmurs, bowing his head over our clasped hands in a prayer of relief.

And it's good that he can't see my face right now and the ugly, murderous expression that I'm sure is on it.

Because he can't know, doesn't need to know, the real reason why I've agreed to help him. And why I will now do *anything* to get Anna out of my life for good.

I thought I'd covered my tracks so well. Everything had remained hidden for all this time. But what Jasper has shared about Anna's true past makes me certain that I've been right to suspect her reasons for moving into the house across the street. I wasn't just imagining things. Though, what I didn't realize was that she might not be here for Louisa—but for me. Because the similarity of her past to my own can't be just a coincidence. She must be here for a reason. I'm sure she must know something about me that she shouldn't.

My eyes snag on a glistening spider's web visible just behind Jasper's head, and I watch a fly flounder in the silky strands. I force myself to quash the mounting panic I'd felt a moment ago, and instead, a small smile creeps across my face as a comforting realization flashes through my mind. I'm on the front foot. Because it might be the case that Anna knows something, and is here to catch me out. But now, she will have no idea that I'm also on to her.

So, as Jasper clutches my hands tight in thanks, I make myself a promise. I will take my time watching her, and I will formulate the perfect plan to get that widow out of our lives for good.

At last, I understand why she's been sniffing around, why she wouldn't have wanted me to discover her lies.

Because Anna isn't who she says she is. But then again, neither am I.

I'm not Jacqueline.

The real Jacqueline died a long time ago.

# PART TWO

# Chapter Eighteen

## Anna

Even though we're two weeks into May, the sun still refuses to shine. I stare out through the rain-soaked panes of my bedroom window, watching the heavy drops batter endlessly down onto the front lawn—and the house across the street.

It's only two o'clock on Saturday afternoon, but all the lights are on, and I squint to try and spot any shadows of the family inside. I can't spy any movement. Instead, I imagine what they might be up to: Matilda with her nose buried deep in one of the books she's borrowed from our library. And Charles—I picture him either preparing for a new case or maybe even doing a few reps on the rowing machine he told me he enjoys using in their basement. Charles—who has no idea that his darling wife is lying to him about who she really is.

And, of course, *she* will be in there somewhere.

"Jacqueline."

But it can't be.

Because the real Jacqueline Kelly was my sister. And she is dead.

I saw her cold body with my own eyes. I know who killed my b
ful sister Jackie. And it wasn't this woman across the street, so why 
she stolen her identity?

I only came across this fake Jacqueline by chance. But since then, I've
not been able to stop thinking about her.

It was around three years before David died. I was still working at
the Drummond Hotel in London, and David and I had started secretly
seeing each other. I was helping out our Events Manager with coordinating some Law Society dinners in the run-up to Christmas, and I
was in charge of the guest lists. A request came in at the last moment
to change a name from Jacqueline Kelly to her newly married name,
Jacqueline Banks. It gave me pause because Jacqueline Kelly was the
name of my dead sister. The coincidence stopped my heart in my chest.

But I told myself it was just that. A strange coincidence and an
unhappy reminder of the dead half-sister that I never really had a chance
to know. We had only connected in the last few months of her too-short
life.

I tried to forget about it—but when the evening arrived, I was ar-
ranging the place card settings, and the name leaped out at me once
more. I told myself there would be no harm in just observing *who* this
other Jacqueline was. If only to put the unease that had slid into my
stomach to rest.

On the night, I watched her closely. She was not my sister Jacqueline. But there was an uncanny resemblance between them. A similar
build and the same curly, rich, hazelnut hair that I'd envied from the
first moment I'd met my half-sister. I could never forget it. It was so
similar to our mother's. I tried to convince myself that it was just that:

similarities. But as the evening wore on, I drifted closer so I could listen in on snippets of her conversation.

And a sensation like fingernails on a chalkboard scratched down my spine when I heard her accent. Her *American* accent—which sounded exactly like how I remembered my sister's.

I told myself that didn't necessarily mean anything. People shifted their accents all the time; I had tried hard over the years to perfect a British accent so no one would know where I was originally from. But all the same, it wasn't entirely a common thing to do. The more likely explanation was that she genuinely *was* from a similar part of America to my sister.

As the evening wore on, I couldn't help listening even more intently to her conversations. I overheard people congratulating her on her recent marriage, and she laughed—in an almost identical way to how my sister had—saying, "Thank you, it was about time. We'd been together for, oh, almost a decade. It was so special to finally tie the knot when our daughter was old enough to celebrate with us."

The woman she was speaking with asked if any of her family had made it over from the States for the wedding, and "Jacqueline" had replied that all her family were dead.

I'd crept away and attempted to carry on with my work for the rest of the night. After that, I tried to forget all about it. Telling myself again and again that it was just a bizarre coincidence. Besides, what use was it, dredging up the past now? There was a reason I'd kept my secrets buried all these years and left my old life behind.

But even after David and I married, the image of that woman's face dogged me. Whatever I did, I couldn't stop thinking about her. I even started having nightmares of my sister begging me to help her. It felt like I was being haunted. Maybe that was why things between David and I started disintegrating. Perhaps I really had been too preoccupied to be a good wife to him, like he accused me of in those final weeks.

At the start of our relationship, I really had fancied myself a little in love. So I guess that's why I agreed to marry him when he asked. He said he wanted to look after Sofia and me, so why would I say no to that? I'd been running for so long, and I needed to give us some security. But as the last couple of years slipped by, and I got to know David even better, I saw that he wasn't quite the man he'd first appeared. I realized that perhaps I hadn't made the best choice...

I squeeze my eyes shut from those intrusive thoughts and focus on the reason why I'm here in this house today.

Because even when David died, and all those terrible rumors started chasing me, I still couldn't forget about this woman. And I realized that the only way to try and move on with my life was to *disprove* that this woman was connected to my sister. Hopefully, I would discover that it was all some bizarre coincidence.

The private investigator that I hired last autumn was discreet. And when he shared with me everything he'd gathered, I almost fainted.

He uncovered that "Jacqueline Kelly" had moved to the United Kingdom eleven years ago from California. But he also verified that this same woman had apparently gone to college in Pennsylvania before that and finished high school in Ohio.

I made him dig to make sure that no other Jacqueline Kellys had been at the college at that time, and they weren't. She was the only one.

I'd covered my hands over my mouth in horror.  Because I knewmy sister was dead. She'd diedover eleven years ago in Philadelphia. But then, how was it possible that this other Jacqueline that I'd met had her *exact* history?

It couldn't be. It *shouldn't* be.

Yet here it was, in front of me. In black and white.

I knew that my sister had never had any social media presence, and the private investigator confirmed it. I wasn't surprised, seeing as one of the few times we met, she'd told me that she abhorred the idea of posting about her life publicly for everyone to see. I had to agree. It is also one of the reasons why I've never created a social media presence. If you're running from your past, you never want anyone to find you, after all.

There was only one last thing I could ask the private investigator to check for me. Any record of Jacqueline Kelly's death on that awful winter's night.

He scoured the records and found there were many deaths that night in Philadelphia. But none of the people had the name Jacqueline Kelly.

According to official records, my sister never died that night.

But I *know* she did.

I *saw* her body wheeled away.

That settled it—it really did seem like this woman had snatched my sister's identity. And I knew what I had to do: I needed to find out who this imposter was and why she was using my sister's name. I understood that sometimes when you're in a difficult situation, you have to make desperate choices. I'd done it myself, after all. Maybe there was a reason why she had taken my sister's identity? Maybe I could find a way to understand...

So I discovered where this "Jacqueline" was living now, and I gave the owners of the house across the street an offer that they couldn't refuse to put their house on the market. I coordinated my plan seamlessly. Because I had to ensure I moved as close as I could to this woman to discover the truth at last.

I owed it to my sister—Jackie, as I always called her. Even though I'd known her for such a short amount of time, she'd saved my life. The *real* Jacqueline had saved me when no one else would.

And I'd lived with the guilt for all these years that in doing that, it had cost her hers.

Because what she'd done for me all those years ago meant that I was able to escape from the one person I feared most in the world. The reason why I created a new backstory for myself and still hid my past to this very day...

These thoughts shatter into me again like shards of glass as I stare unblinkingly at the house that holds all the answers to my questions.

All I have to do is uncover the secrets of the wife across the street at last.

# Chapter Nineteen

"Muuuuum. Can we go now?" Sofia cries at me through my bedroom door. I pull myself away from the view and my maddening, circular thoughts. Because even though we've been living here for around two months now, I'm no closer to any answers.

The large wooden door swings open to reveal my girl: her raven black hair, the same shade as mine, but cut into a short bob. She's dressed in a bright yellow raincoat and her favorite denim jeans.

"You said we could go and get some hot chocolate in Clifton Village with Matilda when it stopped raining. And it has!" She gestures toward the window.

I can't help but laugh at her attitude. Twelve going on thirteen, certainly. In front of other people, my Sofia can be very quiet. I suppose my own careful habits have accidentally slipped through to her. But in front of me, and apparently her new best friend Matilda, she can be very confident—bordering on demanding. I'm glad. I don't want my secrets and lies to mean that she won't ever trust anyone. That she will be too scared to make true friends.

Just because I can't be too close to anyone, it doesn't mean my daughter should suffer the same fate. That's one of the reasons why I ran from America and gave us a new life here in the UK in the first place.

"So it has," I say, standing up from the little plush window seat I've been perched on. Even though I mostly moved to Bristol to find out who this "Jacqueline" truly was, I really had wanted a new start for my daughter, too, away from all the chaos of our lives in London. She deserved that after everything we'd been through with David's death.

I'd spent a good few months redecorating everything, making it comfortable. Sometimes, I feel a bit guilty about not sharing with Sofia the real reason why we've moved here, but at least she seems happy.

Anyway, hopefully, discovering the truth about the imposter Jacqueline across the street won't necessarily mean that we will have to leave our new home. Perhaps there might be a simple explanation for all this. Because ideally, there is a world in which once I know *why* she took my sister's identity, I'll accept or understand her reasons. I know what it is like to run from danger, after all. I understand that when you're in a desperate situation, sometimes you have to make desperate choices.

But that's why it is crucial that I discover the truth without her realizing that I'm on to her. I first have to know whether her actions could be justified or not. I don't want to put Sofia in danger if I realize that the fake Jacqueline might do anything to keep her secret safe...

I've been trying hard to get close to the whole family to sniff out the facts. But so far, I haven't had much luck with "Jacqueline" herself. I've wracked my brain for reasons why. There's surely no reason why she would suspect me?

The biggest reason I can think of is simply how we started on the wrong foot when I found her and Matilda "lost" in our home. I reacted badly, I know that. But I'd been so shocked and terrified to find them in the library, of all places, with the safe wide open. The place where all my secrets are kept under lock and key.

But I'd tried to make up for it—going over to apologize the next day. Even though I didn't see her for a couple of weeks after that because she'd been so busy at work, I thought we'd made a fresh start. Charles certainly seemed to think so. I shared with him in those weeks that I'd love to become better friends with his wife. He was the one who suggested I help her out by finding a new venue for the charity fundraiser—he said that she hated asking for help, but if I offered up a solution on a silver platter, she'd be so grateful. Unfortunately, that seemed to have backfired too. She never thanked me for it and even looked mad when she found out. If anything, she has become more distant from me ever since that Saturday at school.

Maybe it got back to her what Sofia and I had accidentally revealed to those two nosey women at the school gates. Even though I'd been married to David for a few years, I never got the hang of navigating probing conversations with those kinds of women. I purposefully tried to avoid spending too much time at any type of "society" event. They made me feel uncomfortable, and in any case, I didn't want any extra limelight. David was fine with that; it was one of the reasons he liked me so much in the first place—that I wasn't one of these women who wanted to use him for extra attention. Whenever David had to go out for the occasional more public-facing event, I stayed safely at home, waiting for him. He thought it showed my love and dedication. But it was mostly because I valued mine and Sofia's privacy. I was pretty sure that after all this time, I must be safe from my past, but there was no point in tempting fate by seeking out any extra attention. I managed to keep our faces out of the public eye over those few years. It was only when David died so dramatically that the newspapers took any interest in me.

So, I wasn't prepared for the gossip queens of Briar Prep. Claire and Caroline had cornered me and Sofia as we were leaving school one afternoon. They'd appeared so nice at first. Asking all about our experience of moving to Bristol. Somehow, the conversation turned toward our neighbors, and I guess they asked how we first met. Sofia had piped up, saying it was a hilarious story because we had run into them lost inside our house. They'd exchanged glances with raised eyebrows, and I knew instantly that Sofia's words had been a mistake. I tried to laugh it off, but all I could see was their excitement at the latest juicy tidbit of gossip. I hoped it wouldn't get back to Jacqueline, but maybe it had because, during the Easter holidays, it had been so difficult to pin her down for longer than the briefest of neighborly conversations.

For the last few weeks, I've been trying to find new opportunities to talk to her. But almost every time I drop over to pick up Sofia, Charles greets me instead, and equally, it's always him coming over to ours to retrieve Matilda. It's taken me a while to figure Charles out. When I first met him the day I dropped over to start again with Jacqueline, he took me by surprise. Jacqueline had been out, and his reception of Sofia and I was a little frosty at first. He seemed to stare at me like he'd seen a ghost. We'd only been invited in because Matilda had appeared from behind Charles's shoulder and bravely apologized for scaring us the day before. That seemed to have jolted Charles out of his stupor. Up until that point, he'd been staring at me with that confused expression on his face as though trying to work out how he might know me. He'd shaken his head and asked us to wait inside for Jacqueline. Matilda and Sofia had slipped upstairs, and Charles brought me through to the kitchen. We might have awkwardly hovered there without speaking for ages, but I commented on the garden that I could see through the window. It was that which transformed the pale expression on Charles's face. He'd invited me outside excitedly, and we'd been swept away in an animated conversation about his gardening.

I thought we'd made good progress to becoming friendly then, but he seemed to change again the next time we saw each other. When I picked Sofia up from an afternoon playdate, he was unusually quiet, barely responding when I asked him about his garden. I couldn't help but ask him how he was *really* doing. His lips twisted into a rueful smile. "You know, no one ever asks me that."

I'd nodded and replied, "Me too. It's like everyone expects you to just say fine—even when you're not fine."

His eyes had widened at that, and he'd managed a shaky laugh. "Exactly."

I hadn't wanted to pry. I could see that whatever was on his mind was a personal pain. And that I understood. It was something he'd hopefully share with me in his own time. But then he'd said, standing straighter. "I've been meaning to say I'm sorry about your husband. I understand what it can be like—I lost my first wife." He looked at me again as though trying to puzzle something out before adding, "It's well... Something I still struggle with."

I'd nodded in understanding—perhaps these small shifts in moods that I'd noticed came down to that. A man still struggling quietly with his grief. Perhaps my appearance as a recent widow had brought it all up again for him. I endeavored to be even more considerate and observant of him. And it seemed to work because, over these last couple of months, we've become ever closer. Whenever we've spoken about what I've been through with David, he's continued to allude to his own struggles. Slowly, I can see that if I'm patient, he might open up. And he's been helpful in filling me in on his and Jacqueline's lives since they met back in California.

But what I have to know more about now is this Jacqueline's time at college in Pennsylvania and high school in Ohio. If she even lived there. Or is she just using that narrative because it was *my* sister's story?

Really, it's still crucial for me to become closer to Jacqueline herself—but she's been proving elusive to spend time with. It almost makes me wonder if she's been trying to avoid me?

Finally, though, we seem to be turning a corner because I caught up with Jacqueline at the school gates yesterday. We had a brief conversation, and she suggested we take the girls for a hot chocolate in Clifton Village today if the rain held off. She said she wanted a chance to get to know me better. I leaped at the opportunity. It was perfect.

I stretch, digging my bare feet into the soft white rug, then look around for my phone. I spot it lying on the bed—an antique four-poster that I adore. Even though I came from nothing, I acquired a slight taste for luxury over the years with David.

Most especially art. Hanging over the walls of my bedroom and many other walls of the house are some of my favorite pieces I've collected over the years. When I was younger, I loved singing, but running from my past meant I had to give it up. My creative bent was translated into loving art and books instead. A much more anonymous pastime.

As well as helping me curate a collection of my favorite books, David encouraged me to take painting lessons in those early days when we were happy, but I never have. Maybe one day I will... When this is all over.

"Alright then," I say, grabbing my phone and pulling Sofia into a tight hug. She tries to squirm away, but I hold her even tighter. "Why don't you go and find your boots? I'll just get myself rugged up."

"Okay," she responds as I let her go. She dashes back down the hall toward the staircase. This house is too large for us, but I like it. It gives me space to breathe.

In any case, it's smaller than the home we shared with David back in London. But there, it felt like all the rooms were pressing in on me. There, I couldn't breathe easily at all. I hadn't been able to for a long time. Even before David's death.

I shake off the thoughts as I head to the walk-in wardrobe I had added during the renovations.

Entering through the arch, I smile at the workmanship. In front of me and along the wall to my left are floor-to-ceiling rails and shelves. All my favorite dresses are lined up and color-coordinated. It ensures I know exactly where everything is at all times. When so many other things in my life have been so unpredictable, I try to do everything in my power to control what I can. In the middle of the room is an oval-shaped chest with a soft padded top. It's the perfect place to sit and consider what to wear today. On my right-hand side are two windows—which look out to the same view as my bedroom: the house across the street.

The walls are painted a shade of pale rose pink, and the carpeted floor is the color of soft vanilla fudge. It makes me happy every time I walk into this room. I know I shouldn't care about such frivolous things when so many more significant problems are whirling around out there. But whatever people might think, I'm proud of the life I've been able to build for myself and my beautiful girl. And I won't let anyone take that away from me. Especially not David's despicable son, Jasper.

I pull too hard on the chest of drawers, holding my cream jumpers as the thought of him pops into my head. That man makes me irrationally angry. I know he hates me; he's made that abundantly clear from the first moment he met me. And that's why it's surprised me so much that since the death of his father, he's only ever been polite and considerate. Even with the revelation about the will, he seemed at ease. To my face, anyway.

His outwardly calm demeanor puts me on edge more than anything. His father always said that he loved his son but that even he wouldn't trust him as far as he could throw him.

But for now, he's been staying out of mine and Sofia's business. Even the emergency meeting that I had to have with the Drummond family solicitors wasn't because of him—it had to do with some greedy cousin contesting the will. So there we are. I guess I shouldn't second guess it and simply be happy that Jasper seems to have accepted everything so readily.

I push the thoughts away and grab the cashmere jumper I've been searching for. I find my favorite soft black jeans—it's best to be comfortable for a rainy day walk. I sit at my dressing table to brush out my hair, which has been up in a messy bun all day.

I tug on the hair elastic, and my long hair cascades down around my face. I stare at myself in the mirror as I brush it through—the shade so dark it almost matches the black handle of the brush. As I study my piercing blue eyes, I thank God that I don't look much like my sister. Our only similarity that you could possibly pinpoint is our eye shape. The shade is entirely different, though—hers had been a light brown. And mine are bright blue.

I'm thankful for that now. At least, there's no way that the woman across the street could have connected me to the real Jacqueline by looks alone.

"Muuuuum," Sofia calls up at me, interrupting my thoughts again. "Hurry up! Matilda says they're leaving their house now."

I replace the brush and jump up from the little stool. It is time to stop getting lost in my thoughts and get outside with my little girl.

Grabbing my raincoat from the hook by the archway entrance, I step out of my bedroom and bounce along the corridor toward the grand staircase.

"I'm here!" I sing theatrically at the top of the stairs, spreading my arms wide.

Sofia, at the bottom, laughs as I hop down.

"You took your time!" she says when I reach the bottom. "Let's go." She starts to walk to where we keep our boots, shouting over her shoulder as she goes. "Oh, and Mum, there's a letter for you. I've put it on the table by the front door."

I zip up my raincoat as I go to collect the letter, finding a small white envelope addressed to me. A first-class stamp in pride of place.

Slitting it open with one manicured nail, I pull out the crisp white note.

I almost faint at the four words stamped along the center of the page.

Four little words that, read on their own, are innocent, but when put together, mean my world could come crumbling down.

Four little words that say:

*YOUR TIME IS UP.*

# Chapter Twenty

My heart thrashes in my chest like a bird caught inside a cage as I stare disbelievingly at the words in front of me.

*Have they found me? Have they found us?*

With a deep breath, I delve into the rational part of my brain and tell it sternly: *You know there's no way they could have found you. You've been so careful to cover your tracks... Except for the photograph that the newspapers managed to snap.*

I close my eyes and breathe in and out to calm my careening pulse.

"Mum, are you ready?"

I crush the note against my chest as Sofia's head peeks out from down the end of the corridor.

"Yes, sweetheart," I say on autopilot, turning away from her. My breath comes out more wobbly than I'd hoped. I clear my throat. "I'll be there in a second."

I whisper to myself that it can't be my past calling. No way, not after all this time. Even with that photograph out there, it's been almost a year since it first appeared. If anyone from my past had found me through that alone, they would have come calling long before now. And they would have found me in London—there's no way they'd know that I'd moved here.

I open my eyes with regained certainty. It's probably some scaremongering from Jasper. He's the only one who knows my new address. It would be just like him to be nice to my face but trying to frighten me behind my back. Shoving the note in my pocket, I march toward the back door. I've been through worse. It's going to take more than a threatening note through the post to scare me.

I find Sofia waiting by the glass doors for me, my boots lined up and waiting.

"Time for hot chocolate!" she announces, grinning from ear to ear.

I can't help but smile back, the stupid note in my pocket forgotten. A walk and hot chocolate on a blustery spring afternoon can only bring good things.

As I put my boots on, Sofia runs along the patio and round to the side gate, disappearing out of view. As I start to slide the doors shut behind me, I hear her singing a Taylor Swift song at the top of her voice as she skips down the path. But her song stops with an abrupt shriek.

"Sofia," I call out. "Are you okay?"

No response.

*Oh my god.*

I run the rest of the way down the path, yelling out her name.

But by the time I get round to the front of the house, she isn't there either.

My body goes numb as utter panic clutches my chest. Was I wrong to ignore that stupid note?

I do the only thing I can and sprint toward the open gate, screaming her name.

"Mum!" She comes running back into view off the driveway and stops abruptly as I crash into her with a big hug. "What's wrong?" she asks a note of terror in her voice.

"You're okay, you're okay," I repeat into her ear, clutching her tight.

"Yes, Mum, I'm fine," she says in a quiet voice as she steps back, allowing me to take in the rest of the view. I look up to see Matilda, Jacqueline, and... My blood boils as I recognize the third person with them: Freddie Banks.

"I just saw Matilda and ran out to meet her," Sofia adds, looking up at me with pleading in her eyes. I know that look—it's her "please calm down, you're embarrassing me" look.

Her shriek must have been one of excitement. I didn't register it. I guess I am more affected by this threatening note than I want to admit. Honestly, ever since David's death, I've become more concerned about our security. I'm anxious that a photograph of me was plastered across the newspapers. I'd been so careful to keep a low profile *on purpose*. I know it is unlikely that, after all this time, my past will find me. But I've always lived by the saying that it is "better to be safe than sorry." I also know, though, that I can't become so obsessed about Sofia's safety that I become the boy who cried wolf.

Especially since Jacqueline and *Freddie,* of all people, are now here—I must pull it together.

"Oh, silly me. That shriek sounded like... like something else," I mutter.

"Like she might have hurt herself?" Jacqueline offers, stepping toward me with a wry smile.

"Something like that," I mumble in response.

"Don't worry," she adds. "You have the Banks family watching out for her—I would never let anything happen to her."

I try to smile gratefully. "I hope you don't mind," Jacqueline is saying. "Charles is busy, so I invited his brother Freddie to join us on our little walk. I believe you've met before?" She phrases it as a question—but I'm certain she knows the answer from the knowing look that passes between them as Freddie steps forward with an outstretched hand.

"Anna, lovely to see you again," he says with a charismatic smile.

For a second, I consider ignoring it, but then I decide to extend my fingers out to meet his. He wraps around my slender knuckles with a vise-like grip and squeezes tight. A little too tight. I try not to squirm.

His sandy blonde hair is windswept around his face on this blustery day, and as I look up into his eyes, I'm startled to see that they appear even deeper and greener than the last time we met. The contrasting gray day must be enhancing them somehow. I obviously didn't know Matilda the first time we met, but looking into his eyes now, I can see the family resemblance between her and her uncle there—Matilda's eyes are light gray-green.

As he lets go of my grasp, he runs a hand through his hair, ruffling it like he's in the middle of a photoshoot. Of course, he's handsome, but he knows it, and he's far too charming for his own good. There's something about his green eyes that I don't trust. They remind me of a snake's, and I can never forget that snakes have the ability to shed their skins when they're not of use to them anymore.

The last time I saw him was at a party Jasper organized at the family estate in Somerset. A party that I really hadn't wanted to go to, but David had insisted. It was only a few months before he died, and I'd been trying to stay on his good side.

I remember observing how Freddie laughed and slipped his way in and out of the conversations around the room and then would return to Jasper to whisper in his ear. It was like watching an eel slide through water.

I was surprised to discover that this fake Jacqueline was related through marriage to Freddie. It was something I only found out when I'd moved here and started to get to know Charles.

I'd started to think of it as yet another puzzle to solve. After discovering that this Jacqueline really did appear to have stolen my sister's identity, I didn't think there was such a thing as *coincidence* anymore.

So perhaps it was a good thing to be joined by both him and Jacqueline on this activity. *Or*, a voice whispers in my ear, *are they laying a little trap for me?*

# Chapter Twenty-One

Matilda and Sofia race ahead down the road of our little cul-de-sac as Jacqueline, Freddie, and I follow at a slower pace. I chew my cheek, searching for something to say, a way in to help me get a sense of this pretend Jacqueline's story.

What I need to know is how this woman had enough access to the real Jacqueline's life that she could take it?

But the private investigator couldn't dig up much to help me in that department. So many personal records he said he was unable to access. The only photos of the real Jacqueline—my Jackie—that he seemed to be able to find were a few group shots in the college yearbooks and a couple of high school photo snaps. But they aren't enough. If anyone else looked at them, they would just assume they were photos of a younger version of this woman walking beside me.

But I know it's not my sister, Jackie.

Before I have a chance to formulate a question, Freddie speaks up.

"So, Anna, how are you enjoying Bristol then? Bit of a change from the pace of London life, I imagine?"

I know he's probably trying to draw out an interesting tidbit to take to Jasper, but I take the bait—if only to figure out why he's really here today.

"It is, but in the best possible way," I say in as breezy a voice as I can muster.

"Yes, good to get away from all the attention, I suppose," he suggests.

I raise my eyebrows. He's not beating around the bush. Well, two can play that game. "What do you mean?" I ask, my eyes wide with innocence.

"Oh, just those terrible rumors," he remarks vaguely with a wave. Jacqueline remains silent beside him as we walk. Listening in.

"Ah yes, you mean the ones about whether I killed my husband or not," I say bluntly. He almost stumbles. This isn't the sweet, quiet Anna that he saw at the party last year.

He coughs and looks up toward the tall trees overhead as though trying to figure out the correct response.

Luckily, Jacqueline pipes up. "Yes," she says in a relaxed tone. "It must have been so difficult. I can understand why you would want a fresh start away from it all."

I nod, trying to dial down my simmering rage. I was gearing up for a confrontation—to justify to Freddie why I've moved to Bristol—because obviously Jasper has sent him to find out.

But instead, Jacqueline appears to be on my side. Maybe this is a sign of growing friendship.

"Exactly," I find myself responding with an appreciative smile in her direction.

She continues, "So you moved straight from your house in London to here?"

I shake my head. "No, we were in some temporary accommodation until now."

"Oh, because it was too hard to be in the house where he died?"

"Yes, I—" I begin, surprised by her direct question. But then I think twice. I don't want to share how I really feel with Freddie listening in on every word. "It's been quite a chaotic period for us. I'm glad we've found a quiet area with respectful neighbors."

Out of the corner of my eye, I see Jacqueline and Freddie exchange a glance. Are they working together to try and draw something out of me? Or has everything made me paranoid?

As we crest the top of the road, the broad, flat parkland of the Downs stretches almost as far as the eye can see. Here, luckily, the conversation steers away from me and toward Jacqueline's favorite subject. She points out a house on the corner overlooking the vast greenery that she's been trying to sell for the last few weeks. She starts telling Freddie that it's such a shame that his American friends were looking to rent rather than buy.

I zone out of the conversation as I try to keep my eyes trained on Sofia's bright yellow raincoat. She and Matilda are far ahead, skipping and jumping through the puddles that have pooled over the path. It makes me smile. I know this is the last year of my Sofia still enjoying the carefree moments of her childhood before she becomes a teenager. Soon, I imagine there'll be far less enjoyment in jumping through puddles and more of an interest in make-up and boys. I have to enjoy it while it lasts.

"What do you think, Anna?" Freddie's voice cuts through my thoughts.

"Of what? Sorry?" I ask in a daze.

"Of that story in the news about a mother trying to disappear with her son, running away from his father? Apparently, he was abusive, but she couldn't prove it. So it was the only thing she could think to do," he explains.

My heart starts to hammer in my chest, but I can't let either of them see that it's affected me.

He goes on, "I'm on her side. Sometimes, you have to do drastic things to protect your family. What do you think?"

I wrap my coat tighter around me, trying to cover the fear that I'm sure is written all over my face. I really don't want to answer this, and thankfully I'm saved from answering by Sofia and Matilda sprinting back toward us.

"Come on, slow coaches," Matilda giggles. And in tandem, Sofia grabs my hand, and Matilda grabs Freddie's and Jacqueline's in hers. They start to pull us faster over the muddy ground, laughing in delight.

After that, they don't leave our side as we exit the park and start the walk along College Road and up to Clifton Village. As we pass the now-closed zoo, Sofia and Matilda start telling us about the excursion that the school is planning to the aquarium and the project that they'll have to complete. I contribute with various ideas where I can. But most of the time my mind is far away, wondering why Freddie brought up that strange story in the first place. I bite my lip nervously as I glance at both him and Jacqueline.

As we turn onto pretty Victoria Square, Matilda and Sofia run ahead through the arch. I know that Primrose Café is on the other side, so I try not to panic when they disappear from view.

When we catch up, they are both waiting impatiently for us outside the café, arms folded across their chests. Though Matilda is a lot taller than my petite Sofia, I can't help but do a double-take at how similar they look with their dark hair and pale porcelain skin.

Beside me, I feel Jacqueline stop short, too.

"Oh, you're both too fast!" shouts Freddie with a laugh.

"You're too slow!" Matilda retorts back, and he tackles her into a firm hug. He appears completely transformed into this "fun" uncle mode, a side to him I haven't seen before. This is a man with many faces. But which face is his true one?

Next to me, Jacqueline whispers in a voice so quiet I almost don't catch it: "Sofia is such a sweet girl. She looks just like you."

I follow her gaze back toward our girls, where Sofia laughs with Matilda.

"Thank you," I reply with a smile of my own. Seeing Sofia this happy fills my heart with joy, no matter what else is going on around me.

"Except for her eyes," Jacqueline adds thoughtfully, pulling me out of my thoughts. "Such a distinctive green color, and that almond shape... They seem familiar to me somehow. Are they like her father's?"

Even though I'm rugged up against the cold, I feel a bead of sweat slipping down my spine. I struggle to talk about Sofia's father. It brings back... a time I'd rather forget. And then there's Jacqueline's casual reference to Sofia's eyes being familiar. What does she know?

But I can't really ignore the question outright. That would be even more suspicious. "A bit," I manage to say.

She turns to look at me straight in the eyes. "I heard from Charles that you were married before. I'm so sorry; it must have been so hard to become a widow twice over. And tragic for Sofia—to have had a stepfather and then to lose him too."

I can't help but look away. The intensity of her stare makes me feel uncomfortable. "Yes, it was," I whisper. That part, at least, is true.

Silence falls for a moment, and I look up to see Sofia, Matilda, and Freddie walking inside the coffee shop. I hate having Sofia out of my sight—especially with Freddie, who I don't feel like I can trust because of his connections to Jasper. So I take a step forward, about to hurry on, when Jacqueline speaks again.

"And do you have any other family?"

I pause mid-step. An innocent follow-up question?

I turn slowly back to see her head cocked at an expectant angle.

"No, it's just us," I say, shaking my head.

I try to walk away again when her voice rings out as clearly as a bell behind me. "Then it's lucky she has you. Imagine if anything happened to take you away..."

Tiny alarm bells start to ring in my head. What a strange choice of words, *to take you away...*

But I shake my head. She can't know the real reason why I had to leave the US, change as much of my identity as I could, and start again. She can't know what really happened between me and David before he died either.

She steps up beside me, taking my hand in hers to give it a squeeze. It feels like ice as she turns to look at me and says, "But don't worry—you have us now. We can be your family. Especially with our girls so close... they're like peas in a pod. Don't you think? In fact, they could even be sisters." She laughs, but without mirth. "So don't you worry, if anything happened to you, you know I'd be here for her. I'm good at that—stepping in when needed."

Her final words cause my stomach to turn over: *Stepping in when needed.* Is she purposefully referring to what she did herself? What she did to my sister when she took her identity? Or am I just reading too much into everything now?

But as I look across at her, I watch her smile. Her white teeth glisten in the weak light, reminding me of a predator surveying her prey.

And I can't help but think that I might be her next victim.

# CHAPTER TWENTY-TWO

I'm sure this Jacqueline has just oh-so-carefully threatened me. But before I can even attempt to respond, I see Matilda and Sofia tumble back through the doors, hot chocolates in hand.

"See," says Jacqueline. "They really are the best of friends. It would be *such* a shame if you both had to leave." She turns and looks me dead in the eyes. There's no mistaking what I see there. She wouldn't think it would be a shame. Not at all.

With that, she walks in front of me to join the girls.

My throat constricts. I want to break down in tears. Why did I ever think that moving here was a good idea? I should have stayed well alone. Because somehow, it seems like Jacqueline is on to me. And she's not happy about it.

She seems to suspect with her clever words that not only do I have an ulterior motive for moving to Bristol but that I have secrets long since buried, too. Secrets that could destroy mine and Sofia's life if anyone knew the truth. What would happen to my daughter if all my lies came to light? If I was taken away from her...

All I've ever done is to protect her with my actions. But somehow, I don't think a jury would agree. They would likely send me to jail.

I need to get home. I need to get far away from here. I need to *think*.

"Sofia," I call out, walking toward her. She looks up at me, her face bright and smiling, so unaware of the danger I might have put her in. "We have to get back now. It's getting late."

Her face falls. "But I thought I could go over to Matilda's for a while."

"No, you need an early night. It's been a busy week," I manage to say.

She rolls her eyes but doesn't protest. She heard the warning in my voice. Behind her, I see Freddie emerge from the coffee shop and stand behind Jacqueline and Matilda, a small smile on his smug face. "Lovely to see you, Anna. I'm so glad you've found a *safe* place here at last."

I want to scream, his words suggesting that I'm anything but safe. But I can't let my worries show. Instead, I nod and force myself to wave farewell. Not trusting myself to speak again.

Matilda calls out a goodbye as we walk away. Jacqueline says nothing, but she knows she doesn't have to. Because whatever game she wanted to play with me today by inviting me on this café trip, she has won. She's put me on uncertain footing now, and she knows it.

We begin the brisk walk back. Sofia chatters beside me, telling me all about what movie she and Matilda want to watch at their next sleepover.

My stomach starts to churn. How can I take her away from all this? She *loves* her life here.

I can't keep running forever... But what Jacqueline said has me rattled.

All the same, the further we get away from them, the clearer my head feels, and my fears begin to dim a little. She clearly might not like me, and she may be throwing out thinly veiled threats, but it may not be as bad as I fear... it might *not* be about my long-buried secrets at all.

There was a clear conspiracy between her and Freddie on the walk today, so her carefully unsettling words could be down to Jasper instead of my long-buried past in America. No one in the UK has ever known about my American past before. I've done such a good job at burying it—telling everyone that I grew up in Ireland and went to boarding school in England. So, I shouldn't jump to conclusions now.

No, it is much more likely that Freddie was doing Jasper's dirty work somehow. And perhaps they'd roped in this fake Jacqueline to help. Maybe they are trying to find something to pin on me for Jasper. Jacqueline didn't outright accuse me of anything. Her words were enough to make me feel scared—but maybe that was the intention? Now that I think about it, Freddie's little story certainly seemed intended to get a rise out of me, too. Perhaps they thought I would let something slip if they got me on the ropes?

But do they actually *know* anything for certain?

As our house draws into view, I remember the note stuffed in my pocket. Could that also be part of Jasper's conspiracy to draw me out? All these things could simply be a careful curation of acts to build my paranoia. If Jasper wants to come after me, he has to keep his hands clean after all.

I walk over to the keypad and put in the four-digit code as my thoughts continue to swirl. The heavy gates let us pass through and we make our way round to the back door to take off our muddy shoes.

I observe the pretty view in front of me. The expanse of sparkling patio tiles and green grass. Soon, the flower beds that Charles helped me plant will be in full bloom. I don't want to leave now—not when this place is just starting to feel a little like home. I throw my shoulders back. I've been through worse.

Sofia runs to the glass sliding door as I continue to admire our garden. I won't let myself be so easily intimidated by, most likely, Jasper and his cronies. I'm probably only jumping to thinking Jacqueline knows something more about me just because I know that she's hiding a big secret, too.

I'm about to turn away from the view and follow Sofia when my eyes snag on a trampled bush right next to the tall brick wall that borders the back of our garden. It's small enough that it might be from a fox. But I've never noticed it before, and it could equally be from a person landing softly on two feet...

Sofia's voice comes hurtling into my consciousness. "Mum!" she declares as she turns around to face me. "You left the door open!"

Sure enough, there's a crack in the sliding panel—only as wide as my foot. But it's there.

Sofia starts to slide it open when I cry out, "No!"

She looks back at me, startled.

"Let me go in first," I say softly. I don't want to scare her, so I flash her a bright smile. "Just to make sure no wild animals or spiders have snuck in."

She shivers—she hates spiders.

"Okay, Mum," she says, flopping down onto one of the wooden patio chairs.

I open the rest of the door. It moves like a knife through butter.

Taking a deep breath, I steady myself as I step inside. My pulse races. Had I not closed the door properly in my haste to rush after Sofia when I'd heard her scream? It's possible. But the trampled bush has set me on red alert. Better to double-check before letting Sofia inside. I know how to defend myself, after all. I've had to do it more times than I care to remember.

Glancing around, everything in the open kitchen-diner looks like we left it. Even my hastily stacked plates by the kitchen sink.

Continuing on, I enter the hallway that takes me through to the staircase and adjoining rooms. Methodically, I race through every room—but it's all exactly as we left it. Even my bedroom. I make my way back down the steps two at a time, searching for anything. But nothing is amiss. Maybe I really did leave the back door ajar in my haste, and that mess in the garden was only an animal. Everything today has got me on edge.

I shake my head at how quickly I jumped to the worst conclusions. But it's always better to be safe than sorry. I return to the kitchen and call Sofia inside. She happily rushes in, declaring that she better go and find this book for Matilda that she promised to give her at school on Monday.

I glance at the large white and gold clock on the wall and see that it's approaching five. An early dinner is what we need. Cooking will help calm my frazzled nerves.

I start walking toward the fridge when a thought suddenly hits me: my safe.

That safe holds all my deepest secrets, as well as the gun that I shouldn't have. The gun that I procured illegally when I moved to the UK many years ago. Like I've always said, it's better to be safe than sorry. And I feel like I need to have it—just in case.

I race back through the hallway to the library. As I burst into the room, Sofia looks up from the bookshelf she's scanning.

I ignore her as I make a beeline for the safe, looping around the door to its hiding place. It was unfortunate that Jacqueline and Matilda wandered into this room when the safe was open because otherwise, you would have no idea that it was there. I had it purposely built into the wall when I bought the house, and then I always have it hidden behind a painting.

Or it should be. Because right now, the painting is lying on the ground.

I whirl around. "Sofia," I say, my heart in my throat. "Did you move the painting off the wall?"

She pauses her search and glances in my direction with a puzzled expression on her face. "No, you told me not to touch it." Then she goes back to the shelf.

My palms start to sweat as I step forward. Maybe it was me? Maybe I'd forgotten to replace it?

Quickly, I spin the dial to input the combination. It releases with a satisfying click. I grab the stacks of photographs inside. Flicking through, I take stock of them all. Nothing appears to be missing. It's all in place. I must be losing my mind. Forgetting to lock the door and forgetting to replace the painting. What is wrong with me?

Distracted, I chew on my cheek as I pause on a photograph.

A photo of Sofia's dad and me. His arms wrapped around me tight. We look young and happy. How did it go so wrong?

I'm gazing so intently at it that I don't notice Sofia's soft footsteps behind me until she wraps her arms around me in a tight hug. "You okay, Mama?"

I clutch the photograph tight to my chest so she doesn't see. She doesn't know who her father is. And I'd prefer to keep it that way. Sometimes, I'm not sure why I keep lugging around—and secretly hiding away—all the history that could damn me so easily. But I think it comes down to the fact that I don't want to forget. I can't ever forget where I've come from or what I've done to be where I am today. It keeps me grounded.

I sigh at my daughter's caring question. I wish I could answer her honestly. I wish I could share with her the truth about why we moved to Bristol and why my deepest fears were sparked because of Jacqueline's questioning today. I wish I could tell her about the threatening note from earlier. I wish I could share the burden. But I can't. What sort of mother would I be then? And after looking at this photo, I'm reminded of *why* I've done everything I've had to do in my life. To protect her—to give her a happy life. So I can't share this. Not yet—maybe not ever.

I spin around and give her a tight hug. "Yes darling, just missing your dad," I lie. All Sofia knows is what I've told her. That I loved him, but he died before she was born. I'd decided a long time ago that if I was going to lie to Sofia about her father, then I might as well make up a lovely fictional one for her. I didn't need to give her my pain.

Sofia hugs me back. My chin rests just atop her soft head of hair. I wonder if there will come a day when she's my height or even taller. She won't be my little girl anymore then. But I'll still do anything to keep her safe.

"I think you need a friend who understands. Like I have," she adds matter-of-factly, patting me on the back.

"What do you mean, darling?" I ask, pulling back from her to replace the secret photographs in the safe.

"Well, like Matilda. She also understands what it's like to not know one of your parents."

I spin back to face my daughter, alarm bells ringing in my ears. "What do you mean, Sofia? Matilda has both her parents."

She opens her mouth to reply, but then she bites on her lip, a worried look crossing her face. She shakes her head.

"Don't worry, Mum..." She turns away to go back to the sofa.

"Sofia," I say in as calm a voice as I can muster. I drop down next to her on the sofa. "Please, you can tell me what you mean..."

She shakes her head. "No, I didn't mean to say anything. You just looked so sad, and I wanted to help."

"Please, Sofia..." I repeat, taking her hand in mine to press her on.

"I promised not to say anything." She pulls back her hand and crosses her arms in front of her chest, sinking back into the deep cushions.

"Well, I understand that," I say evenly. "But I'm not going to tell anyone anything, am I?"

Her brows furrow as she considers. I press my advantage. "And we promised we wouldn't keep any secrets from each other—didn't we?" I push away the guilt I feel. I know that I'm keeping a million secrets from my daughter. But I can't have *her* keeping any from *me*.

"I suppose so..." she says, hopping up suddenly. "But you have to promise to not say anything to anyone. Especially not Mr and Mrs Banks!"

"I promise," I say, sticking out my pinky finger. It's always been our way of confirming our promises. She takes it gratefully in hers, and we complete our vow. I can't help but cross my fingers on the hand behind my back.

"Okay, it's a big secret—but Matilda went digging through her dad's papers this week," she says sheepishly. "I guess it was because I mentioned a while ago that her birth certificate could tell her whereabouts in America she was born. I didn't *tell* her to snoop, but she decided to anyway. She said that she'd tried to ask her dad about it, and he got all weird." She shrugs.

I try not to frown at this admission; I don't want Sofia to clam up now.

"So, Matilda found her birth certificate in his study. But it didn't only tell her where she was born. It told her something way crazier. Because in the box for her mother, it doesn't say Jacqueline's name... it says someone called Louisa Huxley."

My heart stops inside my chest. I bring Sofia into a quick hug so she can't see my face. Through the dark window panes, I watch as it drops into an expression of horror.

Because I know that name.

I heard it spoken on my sister's lips the last time I saw her alive.

# Chapter Twenty-Three

I hug Sofia tighter as I register her words. She can't see the fear and shock etched across my features.

When I close my eyes, I can still picture that final meeting between myself and my sister. We'd gone back to the little diner on the fringes of Philadelphia. Our safe spot, away from any prying eyes. My true Jacqueline—Jackie, as I always called her—was helping me coordinate my escape from the terrible situation I'd found myself in.

We didn't have long on that cold winter's day in early December—I had to get back, or I'd rouse his suspicion. I hadn't seen Jackie for a few months. We never wanted to get caught. But the final stages of our plan were together. My first ever American passport had been delivered to her address, she'd handed over our shared mother's proof of Irish ancestry to help me secure dual citizenship, and on that day, she'd handed me the money to help with my escape. I was going to go to Ireland, and then I would start again. *He* would never find me, and it was all thanks to her.

Her eyes were a beautiful brown. The opposite of our shared mother's frosty blue ones that I'd inherited.

Well, at least our terrible mother had given us one thing: each other. Now that we'd been connected at long last. As I looked at Jackie more closely that day, though, I could see that she wasn't the same woman that I'd met a few months before. Her father had recently had a heart attack, and I could tell it was on her mind. Everything about her was smaller. I was worried about her—but I also knew I didn't have much time. I promised myself that once I was far away and settled with my new life, I would reach out to her and only her. She'd promised that she would never tell a soul about my existence, and I believed her.

"I can't thank you enough," I said through tear-filled eyes as she passed over the money. "It's like a guardian angel sent you."

Until only a few months before, I hadn't even known I'd had a half-sister, and now she was saving my life. Helping me escape from the man that I'd been inextricably tied to.

Jackie shook her head, her hazelnut curls tumbling over her face and covering her tired eyes.

"Don't worry about it. It's what sisters are for. And I have a lot to make up for."

"What do you mean?" I asked, tucking my goods safely away in my bag. I glanced at the clock on the diner wall. I had to get going. But there was something in her tone that had made me pause.

"Well," she sighed heavily, "there's something I haven't told you yet." She avoided my gaze, playing with the edge of a fraying laminated coaster on the table.

I watched as she started bending the edges back and forth. "And there's no easy way to say it. But... we have... another sister."

"What?!" The word echoed around the diner. We were hidden in a booth at the back, but I clamped a hand over my mouth. I didn't want to attract any attention. There could be eyes and ears anywhere.

Jackie shook her head and flicked the coaster away. It slid off the table and onto the floor. "I'm sorry I didn't tell you before. I wanted us to get to know each other first. And the story is a painful one. That seems to be my life at the moment. But you should know... Her name is Louisa."

***

Sofia tugs on my arm, and I blink myself back to the present. "Muuum, you're squishing me."

"Oh, sorry," I say on reflex, stepping back as I let her out of my arms. "You've just surprised me, that's all."

She looks up at me intently, her green eyes flashing in concern. "Please don't say anything. Matilda says she's going to talk to her dad about it soon. But all I'm saying is it's been so nice having a friend like her. We understand each other. You need that, too."

"When did you get so old and wise?" I try to force a smile, shoving down the careening questions that are bombarding me. Could it be another bizarre coincidence that Matilda's birth mother's name is Louisa Huxley? Surely not.

Jackie said that Louisa had changed her surname because she didn't want to be connected with the Kelly family anymore... And Huxley is quite a rare surname... My stomach churns. What had this fake Jacqueline done to *both* my sisters?

"So, I'd better get dinner started," I say with attempted cheer.. I need to get out of this room to think everything through and away from Sofia's observant gaze. "How does spaghetti carbonara sound?"

"Yum," Sofia says with a smile, turning back to her search on the bookshelf. I quickly shut the safe and spin the lock before racing out the door. I try not to breathe a sigh of relief as I close it with a click behind me.

I lean against the wood, pressing my weight into it. Could I just lock her in there? It might be the only way to keep her safe.

I push myself off the door and march into the kitchen. On autopilot, I fill the saucepan with water and slowly let it start to boil. I methodically start preparing dinner as I try to process what this all might mean for us.

Charles told me that his first wife died tragically. He shared this openly with me to show kindness. But he's never told me her name. Why would he?

But now, with this latest revelation, I'm starting to wonder what other secrets this fake Jacqueline might know about my family... I never knew Louisa, my other mystery sister. Jackie was killed, and I had to disappear before I had a chance to try and track Louisa down. I had to erase my past and create a new one when I moved to Ireland and then London soon after. So Louisa's identity was a mystery I'd come to terms with. Especially as Jackie had told me that they'd had a terrible falling out and that Louisa had wanted nothing to do with anyone from her birth family.

When we spoke in that diner, Jackie showed me one photo... I close my eyes as I recall the image seared into my brain. I know that if I see a photo of Charles's Louisa, I'd be able to know for certain if they're the same woman.

I blink my eyes back open. Jackie had said she'd been hopeful that one day they might reconnect. Had they managed it? Jackie had died not long after our last meeting, but perhaps our conversation spurred her to track Louisa down straight away?

Something occurs to me, and my hand grips the wooden spoon above the simmering sauce. How did Charles's wife, Louisa, die? Did fake Jacqueline see Jackie's sister, someone who would have known and loved her, as a loose end that needed to be tied up? Did she take the identity of one sister and the husband of the other? It's a possibility.

The fake Jacqueline, whoever she really is, must have known my Jackie very well to adopt her identity so successfully, and it seems now that she may have known about Louisa too. But if that's true, could she know about me?

My heart pounds in my chest. If she knows I'm Jackie's sister, am I another loose end to be tied?

The hot water boils over the saucepan, splattering all over the hob as these questions hurtle through my mind. I reach out to turn the temperature down, but a small splash flies out, burning my hand.

I'm so distracted I'm making stupid mistakes.

I breathe deeply, calming myself down as I run cool water from the tap over my burning skin.

No, this woman across the street can't know who I am. Jackie kept our connection a total secret from everyone in her life. I know that. We'd agreed that it was too dangerous for me for anyone to know that we were meeting up. I'm sure she would never have betrayed my trust.

Maybe there's another, less insane explanation for everything? I know that this fake Jacqueline wasn't responsible for Jackie's death, after all, even if she *did* take her identity after it happened. Perhaps I'm leaping to conclusions about Louisa, too. Maybe Charles's first wife having the same name as the other sister I never knew is just an awful coincidence. I suppose there's only one way to find out.

I need to see a photo. That way I can connect the two—or not.

Because one thing is for sure: I need the truth now more than ever. Not just for the sister that I knew but also, potentially, the sister that I didn't.

# Chapter Twenty-Four

The next week feels like a month. Charles is away in London the entire time, so I'm not able to speak with him. I know he's my only chance of discovering if my sister, Louisa, is also his dead wife, Louisa. There's no way that I can risk asking that woman across the street for anything. I can't involve Sofia and Matilda either. I don't want to put them at risk, nor do I think that they will be able to find out successfully without rousing "Jacqueline's" suspicions.

Charles is back tonight, though, and hopefully, I will see him tomorrow if he comes to collect his daughter after Sofia and Matilda's planned playdate.

Despite the delay and new questions that have been thrown up by Sofia's Louisa revelation, I'm hopeful that I can get everything back on track. I'm sure I'm *this* close to getting my answers at last. I can't stand to wait much longer.

But when Sofia gets home from school, she's unusually quiet. Normally, on a Friday night, we have a bit of a singalong while we decide what to eat for dinner. We both love to sing. There was a time when I even wanted to be a professional, but that ship has long since sailed.

I try everything to draw her out of her shell, even offering to get a takeaway as a special treat. But she barely responds. I decide to order her favorite pizza, but when it arrives, she hardly touches it.

"Sofia, darling," I say softly after half an hour of watching her nibble at her margarita pizza. "Please tell me what's wrong. Did something happen today?"

She sighs heavily as she drops her half-eaten pizza slice on to her plate.

"It's nothing, Mum. If I tell you, I know you'll freak out."

I bristle at that, but I try to keep my voice calm. "I promise you—I won't. Just tell me."

"Okay, fine," she sighs. "So you know we had an excursion to the aquarium today."

I nod, pursing my lips as I try to encourage her.

"Well, when I was there, something weird happened…"

I frown. "What kind of weird?"

"Well, we'd just watched a show at the coral reef, and then we were all starting to file out when a man in a baseball cap came up to me and blocked my exit." My heart starts to beat faster in my chest, but I try not to let my panic show. "It was strange because he said that he knew me."

"What?" I try not to shriek, but I know my voice squeaks.

"Yeah, then he said that I looked just like you."

"What did he look like?" I choke. I have to remind myself that she's safe. She's sitting here right in front of me. Nothing bad happened.

But who was this man? It can't be... No, I push back at the thought before it can finish that sentence. He's dead, I remind myself. He has to be...

"Did he tell you who he was?" I manage to ask.

"No... I was too surprised to ask. And I dunno, he was wearing a cap, and he was kinda in the shadows of the aquarium light. I was a bit too freaked to notice properly because then it looked like he was about to grab my hand as though to pull me away. But just at that second, Jacqueline came running back up the stairs. She called out my name, and that made the man slip away." Sofia shakes her head at the memory. I rush around the table and sweep her into a hug.

"It's lucky Jacqueline was there," she adds quietly.

"Did she know him?" I ask quickly.

"No, she said that she hadn't seen him properly—but I told her what happened." Sofia shrugs, crossing her arms around herself to say, in a small voice, "I was quite shaken up, and she looked after me. I guess I was a little scared to be stopped in the crowd like that."

"Of course, you were, darling!" My heart thunders in my chest. It sounded like this man knew *exactly* who Sofia was... and wanted to take her.

"So Jacqueline came in at the right moment?"

"Yeah..." she says into my shoulder. "I guess she scared him off by crying out my name. I dunno what might have happened next if she hadn't... But anyway, I'm fine, Mum, really I am." She tries to smile at me with a brave face. But I can see through it. The whole experience has made her worry.

My mind races. *God*, it could have been anyone. I always jump to the worst conclusion: that it could be someone from my past. In all these twelve years, I've never been able to shake the feeling of watching over one shoulder. Even though I know after all this time, I should be less paranoid. It's hard to stop, though. And if I am being completely honest, I know I've imbued that sense of "stranger danger" perhaps a bit too deeply into Sofia, too.

I sigh, frustrated. There's no way of knowing if the man was truly dangerous or not. No matter what, though, it scared Sofia. It always seems like I can't seem to keep Sofia feeling fully safe.

But this "Jacqueline" has.

It doesn't change the fact that she isn't who she says she is or that I'm starting to suspect that she might have done terrible things to ensure that no one ever finds out. But she helped Sofia today. And that is something. Maybe that suggests she isn't as terrible as I was starting to believe?

"Well, darling, it's good that Jacqueline was there then," I say, trying not to let my deep-rooted anxieties show. She nods slowly as I continue. "And you are so good at being cautious around people, too. Just like I taught you. But I'm sure everything is *fine*."

Sofia looks up at me with her deep green eyes—the mirror image of her father's. I can't help it when a shiver runs up my spine.

"I guess you're right," she says at last, returning to her pizza slice, but her face still looks heavy with unshed fear. I need to take her mind off it.

"I know… how about we have a bit of a *Harry Potter* movie marathon in my room tonight with some ice cream? It's just what the doctor ordered!"

She offers a small smile, tucking a strand of hair behind her ear. "That sounds great."

As soon as we finish up our pizza, I tell her to get everything ready upstairs while I gather the ice cream supplies. My mind wanders back to the strange man. Who *was* he?

On autopilot, I stand up and make my way methodically around the ground floor, checking every single lock and bolt.

Once I'm convinced that everything is safe and secure, I pull myself together. Pausing on the way to the kitchen, I glance in the hallway mirror. My normally sleek dark hair is matted, clinging to my face at odd angles. My face is always pale, but today, my fair skin looks ghostly, and my eyes look haunted. I run my fingers through my hair, pulling the mass back into a low ponytail, and pinch my cheeks to try and get some color back. It somewhat works, but there's no way of hiding my traitorous eyes and the fear plainly showing in them. I guess the stress of the last year of being hounded by the media, and then these last few weeks of constant surprises, is starting to get to me.

Grabbing the ice cream, I make my way up to my bedroom. As we snuggle together on my bed, I try to forget about this latest horror.

But questions keep rolling around my mind.

Are we safe here?

Do we need to disappear again?

I'm so exhausted by running. I don't want to anymore. It's not fair to either of us. But it feels like someone is threatening us between the letter, the trampled grass, and now this strange man.

I try to lose myself in the movie, and beside me, Sofia falls asleep on my soft down pillows.

I pull a stray lock off her porcelain skin. Her face is a picture of angelic innocence, and I will do anything to protect her. Maybe I should call Jacqueline and ask for her side of the story? Perhaps she could describe the man better to me than Sofia could.

As I press pause on the movie and step out of bed to stretch my legs and clear away the ice cream, my phone starts to buzz on the nightstand.

Looking down at the caller ID, I do a double take: it's Jacqueline. She must have read my mind.

In a swift movement, I grab the phone and stride into my walk-in wardrobe, silently pulling the door closed behind me.

"Hello, Jacqueline?" I take a seat on my bench in front of the window and gaze across at Jacqueline's house, imagining her there looking straight back at me.

"Hi, Anna. I hope you don't mind me calling so late," she says, her voice smooth as butter. "I wanted to check in on sweet Sofia after an incident today at the aquarium... I'm not sure if she told you..." Her voice trails off.

"Of course she did," I interrupt a little too quickly. "I mean... yes, she told me about the strange man and your help. Thank you. I'm not sure where the teachers were—I'll be having some words on Monday!"

"Oh, that's why I like to go on these things when I can. The teachers have far too many children to keep track of—and in a maze like the aquarium. You know how easily children can wander off…"

I frown, even though I know she can't see me. Is she accusing Sofia of getting *herself* into this situation?

"Anyway," Jacqueline continues. "I thought I'd call to tell you in case she hadn't. She was pretty shaken up by the whole thing. I'm not sure what was said between her and the man exactly, but they can't have spoken for more than a few seconds. I was at the back of the group as we left the room and noticed right away we had a straggler. I ran back into the last room and saw them close together. I didn't get a good enough look at his face because as soon as he saw me, he bolted. Hopefully, it was a simple misunderstanding. But I don't know—these things can be very scary. I wanted to let you know right away."

I twist my necklace with one finger. Jacqueline really did seem to have helped out my darling daughter today. I'm grateful. I swallow a lump in my throat at the idea of the danger Sofia might have been in if Jacqueline hadn't been there to save her. "Thank you for your help." I know I need to ask more questions and see if Jacqueline can recall anything more about the man. I pull myself together.

"Can you tell me anything else about what he looked like?" I manage thickly.

"Oh, I wish I could. But he was wearing a cap—and you know those aquarium lights, so many shadowy places. He ran off before I could get close enough."

My heart sinks at her words. It seems like I won't be getting any more answers about the description of this man.

"Okay... well, thank you again," I add quietly.

"Like I said to you before, we're practically family, with our girls being so close. I'll do anything to help Sofia—you know that."

Her words don't calm me, though. I'm certain it's no accident that they're reminiscent of what she said outside the coffee shop. I could never forget those words, and they play once more in my head: *We can be your family. Especially with our girls so close... they're like peas in a pod. Don't you think? In fact, they could even be sisters... Don't you worry, if anything happened to you, you know I'd be here for her. I'm good at that—stepping in when needed...*

I force myself back to the present. It reminds me that even though she might have helped Sofia today, I can't truly trust her until I know the truth about how she took my Jackie's identity and if she's connected to Louisa too.

Before I have a chance to respond, she changes the subject completely. "Oh Anna, while I have you on the phone, I also wanted to check if you received my invite to the PTA drinks at mine next Saturday early evening?"

I shake my head in confusion. "The PTA drinks?"

"Yes, didn't Sofia give you the invitation?"

"No..."

"Oh, how strange. It must have been lost in her bag then. I coordinate it every year before the half-term school break. It's crucial for future planning. So, do you think you'll be able to make it? Everyone will be there!"

"Well, I…" I start, trying to think of a good excuse. I don't really want to leave her after what happened today. I opt for honesty. "I'm not sure with Sofia…"

"Don't worry about that. Charles can take her out with Matilda. He does it every year."

I purse my lips. I can't exactly refuse that offer. "Oh, okay, well, thanks," I manage.

"Perfect! I'll mark you down as a yes! Sleep well, neighbor." The line goes dead.

Gazing out the window, I see at least three lights still on in the house across the street. As though on cue at my noticing, two go off, leaving a singular light at the top of the house.

I tuck my knees into my chest as I watch the beam of light and reflect on our conversation. This woman keeps surprising me. She really did seem to care about Sofia today and had saved her from potentially a terrible situation.

Maybe I've jumped to conclusions about her connections with my other sister, Louisa? It might not even be the same person. I shouldn't cast aspersions until I know for certain.

And could it be possible that I've just interpreted everything she's said in a negative light because I know she's pretending to be someone that she's not? Don't I know better than anyone how you can still be a good person but occasionally have to do what the world might perceive as a "bad" thing to survive? Isn't that precisely what I had to do to protect my baby girl?

I bury my face into my knees to block out the memories. I can't let myself go back there.

I chew on my lip, trying to think back. Maybe this fake Jacqueline *isn't* my enemy. But if she isn't, then who is?

# Chapter Twenty-Five

I barely sleep—tossing and turning all night as my recurring nightmare of Sofia being stolen away by hooded figures chases me.

By the time the light at last creeps through the curtains, it's a relief not to have to pretend to sleep anymore.

Turning on my side, I watch Sofia's sweet face, peaceful in sleep. Not a worry in the world.

As though she senses the direction of my thoughts, she blinks her eyes open. She squints, trying to remember where she is. Then, recognition dawns on her sleepy face. "Mama?" she yawns. "Why are you staring at me?" She scrunches her face into the pillow before turning back to face me.

I laugh, leaning over to lift a dark, silken strand off her face. "Oh, just the usual—I'm thinking how it is possible that you can look so angelic in your sleep and then instantly transform into a devil!"

"Hey!" she declares, sitting up. "Well, I learned it from you then," she retorts with a cheeky grin. But her words don't fill me with joy. No, instead, it makes me worry as she starts chattering away. How much of my darkness is actually embedded in my sweet daughter?

She throws a pillow in my face. "Hello... earth to Mother. Did you hear what I just said?"

I blink and force a laugh. "Ha, sorry. What was that?"

She rolls her eyes, tucking her loose hair behind her ears. "Is it still okay for Matilda to come over today?"

I nod. "Yes, of course." I need her to come over so I'll have a chance to talk to Charles at last.

"Great," she says, leaping out of my bed and padding to the door. But her mention of Matilda has brought the conversion I had last night hurtling back to me.

"Hey, wait," I say, stepping out of bed myself. "What was this about Jacqueline giving you an invitation to share with me for the PTA drinks?"

Sofia looks down at her bare feet. My gaze follows as she fidgets her toes into the plush carpet. "Oh, I didn't think you'd find out..."

"What do you mean, you didn't think I'd find out?" I demand, stepping toward her.

Her head flicks up to meet my narrowed eyes. "Well," she crosses her arms in front of her chest. Her too-long pajama top rolls over small hands, covering them. "I mean that I didn't think you'd want to go. You're always saying how you hate those kinds of things. So I was hoping you'd take me and Matilda to the cinema at the start of half term instead, like you promised."

My mouth drops open. "You mean—you wanted to *trick* me?"

"No!" she declares, shaking her head furiously. Her bob haircut flicks once, twice across her face like knives being thrown across a room. "I just..." She sighs and looks up at me once more, her green eyes full of pleading. "I knew you wouldn't like it anyway. And would have more fun with us. So why even bother telling you?"

Now, it's my turn to shake my head in disbelief. "Sofia, you lied to me!" I can't help it when it comes out more like a strangled yell.

"I, I..." she starts, her voice starting to wobble at my tone, and her eyes fill with tears. I *never* raise my voice at her. I never need to. "I'm sorry!" she wails, bursting into sobs.

"Oh, Sofia," I say, pulling her into a hug.

"I'm... I'm... sorry," she manages. "But I know how you hate parties after everything that happened... I was trying to save you. I didn't mean to lie or trick you!"

My heart breaks at her words. In her own misguided way, she's interpreted my hesitation at being in big groups or going to parties as me hating them because David had died at one. Not because of the real reason that I like to be careful about who I let into our lives.

"Sweetheart, it's okay," I soothe, stroking gentle fingers over her head. Eventually, her sobs subside, and I pull back to see her tear-stained face. "I understand now why you hid this from me. But please never do that again, okay?" She nods slowly, but I go on. "Even if you think you're trying to protect me. That's not your job. I'm the mother. It's my job to protect *you.*"

"Okay," she says in another quiet voice, grabbing me once more for a hug. I bite on my lip as I pull her close, considering my next words carefully. I want to tell her she's right. I don't really want to go to this drinks party next Saturday, and I'd much rather have a girl's movie night with her and Matilda. But I can't. I can't let her think she did the right thing by keeping this from me.

I sigh as I feel her tug me even tighter, and I smell her familiar scent. My sweet girl.

"Mum, you're squishing me," she squeaks. I let her go.

"Okay, now, off you go. And remember. No more keeping secrets."

"I promise," she says solemnly and then turns to leave.

As I watch her retreating figure, I feel guilt ripple through me. I'm keeping so many secrets from her. And I know that later today, I will betray her trust. Because to find out about Louisa, I'm going to have to tell Charles that I know the truth about Matilda's mother.

I sigh, walking toward the bathroom to start getting ready and telling myself all the while that I'm doing it for the right reasons.

The rest of the day, I start planning my approach with Charles. I hate to resort to any kind of trickery, especially when I'm sure he's already being duped by his current wife. But I must do whatever it takes to get him to tell me about his *first* wife. And show me a picture.

When Matilda comes over as planned, and her and Sofia's laughter echoes down every corridor of our house, guilt churns even deeper in my stomach. As the hours tick by to when Charles will come and collect her, my mind wonders whether this will hurt Matilda or help her? I hope the latter.

When the girls are occupied with popcorn and a movie, I start to make dinner—the sun has almost set overhead. Soon, I'm sure Charles will be popping over to pick Matilda up. Almost as though my thoughts have summoned him, the gate notification on my phone chimes. I look down at the camera to see a man's face bathed in shadow. I can't help it as my heart starts to race at the threatening image. But then I hear his voice come through the intercom. It's a little muffled, but it's definitely Charles.

"Come on around to the side gate," I say in relief and buzz him through.

I'm trying to concentrate on chopping the carrots in front of me, but my thoughts keep distracting me. And then I feel a familiar wetness prick at my eyes. I look up at the ceiling. Oh no, I can't be crying when he arrives. But it seems as though all the emotion and fear I've been keeping under lock and key has decided to escape at the worst time. Hiccupping, a sob erupts, and I bury my face in my hands. *Come on, Anna, get a hold of yourself.*

Breaking apart now isn't going to solve anything. I breathe deeply until I feel under control again. But as I come back down to earth, there's a knocking on the paned glass leading to the back garden. It's Charles.

I turn around, grabbing a tea towel to wipe my face free from stray tears. Throwing my shoulders back, I stride over to unlock the doors and sweep them open.

"Hello," I begin, forcing a smile.

"Hey, Anna," he says, flashing his kind grin back at me. "Have the girls been behaving?"

"Oh yes, they're deep in another movie marathon. I think they'll be a little while yet if that's okay!" I say, stepping back onto the cool marble floor to let him pass through.

"Of course," Charles laughs as he follows me inside. "It'll be nice to catch up for a bit." I watch as Charles looks around appreciatively at the modern space. He's been here a few times now, as we've started to become closer over the last couple of months, and each time, he's become more and more relaxed in my home.

"You've really done a lovely job here," Charles compliments me. "I remember what a hodgepodge it was before from the photos Jacqueline showed me of the listing!"

"Thank you," I reply softly.

"You have a great eye for interior design." He gestures around the room, and I follow his gaze, taking in the white kitchen cabinets with a light green splash back, the soft cream rug interweaved with matching green, the teak dining table, and the overhanging modern chandelier. Opposite the floor-to-ceiling windows are three oversized art deco prints, tying the room altogether.

"I wish I could take some lessons from you." He looks down at me, and his deep brown eyes feel like they're staring straight into my soul. I try to laugh off his words and step away from his intense gaze.

"Oh, I had lots of help." I wave it off, walking back toward the oven to pretend to turn off the stove.

"Anna." My back is still to him as he says in a quiet voice, "Are you okay? I saw you crying just now. And I wanted to ask if everything is alright?"

I spin around, my eyes wide.

He steps forward, only the marble island bench separating us now. "You don't have to tell me, of course. But I remember when we first met, and you asked me how I was *really* doing. That's stuck with me. I wasn't in the best headspace then. I was going through quite a tough time at work a couple of months ago. Every single case seemed to be collapsing. I was keeping everything to myself—I was probably being quite moody. But I didn't want to worry Jacqueline, she was so busy with work herself. And we've been trying to stick to only positive things this year after well... Never mind." He shrugs his shoulders, moving on from whatever he was going to say. "So, I only wanted to return the favor and ask if you were *really* okay?"

I feel tears spring to my eyes again at his kindness. I know I can't share the whole truth. But I will gently try to tell him about his daughter.

"There's something I should tell you," I say, eventually. "Do you want to sit down and have a drink?"

"Okay," he says, confusion flitting across his expression. I gesture to the bar stool under the island bench. He pulls it out and sits down with a thud.

I turn and grab the two wine glasses and a bottle of Napa Valley Pinot Noir that I'd placed out earlier. I remember Charles telling me before that Californian reds were some of his favorites, and luckily, David left me a large collection. I'm hoping it will soften the blow of what I have to tell him.

Once I've filled the two glasses, I hand one over to him and sit on the stool next to his. He's looking so nervously at me that he hasn't even registered the good wine.

"So," I begin, "I'm really sorry to have to be the one to tell you this because I know that it's something that you've obviously chosen to keep private..." Charles stares at me, hanging onto my every word. "But it seems that Matilda, umm, found her birth certificate."

"What?" Charles blurts, his eyes wide in disbelief. "But that means..." he shakes his head in shock.

"I'm so sorry," I say again.

He looks up at me now, a deep frown etched through his forehead. "Did Sofia tell you this?" I nod wordlessly. "Oh god, how did Matilda seem?"

"I... I'm not sure. I haven't spoken to her. I think she's okay. Just quite confused. Sofia didn't mention anything specifically."

He runs a hand through his hair in worry. "What am I going to do? How do I talk to her?" Before I have a chance to respond, he continues, "And I guess you know the whole truth then... about Matilda's birth mother?"

I nod again. He sighs deeply. "I hope you don't think badly of me and Jacqueline."

"Of course not," I say quickly, "it's not my place to have an opinion." Except, of course, it possibly is if Louisa is my actual sister. But I can't let him know that.

He shakes his head. "It was never meant to be a secret forever. We always planned to tell Matilda one day about her birth mother. But now, I've completely messed it up. Matilda did ask me the other week about her birth certificate. I waved her off, saying I wasn't sure where it was. But really, I wanted to talk to Jacqueline first. It was clearly time for us to tell her. But Jacqueline has been so anxious lately. I don't know what's up with her. It must be work. So, I've kept putting it off until a better time. But now... now Matilda already knows and hasn't even spoken to us. I'm the worst parent in the world." He buries his head in his hands.

The man is distraught. I need to comfort him somehow. "Don't say that. I'm sure you were acting in Matilda's best interests at the time.

That's all we can do as parents. And now you can talk to her and explain everything. I'm sure she'll understand."

He looks up slowly. "I hope you're right. Louisa's death... it's not an easy one to explain." I try not to jolt at him saying her name. It's the first time I've heard him say it. But he's distracted, as at last, he appears to have noticed the wine in front of him and takes a long gulp, almost finishing it in one.

"Louisa," he says to himself, his voice breaking slightly.

"Are *you* okay?" I can't help but ask him—echoing his words from earlier.

He laughs bitterly. "No, certainly not." He takes one more comforting sip of his wine before adding, "Oh Anna, Louisa's death is so hard for me to talk about."

"Then don't," I say on reflex. I want my answers, but I don't want to send this man who is clearly struggling off a cliff.

"No, I want to tell you. You're a widow. You might be the one person that can understand. And in some ways, it's been particularly hard the last couple of months because of you." I can't help but flinch at his words. He hurriedly says, "Sorry, it's not your fault... but well, it's hard for me to talk to Jacqueline about my grief. I've always been worried that she'll think I'm harboring after my ex-wife. Jacqueline saved me at a time when I needed to be pulled away from even thinking about Louisa. For years, I didn't speak about her at all. I guess also because I realized that Jacqueline can be a little... insecure. But honestly, these last couple of years, I've recognized that I'm still not over what happened. Louisa died so tragically, and it still sometimes feels like it could be all my fault." He looks away from me as though to stop the tears.

Before I have a chance to say anything, he continues, "And... I guess your arrival kind of brought it up a bit for me, too." I frown at his words as he explains, "When I first saw you on our doorstep, I thought for a split second that there was something about you that reminded me of Louisa. Clearly, I told myself that was insane; it was just the guilt talking..."

My heart skips a beat. "Really?" I manage to interrupt him. "Why would you think that?"

He blinks at my interruption. "Honestly, I don't know. When I looked at a photograph of Louisa later, I saw that you really are nothing alike. There is maybe a little something in your eyes. But anyway, it felt like a bit of a wake-up call, and I realized it was my long-buried grief and guilt talking. I've been trying to process it better quietly over the last few months. Anyway, when Jacqueline said the same thing to me, I denied it. Her imagination can run quite wild, and I didn't think it would be helpful for our relationship for her to become obsessed with something fictional. You're obviously *not* Louisa." He forces a laugh, but it sounds hollow. My palms feel sweaty.

"Look,' he says, fishing his phone out of his pocket. "I'll show you a photo." He scrolls for a moment, and I watch with bated breath as he at last finds an image and slowly, oh so slowly, turns to show me.

And it takes everything in me not to fall off my chair.

Because she might be a bit older in this photo that he's showing me. But without a doubt, the blonde-haired woman is the same one in that photo Jackie showed me all those years ago. And even if I couldn't remember that photo, I'd be able to confirm that this Louisa was definitely my sister. Because those eyes—she has *my* eyes. Our *mother's* eyes. The only small resemblance that could tie Louisa and me together. But a small enough similarity that it can also be dismissed as a strange coincidence.

I have to make a snap decision. Do I tell Charles everything I suspect or deal with Jacqueline myself?

"No, I'm obviously not her. I guess we just both have blue eyes," I manage to say. He nods in agreement. "I'm sorry that I brought this all up for you," I add, finally.

I decided that I couldn't tell him anything just yet—not when I don't have any idea of the actual reasons why his current wife might be so connected to *both* my sisters. There's no need to land this poor man with this too.

"Not at all," he says with a heavy sigh. "It's about time we talked to Matilda properly. I'm only sorry that she's discovered it for herself secretly and hasn't felt able to talk to us yet. I'll try to figure out a way to talk to Jacqueline about it as soon as possible, and then we'll speak to Matilda together. It'll be hard breaking the news to Jacqueline. She hasn't really been herself lately..."

Hasn't been herself? I want to latch onto that sentence and ask him about specifics. But before I have a chance, Charles gets to his feet.

"Thank you, Anna, for everything. You've been such a good friend to me."

A sickness churns in my stomach at my deceit. If only he knew the whole truth.

I avoid looking him in the eyes as I get stand, too. "Anytime."

Then he stretches his arms out wide. "Can I give you a hug?" he asks.

"Of course," I say and step into his embrace. I allow myself to feel safe in his friendly warmth for one moment before I wriggle away. "Let me know how you go," I say finally. "I'm just here."

"I know," he says with a small smile. With that, he turns away, walking toward the corridor to call out for his daughter. I can't help but feel a chill at the absence of his warmth. It was nice feeling supported for a moment. I'd forgotten how that feels.

But as I turn back to the countertop and see the last remnants of my blood-red wine, I can't help the shiver that rushes down my spine.

Because all this has proved one thing: Charles's late wife, Louisa, was also *my* Louisa. And that means that Matilda is also my niece… My mind whirls.

What has that woman across the street got to do with both my sisters?

I clench my fists tight in frustration. Enough is enough. I have all the information I can possibly find out for myself. Now, my only option left is to demand answers straight from the source.

As I hear a mingling of Charles, Sofia, and Matilda's voices down the corridor, an idea dawns on me. And a promise.

Because now, I have to be brave. I have to be brave for all of them.

Next Saturday at the PTA drinks, when both Matilda and Sofia will be safely away with Charles, will be my perfect chance.

With Jacqueline busy entertaining, I might have a chance to search the house properly for any scraps of evidence without her noticing. And then, by the end of the night, Jacqueline should have had quite a few drinks—*that* will be my moment to strike. To demand the truth.

So I pick up the wine glass and take a long sip.

I am going to make sure that this party will be my chance to catch her out at last.

223

# Part Three

# CHAPTER TWENTY-SIX

## JACQUELINE

Today is the day of my annual PTA drinks, and I think it's going to be the best one yet. Well, for *some* people, not for others. Specifically not for that deceitful widow across the street.

Because tonight, I will force the truth out of her at last. Now that she has done everything possible to ruin my life. Most recently, her role in forcing Matilda to find out the truth about her birth mother. I don't care that Charles says it was Matilda's idea to go searching for her birth certificate. I'm sure that Anna's behind it somehow. She must have put the idea into Sofia's head in the first place after I overheard that conversation between her and Matilda all those weeks ago. Sofia clearly encouraged Matilda to go looking at her mother's request.

Luckily, when we sat down and spoke to her a few days ago, Matilda appeared to accept our explanations, but it was heartbreaking listening to her ask questions about Louisa. This woman gave birth to Matilda and then abandoned her. *I'm* the only mother Matilda has ever known.

I am now certain that Anna is somehow connected to Louisa. I thought Louisa had been the only family left in the real Jacqueline's life. But I guess I was wrong... because why else would Anna have coordinated all this? I just don't know how she's connected to them yet. But tonight will be the night I find out. And it will be the night I get even.

I can't undo what that woman has done to my perfect family. But I *can* get her out of my life for good.

Watching my reflection in my vanity mirror, I twirl my curly locks up into an elegant bun. I stick careful, sharp pins in one by one as I think back over the last six weeks. Everything I've done. All the little bits and pieces I've coordinated to lead me to today.

Because at that fateful Easter party in the Drummond mansion, I realized that Anna might know something about my darkest secret: that I'm not really Jacqueline Kelly. I never have been.

When Jasper told me that she was from Ohio too but had been lying about it, pretending to be British-Irish, I suspected that it couldn't be simply a coincidence that she'd moved in across the street from us. It seemed clear that Anastasia Drummond—if that is even her real name—could potentially know my secret. I didn't know how, and I didn't know *why,* but it all made sense now why she'd been so intent on hanging out with Charles and getting to know the other mothers at school behind my back. To get information on me.

I have no idea what she might do with the knowledge that I'm not who I say I am, but waiting to find out wasn't something that I could risk. So, I had to take matters into my own hands to discover if she really did know my secret, without, of course, asking her outright.

Over the last few weeks, Freddie and Jasper have thought that I agreed to help them find proof of her hand in Sir David's death—but really, I need to know who she is for my own sanity and safety. After all, as I always say, knowledge is power.

Charles and Matilda have both been feeding me useful tidbits of information, unaware, but the real breakthrough moment of clarity came with our coffee shop trip.

Freddie tried to start off by finding out about Anastasia's "morals". He attempted to get a nibble through that news story of the woman who ran away with her child, his theory being that it might reveal some of her true nature. I honestly didn't think it would do anything. If Anna had been clever enough to kill her own husband and not get caught, she wasn't going to get caught out by Freddie's clumsy questioning.

However, observation is a key skill when trying to pick up things that someone is hiding, and what I witnessed was *very* interesting indeed. Because I saw quite clearly that the story terrified Anna. It got me thinking on the spot—could Anna's fears around Sofia's safety stem from a similar situation? A situation where Anna had to steal her own child away from someone else? I turned my phrasing over carefully in my mind for the rest of that walk. I wanted to confirm two things: had she run away from a similar situation? And did she really know my secret?

When we were about to arrive at the café, and Freddie, Matilda, and Sofia were all out of sight, I pounced. I did it so carefully that if you were overhearing the conversation, you wouldn't think that there was anything amiss in my words at all. But, if there was something you might be trying to hide about your past, then it would definitely make you uncomfortable.

I began with a subject that I knew would make her bite: her daughter. I set the perfect trap with an easy compliment about her being *such a sweet girl*. Then, I commented on Sofia's eyes. The one feature I'd noticed that is nothing like her mother's, who has the ice blue eyes that first brought Louisa to my mind. Though, of course, I still don't know if Anna *is* connected to Louisa...

But in that moment, I wanted to discover whether Sofia's eyes were similar to her father's in any way because if Anna's reaction to Freddie's question was at all to do with Sofia's father, then Anna would likely become edgy about answering. And she did. She could barely speak as she confirmed it, and when I offered my apologies about her loss, she was unable to look me in the eyes.

Bingo. Questions about Sofia's father made her nervous. My first question was somewhat answered. Perhaps she had run away from a similar situation...

It was the ideal lead for asking an innocent enough follow-up question about whether she and Sofia had any other family. This also was a resounding no. I wasn't surprised. If Anna was related to the real Jacqueline and Louisa, then she wouldn't exactly tell me.

But all the same, I was pleased. Because I knew that I was under her skin when she tried to walk away from me.

Next, I spoke what I now knew must be Anna's deepest fear. "It's lucky she has you. Imagine if anything happened to take you away..."

Anna had paused her retreat, shaking her head, clearly seeing the threat inherent in my words.

I'd stepped forward, taking her hand in mine. It was clammy with fear.

And then, it was the time to land the killer blow. To find out for sure if she knew something about *my* secret. "So don't you worry, if anything happened to you, you know I'd be here for her. I'm good at that—*stepping in when needed.*"

My last words were purposeful—I wanted to reference taking the place of someone else without saying it outright. And it paid off. I watched as her composed mask fell away entirely. Her pale face was ghostly in the grey light. It was only for a moment, but I knew, I just knew that I'd caught her. I'd spent long enough covering my tracks. I had learned how to read people well over the years. And my words hit home. She knew about me, alright. She wouldn't react like that if she didn't. I just didn't know how she knew.

From that moment on, I could only assume that the real Jacqueline and Louisa had more family members that I didn't know about. I didn't know how it was possible. I thought I'd been so careful. But I'd have to figure it out now.

She'd glanced across at me, her piercing blue eyes flashing at me like shards of ice. I could see the fear and revulsion in them clear as day. The eyes that I was now convinced must be connected to Louisa's. Even if Charles kept dismissing the connection for some reason.

At the time, all I did was smile. I would bide my time for the right moment.

But now, after Anna's final parting shot by exposing Matilda's real mother, the time has definitely come. Tonight is the night. And I have the perfect plan.

I pout with steely determination as I finish applying my dark red lipstick in the mirror.

I won't let her have a chance to destroy my carefully curated life by exposing my secret. Before the end of the day, Anna will be little more than a footnote, and I will be safe at last.

# Chapter Twenty-Seven

## Anna

As I stare at the doorbell, it takes everything in me not to turn and run away from the house across the street. I know this is a solid plan, and it's about time I took a risk, but I'm still nervous.

I spent ages getting ready, straightening my hair, and applying my lipstick perfectly. I'd planned just the right outfit: my favorite green and white long-sleeved maxi dress. Nice, but not too nice. I don't want to leave anything to chance.

It was only when Charles and Matilda came to pick Sofia up that I hesitated. I saw Freddie in the front seat of the car, and it made me squirm. I told myself I was being silly. If Charles trusted Freddie enough to hang out with him, Sofia would be fine with them. I was only feeling jumpy because of what I had to accomplish tonight.

Charles said they were off to go and watch some movies. These two girls—they love their stories so much. Whether it is books or films, they can't get enough of them. I knew they'd have a fantastic time.

Now, I have to let go of worrying about Sofia for a few hours and concentrate on what I've come here to do.

Because it's time. Time to get the truth at last.

I press my finger down onto the cool metal of the bell. I can't help but think it feels like the cool blade of a knife, and I step back quickly.

A few moments later, the door swings open to reveal my lying neighbor. She's dressed in an elegant white jumpsuit. A wolf in sheep's clothing?

"Come on in," she says. Her smile is wide and pleasant, but it doesn't reach those light brown eyes.

I swallow audibly as I step over the threshold and walk past my host.

As she shuts the door carefully behind me, I realize that there is something a little odd.

The house is completely silent. Not a splinter of sound breaks through the empty corridor. I thought this was supposed to be a party, but it seems like I'm the only one here.

My heart starts to pound in my chest.

Where is everyone?

# Chapter Twenty-Eight

## Anna

I whirl around. What is going on?

I turn back to Jacqueline, who smiles at me once more. She's blocking the door. My exit.

"What's wrong, Anna?"

"Umm... Where is everyone?" I force my voice to sound calmer than I feel.

"Oh, don't worry, they're coming," she says with a twinkling laugh. "You're just the first to arrive."

I frown. I don't know whether to believe her or not. The grandfather clock in the hall says six-thirty, the time the invitation said to arrive. Maybe everyone else is running late.

Jacqueline follows my line of sight. "Everyone else is coming at *seven*-thirty. I thought it might be nice for you to come a little earlier so we can have a neighborly catch-up. Sorry if that wasn't entirely clear."

She brushes past me and down the corridor to their kitchen.

I look back at the front door. Do I believe her? Or do I run instead? I could escape right now. But I've come here tonight for a purpose. And

233

just because she's taken me by surprise, it doesn't mean that I should back down from my plan.

I make a decision. Walking inside the airy kitchen, soft music greets me.

Jacqueline is placing a series of canapés on trays, ready to be put into the oven. There really must be people coming over, then. I hope.

But the vision makes me pause. From this distance, it is crazy how similar she looks to my sister. It's only when she gets closer that the wrongness becomes clear, just like that first time I saw this woman at the Drummond Hotel in London.

A small, naïve part of me still can't help but hope that there's a simple explanation for this whole situation. But I doubt it. And if not, I just hope I can take on the woman in front of me.

When I first came up with my big plan and decided to move to Bristol to find out the truth for my poor sister Jackie, I'd weighed up how dangerous it might be—weighed up how much risk I was potentially putting myself and Sofia in by moving across the street from this usurper. I'd convinced myself that it would be fine because this woman would have *no* idea of my real reason for being here and that because she had a family, she wouldn't do anything to physically hurt us.

But maybe I was wrong.

Because if she has figured out why we really moved here and if she knows how closely connected I am both to the real Jacqueline and Louisa, then it might be more likely the case that she will do *anything* to protect the life that she's built.

As I step further into the kitchen and I see her cold, calculated smile, I'm convinced that maybe this whole time she's orchestrated the strange things that have been happening: the threatening note saying "YOUR TIME IS UP", the trampled grass—perhaps she'd even tried to scare Sofia on purpose at the aquarium. Who knew what kind of mind games she might be capable of?

Because all these things serve a purpose of scaring us away—and who else would want to do that?

But she will not frighten me away now. Because enough is enough. I need to stop running. I need to show Sofia that I can be brave. That I can protect this new life for us. This woman has already taken one Kelly sister's identity and another's husband. I'm not going to let her take anything else from our family. I'm going to be brave.

I'm going to stick to my plan and force the truth out. Tonight.

# Chapter Twenty-Nine

## Jacqueline

Anna appears awfully confident for someone who's walked into a lion's den. Maybe she doesn't realize it yet? But there's no way she's leaving here tonight without agreeing to what I want. For her to leave Bristol and never come back.

I'll do that by catching her out in her little white lies. Then, I'll be able to scare her enough to leave. I've been working up to this moment... Now, I just have to set my final trap.

"So," I say. "I think we need some wine." Before she has a chance to refuse, I march across to the tall oak cabinet and retrieve two glasses.

Anna watches silently as I claim an open bottle of rosé that I'd left chilling in a large ice bucket. Filling our glasses, I hand one over to her.

I watch as she frowns at the offering, carefully considering it. But at last, she accepts the glass and takes a gulp. I sip as I study her.

She is still stunning, but her naturally pale complexion has turned sallow over the last few weeks, and there are some blue-black shadows under her eyes. I take cheer—my plan is working. It seems it hasn't taken much to cause her some sleepless nights. All I needed to do was send her a threatening note, ask her a few leading questions, and make her think that Sofia was in danger from a strange man...

"Thank you," she says at last, as though remembering her manners with a nervous smile.

"Not at all. Why don't you follow me through to the sitting room? It'll be more comfortable." She nods as I lead the way out of the kitchen and back down the corridor. At the front door, I veer left into the sitting room. I survey the scene—the white sofa and two matching armchairs facing it, the Liberty print cushions plumped perfectly on top. I gesture her in and toward the most comfortable armchair by the window. I want her to feel at home. For now.

She floats through with that irritating grace of hers and folds neatly into the seat, looking up at the artwork above her. I walk past her, sit down on the opposite sofa, and swirl my wine.

"This is a lovely room," she says, studying the paintings lining the walls. I follow her gaze, taking in the collection we've accrued over the years.

"Thank you. I only tend to use it for special occasions—otherwise, we're mostly in the kitchen or the living room next door. I'm glad you like it. I thought it would be nice for us to chat for a bit before the others arrive. I feel like we've been neighbors for two months, and I hardly know you. I mean, I don't even know where you're from..."

She visibly stiffens at my words and drags her eyes away from the paintings to lock onto mine. I know she must be trying to hide it, but I can see the fear in her eyes. Now, I'm sure it won't take much for me to scare her enough into leaving—which is my ultimate aim tonight. Because, of course, I know where she's from now, thanks to Jasper, but

Anna doesn't know that. She's never told me herself. This is the perfect place to start my questioning... where I'll back her into a corner and make her see that her only option is to leave Bristol for good. Because, over the last few weeks, I've been steadily building up to this moment.

After Jasper's party, as well as stealthily gathering as much as I could from her, I knew I also had to come up with a plan to shake her up and make her think that she wasn't safe here anymore. To make her realize that her only option was to leave.

Step One was that letter suggesting her *time is up*. Of course, I wasn't sure why she had hidden her past from the Drummond Family, but a person only does that if they have something to hide. I know that better than anyone. I thought it would help make her feel potentially anxious about something—or someone—coming back from her past. And it was perfect timing for that letter to arrive on the same weekend as our little coffee excursion.

Step Two was carefully questioning her during our walk. That's when I learned that whatever she was hiding about her past might have something to do with Sofia's father. That was *very* interesting to me. It provided me with a clear route to build her paranoia around Sofia's safety. Something that, if she felt was under threat, might be enough to force her to leave.

Step Three was making her believe that Sofia might actually be in danger at that aquarium excursion. I enlisted the assistance of Nathaniel, Freddie's friend, and my client. I needed a man that Sofia had never met before and someone who was on Jasper's side. We met for a coffee before I joined the school group, and I asked if he could do me a favor. I asked him to briefly speak to Sofia and hold her back from the rest of the group for a few moments. He was a little confused and hesitant, but when I said it was all part of my plan to help Jasper and Freddie out in their quest to catch Anastasia in her lies, he agreed. And then I got to be "Sofia's savior", which I now hoped was enough for me to have gained Anna's trust—even a little—all to lead up to tonight. Where I hope I'll put the final nail in the coffin that is Anna's time in Bristol.

Because, of course, all these small things have served the purpose of making Anna worry about Sofia's safety. While over the last few weeks, I've played my part, being friendly and not doing anything outwardly to arouse suspicion—I hope. Potentially friendly enough to make her think twice about what she thinks she might know about me. Because the fact that she hasn't exposed me yet over these last couple of months has made me think that she can't really have any proof. And, of course, I'm not entirely surprised: I have been so careful in making sure that no one can prove that I'm not Jacqueline Kelly.

But even if I know she might struggle to prove my secret, I don't want her hanging around anymore. I want her gone. And tonight, I also want to try and discover *how* she might be connected to the real Jacqueline and Louisa—*why* she knows about me in the first place. I have to be sure that after her, there isn't anyone else left who might know about me. She likely won't tell me anything, but maybe I can get a little out of her. Either way, it will make her feel anxious, which suits me fine, too.

So now, first, I'll gently start to unpick her lies about where she's really from through careful questioning. And then, when she appears nervous enough, I'll tell her that I've seen someone snooping around her house. I'll build up such a picture that she should hopefully realize on her own that her only option is to leave. If she wants herself and Sofia to be safe. I hope.

Honestly, it doesn't have to become messy. Not if she realizes the safest thing for her to do will be to just disappear. If she doesn't... Well, then I might have to resort to other more *bloody* tactics... But I'd rather not.

My thoughts dart away from my careful plan and back to the present as she says, "Oh, I thought Charles might have filled you in. I'm British-Irish, I suppose..." She takes a mouthful of her wine.

"That's so interesting," I respond, timing my next sentence perfectly. "You know, I've often wondered about your accent. Occasionally, I think it sounds American, a bit like mine. But maybe that's just the Irish twang." I watch Anna choke on her wine, spluttering as she swallows.

I go on, ignoring her gasps for breath. "Irish ancestry must be so handy for dual nationality," I say conversationally. "Do you have it through your mother or father's side?"

Anna wriggles in the armchair. I try not to laugh. Oh, it is so easy to mess with her. She should really take lessons from me about hiding your past. Her lies are written all over her face. I'm surprised Sir David never saw through them.

I'm enjoying my show so much that I almost miss her quiet response. "My mother's," she says softly.

I smile at her discomfort. Gosh, this is going to be even easier than I thought. But then she looks up, her ice-cold eyes glacial. Maybe I was wrong about this going my way because then she says, "My sisters were proud of their Irish ancestry, too."

Her eyes narrow onto mine, full of deliberate meaning.

Her sisters? Do I dare consider what I think she's implying? My glee evaporates in an instant, and I suddenly feel like I'm on the back foot as my mind races to fill in the blanks.

I thought Jacqueline only had one sister: Louisa.

I thought *that* was taken care of. And that there was no one left that could call me out on my bluff.

But maybe not... My thoughts whir, trying to piece it together any other way. But Anna's meaning seems clear to me: she could be the *real* Jacqueline's other sister.

How is that possible? I'd been so careful in my research when I did what I had to and became Jacqueline. But clearly, I had been wrong.

I've been right to be suspicious of Anna these last two months, though. Because there had been something familiar about her, something about those ice-blue eyes that reminded me of Louisa. It's because they were sisters, too.

I curse myself for not being thorough enough in my search, not thorough enough in my questioning of Charles. But equally, maybe he'd never known anything about another sister either.

This woman in front of me had been hidden in the shadows of the real Jacqueline and Louisa's lives.

I throw up my walls on instinct, shoving my mask back into place. There is no way that she can know that she's gotten to me.

I have to stay in control. I have to get rid of her—no matter what.

# Chapter Thirty

## Anna

Well, it certainly looks like I've got her attention now. I watch as she stiffens, and her eyes dart over every inch of my face as though trying to figure it out. Clearly, my words have taken her by surprise. She doesn't know *everything*, then.

I let out a small smile. It's now time for me to be in the driver's seat. And I'm going to start with Louisa.

After my conversation with Charles, when I discovered for certain that Matilda is my sister's child—and so my biological niece—I'd felt even more responsibility to keep her safe and find out how this con artist weaseled her way into Charles and Matilda's life. Charles had texted me earlier in the week to say that he and Jacqueline had spoken with Matilda and it had gone as well as could have been expected. I was happy for him and for Matilda. But I wanted answers from this woman now.

"It must have been a stressful week for you," I say carefully, "with telling Matilda about her birth mother. Louisa, was it?"

I watch her intently. I wish I could read her mind. But she's replaced her momentary surprise with practiced calm. I try not to gulp—she is clearly much better at these kinds of games than I am. But I have to try.

The silence stretches between us. I'm waiting to see if she will offer any sort of explanation or if I'll have to say more. As I observe her, I notice that she's a little less put together than when I saw her last week. Only small details: her excessive makeup, her taut cheekbones. But the smallest details are the most important.

Then, at last, she speaks, and what she says surprises me, "I wish we'd had the chance to tell her ourselves, but she's doing okay with it. Because it doesn't change anything. Matilda *is* still my daughter," she says emphatically, looking me straight in the eyes. "She might not biologically be my child—but I love her with every fiber of my being. I love her just as much as any mother could—maybe even more."

I blink, taken aback. I wasn't expecting to hear something like this. I could think that it's simply another lie. But I can see the fierce depth of love in her eyes. A mother's love.

I'm about to speak when a loud ring cuts through the silence like a knife, and we both jolt in surprise. Realizing it's my phone, I fish it out of the pocket of my dress. An unknown number. I send it to voicemail.

"Don't you want to get that?" Jacqueline asks, cocking her head to one side.

"Unknown number," I say. "I never answer those. And besides, I think this conversation is going to be more important."

She nods once and opens her mouth to say more when my phone erupts again. The same unknown number. Strange.

"Someone is very persistent," she says with a sigh. "Maybe just answer it, then we can carry on?"

I reluctantly admit to myself that she's probably right. Standing up, I walk toward the window to take the call. On the final ring, I pick up.

"Hello?" I say down the line.

"Why, hello there," says a deep voice. A voice I would know from anywhere. The voice that haunts me when I'm both awake and asleep. A voice that I thought I would never hear again.

Because it's the voice of a man I thought I'd killed.

# Chapter Thirty-One

## Jacqueline

I watch as every last scrap of color drains from Anna's face. I can't hear the words she's listening to, only a rumbling voice, like a roll of thunder.

And then I see it—I see the whip of panic lash through her.

She screams, the half-drunk glass of wine she'd been clutching falling from her hand and shattering across the floor.

I leap up in shock, jumping out of the way as the shards scatter around her.

I watch in horror as Anna clutches the phone even tighter and screams again, screams at the person on the end of the line. But it's too late; they appear to have hung up. She stares at the phone in disbelief, in utter shock, as she starts to shake all over.

Anna crumples to the floor as she mutters so low I almost can't hear the four little words: "What have I done?"

I grab her, pulling her up onto her feet. She's trembling like a leaf tumbling through a gale-force wind, but I drag her back onto the armchair. She flops onto it like a doll. I turn abruptly and carefully step around the glass to close the curtains. I don't want any prying eyes at this moment.

"What's going on?" I say, kneeling down next to her. "Who was that on the phone?"

Anna covers her head with her hands and keeps muttering, "No, no, no, no. What have I done?"

I grab her arm and shake her, injecting as much fear and command into my voice as I can. "Anna, please tell me what's going on?"

She looks up at me then, a tinge of green to her face, as though the sight of me makes her want to be sick.

"Oh, god," she mutters. "I'm so sorry."

That makes me pause. Why would she be apologizing to me?

"What do you mean?" I demand. "Why are you sorry?"

"It's... it's all my fault," she manages through clattering teeth. She must be having a panic attack. Her body is refusing to stop shaking.

I grab a blanket and throw it over her knees. Then I drop down next to her. "Tell me, please." I implore. "What's happened?"

"He... He... He has them."

"Who has them? And who does he have?" I ask, frowning as a sense of dread starts to creep through my bones.

"He... he's taken..." Her voice breaks, but she manages to say, "Sofia and... Matilda." She rocks back and forth. "He says no police. Or he'll, or he'll... Oh god. I'm so... so... sorry."

I freeze, unable to process what she's said. The horror of her words. "Sofia and Matilda... have been taken?" I scream and then shake her hard in desperation. Trying to make her look at me.

But it's as though she doesn't hear my words. It's as though that moment of lucidity was too much for her. And now, she stares into space, eyes unseeing as she rocks back and forth, shaking in absolute shock.

I leap up, running my hands through my hair. What is going on? Matilda's been taken?!

But before I get any further through my thoughts, I feel my phone begin to buzz in my pocket. I slide it out and frown at who's calling.

Nathaniel. What does he want? I wonder if something is wrong with his rental, but I can't deal with that right now.

Now is not the time to talk; I need to figure out what's going on. So I send the call to voicemail, and instead turn back to Anna, who is still lost to her shaking. I take a step toward her when my phone buzzes again, this time with a text message from Nathaniel.

> I'm the one you're looking for. You'd better call back.

My blood turns to ice in my veins. No. It can't be.

I rush to unlock my phone and press his number.

It only rings once before the call is answered.

"Nathaniel?"

"Why, hello, Jacqueline ... if that is your real name."

And it takes everything in me not to collapse to the floor at what he says next.

# CHAPTER THIRTY-TWO

## JACQUELINE

A throaty laugh echoes down the line. "Oh, you're good," he observes. "Almost as good as me at deceit." I don't have the words to respond. But he goes on. "Now, I'm going to make this really simple for you..."

Staring out the window to the quiet cul-de-sac beyond, I can't believe this is happening.

"Come to my new home—you know where it is, of course." He chuckles. It sends ice shooting down my veins. "And bring *her*. No police. No one else. Not if you both want your girls back safely. And if you don't care about that—maybe you'll come because otherwise, I'll reveal your little secret. I know who you *really* are and what you've done. And you don't want that getting out... do you? All I want is for us to have a little chat. You have an hour. Don't be late."

The line goes dead.

I'm frozen. Utter panic grips every fiber of my being as I stare out the window, unblinking, trying to process what I've just heard.

That was Nathaniel—*Nathaniel*! Freddie's kind friend, who I'd welcomed into our home with open arms. But it seems like it was all just a *lie*? How does he even know my secret?

Anna somehow thinks this is her fault—but I know it's mine. Because *I* let Nathaniel into our lives. And if Matilda or Sofia get hurt, it's all because of *me*.

I might be many things—and I might still want Anna gone—but I cannot allow that to happen.

We need to save them.

# Chapter Thirty-Three

## Anna

I vaguely hear Jacqueline on the phone, but my eyes are squeezed tight shut as my breathing comes thick and fast. *Calm down, and get a grip on yourself.* But I'm having a full-blown panic attack, and there's no way to rein it in.

Because after hearing the voice that haunts my sleep, all my nightmares have been realized.

I thought that Nate was dead. I thought that I'd *killed* him after what he did. Because it was Nate who killed my sister, the real Jacqueline Kelly.

But it turns out I was wrong. He's still alive.

Maybe this is the reason he's haunted my nightmares, why whenever something bad happens, I've always jumped to the thought that it could be him or his cronies trying to frighten us and plan their revenge.

Perhaps, on some level, I *knew* that I hadn't finished the job. That he had simply been unconscious and not dead. I knew my new life was too good to be true.

It was because of Nate that I had to plan my escape. And it was because I thought I'd killed him that I didn't want anyone from my

250

old life to ever find me again. I couldn't risk his dangerous accomplices from our old life finding us. And I couldn't risk going to jail either. What would have happened to Sofia?

I run my fingers—damp with sweat—through my hair as I try to think of what to do. I need to pull myself together, I have to, *I have to*. If I want to save Sofia—my daughter. And Matilda—my niece.

And I will. No matter what.

Because this is all my fault. I'll do anything to save them.

I blink up at last to see Jacqueline stooping over me. A look of terror in her eyes. No matter the truths still left unsaid between us, after what she's just told me, I know that she'll do anything to save Matilda, too. I hope.

At last, I register Jacqueline's words. "I've spoken to him on the phone. I know where they are. We have to go and save them. There's no time to waste."

And with that, she turns on her heels and races out the door. I'm thankful that at least one of us has some idea of what to do. I feel frozen, blinking after her, my mind pushing past the shock at last to wonder how this even happened? Where are Charles and Freddie? Weren't they supposed to be looking after Sofia and Matilda?

I force my limbs to move and bump into Jacqueline outside the entry. "Here, take this coat," she says, thrusting a jacket into my hands. Then she pushes me out the front door toward the car.

In a daze, I become aware of the cold early evening breeze, tangling my hair around my face. She opens the car door, and I fall inside.

"I've texted all the PTA mothers and told them I had a family emergency," Jacqueline tells me as she hops into the driver's seat and reverses out of the driveway and onto the road with a sharp spin. She presses her foot on the accelerator, and we speed out of the cul-de-sac and onto the main road, which winds up toward the gorge.

I don't say anything, not trusting myself to speak. My mind is too wired with fear, thinking about Sofia and Matilda. What he might do to them... And how does he even know that Matilda is my niece, too?

*Don't think the worst.* I tell myself. *He only wants you. It's always been about you.*

I don't know what we're going to do when we get to wherever we're going. This woman next to me might be able to stay calm and think this can be talked through. But I know how dangerous Nate can be.

As Jacqueline zooms over the Clifton Suspension Bridge, I chance a look across at her. Her eyes are locked on the road ahead, her curls falling over the side of her face like a curtain.

She seems calm. Too calm.

As she drives past Ashton Court and further into the quiet countryside surrounding Bristol, I realize that I haven't even asked her about how Nate could have gotten to the girls if they were supposed to be safe with her husband.

I manage to find my voice. "How did this happen? Weren't the girls supposed to be with Charles and Freddie at the movies?"

She doesn't take her eyes off the road as she replies. "Yes, they were. I have no idea."

My stomach twists at her words.

Another thought hits me—in my daze, I'd assumed she'd used my phone to talk to Nate and get the address. But actually, my phone had been with me the entire time. So, he called her directly. He had her number.

My heart starts to beat an erratic rhythm in time with the windscreen wipers that are bashing away the falling rain.

She must know Nate already. But how?

It can't be much past seven-thirty now, but the grey storm clouds and rain are making the deserted country lanes as dark as if it were the middle of the night. A lone headlight flashes at us, causing Jacqueline to swerve out of the way as she continues to barrel along as fast as she can.

And then the car turns sharply and stops, sudden as a slap. I slam against the seatbelt.

Jacqueline clears her throat, and when I turn, her face is in shadow, her expression unreadable.

She speaks in a low voice. "It's time."

My breath catches in my throat.

I know that right now, I don't have any other choice but to go with her. To trust that she wants Matilda and Sofia back safely as much as I do. I know I can't go to the police. Facing the man that I ran from is my only chance to save my little girl.

But all the same, I can't help it as one question echoes through my mind: Am I about to save my child, or have all my lies led me to the biggest trap of all?

# Chapter Thirty-Four

## Jacqueline

As I turned down the dark lane, I felt every single one of the cattle grids that we bumped over on the long driveway. There isn't another neighbor for miles.

I gulp. We can't really get much more isolated than this old Victorian vicarage, located in a forgotten village on the far outskirts of Bristol. When I helped Nathaniel find this house, he said one of the big appeals of Bristol was that he would be able to live in the countryside but not be more than a half-hour drive into the city center. He said he wanted to find a house with "lots of character", surrounded by a vast garden and fields as far as the eye could see so his girls could run around... Had he lied about that, too? It seems he's lied about everything.

When we'd come to view the property together, and I'd remarked that the cell phone reception was practically non-existent, he'd laughed and said, "Perfect." I'd thought it was because he preferred a simpler life and wanted to enjoy the joys of the countryside.

Now, as I step out of the car and stare through the enormous canopy of trees framing the old house in the distance, I think that his apparent happiness at the lack of signal might have been for a very different reason entirely.

But why has he taken Matilda and Sofia? What does he want with me and Anna? That's what I'm not sure of.

I wrap my raincoat around me tighter, tucking the hood over my head as the rain continues to pour in a steady stream. Sunset is still around an hour away, but with the overhanging woods and dark clouds, it almost feels like it could be night.

I glance up at the house. It looks like something from a gothic novel, the stonework of each pointed arch window twisting into ornate knots. The house sits in the middle of an enormous garden that abuts rolling hills on one side and stretches up into a tangle of hooded and gnarled trees on another. A singular rope swing floats in the perches of an old oak tree on the lawn. I shiver.

When we'd looked around here in the daytime, full of sunshine, I'd thought it idyllic. But now, as I watch the shadows leering over the house and listen to the swing creaking in the wind, dread creeps into my bones.

I tap my coat pocket for reassurance, feeling the sharp kitchen knife I've stashed away for safekeeping. Nathaniel might have said that he only wants to talk, but I'm not taking any chances.

Anna sniffles next to me, snapping me back to the present. She's emerged from the car and come to stand beside me. She wraps her arms close around her chest and looks nervously up at the house.

"Okay, Anna, let's go," I say, grabbing her arm. She follows me, bewildered. We've only exchanged a few short conversations during our car journey. Anna seems to still be in shock.

We start across the pebbled path leading to the house. The only sound that greets us is the crunch of our feet. My heart beats an erratic rhythm, but I tell myself I've been in worse situations. I'll have that little chat with him; we can give him whatever else he wants, and then we'll all be on our way with our daughters. I hope.

We step up to the front door, and I slam once, twice, on the heavy iron knocker. It echoes around the valley of the house, and a stray bird flies from the trees with a squawk. I turn to see Anna jump back.

I try to hide my frustration. We haven't even gotten inside yet, and she's terrified.

Nobody comes to the door. Is Nathaniel just playing games with us?

Frantically, I try the handle, pushing hard. The door flings open, and I stumble inside with a crash.

Swiveling around, I see Anna framed in the doorway, looking like a rabbit caught in headlights. She looks like she's about to bolt.

I grab her hand firmly before she makes a stupid choice. We need to save our children. "Come on," I mouth at her and open my jacket slightly. In the dim light of the hallway, the glint of the metal is minimal, but it's enough for her to see. She opens her eyes wide in understanding, then nods.

We creep down the dark hallway. I don't bother to shut the front door. It will be helpful to keep it open. Hopefully, it will make for a quicker exit.

We reach the first door on the left, and I take a deep breath, preparing to open it. Before I have the chance, the door creaks open, revealing the person on the other side.

And now it's my turn to jump back in shock.

Because before me isn't Nathaniel.
It's my husband.

# Chapter Thirty-Five

## Anna

My knees almost give out when I see Charles standing on the threshold. As we'd walked along the pebbled path, it was all I could do to keep my nerves under control, preparing my mind to see Nate again. I almost couldn't step through the door, but seeing Jacqueline's forethought in bringing a knife reassured me. She's on my side—she must be. She wouldn't have shown it to me otherwise.

But now, the shock of seeing Charles threatens to undo me once more.

For a moment, I'm unsure what to think—is he in league with Nate, too? But there is utter confusion etched across his face.

"What are you both doing here?" he demands. "I thought you were at the PTA drinks?"

Jacqueline steps past him into the room, and I follow suit—my stomach rolls when I see Freddie Banks perched in one corner of the room, his eyes wide in sudden fear. Why is he scared at the sight of *us*?

I look across to see Jacqueline's previously calm mask start to crumble as she demands, "Where's Matilda? And Sofia? We have to get out of here."

I'm about to scream at them both to tell me where my Sofia is, when behind me I hear a low chortle that sends every rational thought scuttling from my mind.

I spin around, and I can't help it when I let out some of that scream in a strangled cry as I lay eyes on the man I thought I would never see again.

He takes up the whole width and height of the door—I'd not misremembered his impressive stature in my nightmares. As he looks at me, it takes everything in me not to cower under his mercurial stare.

Those mesmerizing green eyes that I once thought I would follow to the depths of the earth but now just wish were underneath it.

"Hello, my darling," he says in a voice dripping with pretty poison. "You didn't think you could really steal our daughter away without saying goodbye..."

# CHAPTER THIRTY-SIX

## JACQUELINE

I gasp in shock at Nathaniel's words. Charles takes a step back in disbelief. Anna is frozen to the spot like she's seen a ghost.

My mind is racing. Everything he told us must have been a lie. Because it turns out he's really Sofia's *father*.

Now, he looks around at this strange gathering of his with a smile on his face.

It's then that I notice that Freddie appears to be the only one of us not surprised by this turn of events.

Freddie steps forward confidently and says to Nathaniel, "Alright, mate. Come on now, what are you playing at?" He walks over to him and whispers in his ear. But in the silence of the room, it is still audible. "This isn't really part of the plan. I thought we had an agreement..."

"Yes, *mate*, I thought we had one too," Nate declares sarcastically. "But that was before you decided to throw me under the bus and showed me your true colors." He slams the door behind him as though to emphasize his point.

"What are you talking about?" Freddie says, throwing his shoulders back, refusing to be intimidated.

Nathaniel stands in front of the door, his arms crossed as he faces Freddie.

"You're seriously asking me that? I overheard you and Jasper speaking last week at his house. You really need to be more careful about what you say out loud. You never know who's listening. You said you were going to get me out of the picture without paying me as soon as I'd done your dirty work of supplying helpful evidence against Anna." He edges closer to Freddie, a snarl on his lips. "I'm so *sick* of betrayals."

Nathaniel laughs bitterly as he adds, "I shouldn't have been surprised, though. It's always the way. Rich people like you looking down on people like me. You always think you can best us. So I realized it was the moment for me to take things into my own hands as I'd always been planning anyway. I could get what I want and have the satisfaction of showing who you really are—who *all* of you really are—to your nearest and dearest." He looks around the room, meeting all our eyes for a fraction of a second. I can't believe I hadn't realized before. The green of his eyes is identical to Sofia's.

"So, it's time that we all told the truth." He fixes his eyes back on Freddie. "Of course, *you* aren't the only one keeping a big secret in this room."

Freddie looks around at all of us as though trying to decide who is most to blame.

"Please," I speak up at last. "Just tell us where Matilda and Sofia are." Instantly, I regret it as Nathaniel's laser-sharp focus falls on me, a smile on his face.

But before he has a chance to respond, Charles jumps in. "What? What does she mean? They're watching a movie in the cinema room, aren't they?"

Nate ignores Charles and says to me, "Ah, Jacqueline... Though I don't think I should really call you that, should I?" He laughs, and it feels like a nail is scratching down my spine. Then he tips his head to one side as though in mock consideration. "Where *are* they, Charles? Don't worry, they're perfectly safe and far away down the hill..."

"Nathaniel, what the hell is going on?" Charles growls, stepping toward Nate. "Whatever it is, I'm going to get them and leave." He tries to push past him, but Nathaniel doesn't budge.

Instead, he whips his hand behind his back, and the next second, a handgun appears.

Nathaniel points it straight at Charles. "I wouldn't do that if I were you."

Charles's jaw drops as Freddie lets out a low whistle. Anna and I exchange shocked glances, and a mutual understanding as we remember the knife in my pocket.

Charles puts his hands up and takes a step back. "Whoa, okay. What do you want? Money? Fine, we can sort that out for you. Just tell us..."

Nathaniel laughs coldly.

"Seriously," Freddie says, stepping forward. "Come on, mate."

Nathaniel turns to him, his voice thick with menace. "I am *not* your mate." Freddie flinches but refuses to back down.

Nathaniel sighs at the sight of the two brothers gearing up for a fight. "Okay, everyone, this doesn't have to turn ugly. Put your phones on the table and sit down like good boys and girls. We're only here to have a chat and for you to be honest for once in your goddamn privileged lives."

No one moves a muscle. But then Freddie moves forward, trying to push Nathaniel out of the way as he heads for the door. "Seriously, you're delusional. I'm going to tell Jasper that you're an absolute joke!"

It all happens so quickly. Nathaniel moves too fast in an expert movement, smacking the butt of his gun up into Freddie's nose. Freddie leaps back with a yell, clutching his hands to his face. Blood gushes through the slits of his fingers.

With a scream, I run over to him as he collapses onto the floor. Charles rushes over, too, grabbing his crisp white handkerchief out of his pocket. In seconds, it's bright red.

In all the commotion, we almost don't hear Anna's quiet words as she buries her face in her hands.

"We should do as he says. It's our only choice."

# Chapter Thirty-Seven

## Anna

"Good girl," Nate says, his voice smooth as velvet. "Seems like you haven't forgotten everything, then. Even if you've completely changed your accent. You've always been a good actress, though, haven't you?" He smirks at me.

My blood boils. I want to scream and rush at him like I did the last time I saw him. The last time, when I attacked him for what he did to my sister Jacqueline. The last time, when I thought he was *dead*.

But I know I can't. Not with Sofia and Matilda, still at risk. And not with him holding that gun. My gun.

How did he get it? It's the one I keep in my safe, in a hidden compartment. I want to be sick as I realize that the day I checked the safe when everything looked like it was as it should be, that was the one thing I *didn't* check. I'd been too distracted making sure that all my precious photographs and documents were there—and then Sofia had revealed that Louisa was Matilda's birth mother. I'd completely forgotten to check the handgun later on.

But it doesn't matter now. We're in this situation—and there's only one way out.

We all have to play it safe if we're going to survive and see our children again. I should have known that Nate's game wouldn't be simple. He likes the theatrics too much. He always has.

The sound of a grandfather clock chiming next to me forces me to look away from his terrible gaze. It's eight o'clock.

I take this opportunity to continue my circle toward the sofas, placing my phone on the small coffee table as I pass as Nate demanded. It's useless anyway—I already checked. No signal in this room.

The walls are painted a dark shade of red and bare of any artwork. The grandfather clock, the two sofas, and the one small coffee table are the only furniture adorning the room. The ceiling is high, though, and I look up to see a chandelier glistening overhead. It's the only source of light as the curtains behind the sofas are drawn.

As I sit down, I realize that the others have followed suit. Jacqueline and Charles are helping Freddie toward the dark brown suede sofa opposite me. They look a mix of furious, scared, and confused. They must never have seen this side of him. However, they do know him... As Nathaniel, apparently. I've never known him by that name—so I suppose if he had ever been mentioned to me in passing, I wouldn't have even noticed.

But it's clear that the others don't know how dangerous Nate can be. I know I have to be brave now. I need to take the lead.

"What do you want, Nate?" I ask calmly. A simple question, but it feels like the start of negotiating my death sentence.

He stands above us all as he collects our phones from the table one by one. He tucks them in his jacket pocket. Then he leans against the door and crosses his arms, letting the gun flop into the crook of his arm. He flashes that dazzling smile once more.

"Isn't it obvious? I want you back."

I blink my eyes closed and allow myself to feel the fear of what that would entail for a flicker of a second. Then I push it away hard. I am not that girl anymore. I can do this. I can play along.

When I open my eyes again, he's lowered the gun. He is staring straight at me, and there are tears glistening in his eyes.

"Anna... My Anna..." he says quietly.

Without warning, he switches again, striding over and grabbing me tightly by the wrist, pulling me up against his chest. Charles cries out in shock and leaps to his feet. The others remain frozen in fear.

Nate laughs in my ear. "Oh, the knight in shining armor to the rescue, I see?" He looks over at Charles. "I'd sit down if I were you."

I feel the cool metal of the gun against my cheek, and I watch as Charles slowly returns to his seat. Jacqueline and Freddie wear expressions of horror.

"Now that I have your attention," Nate says in a confident voice, "I want the three of you to sit quietly right there while I take my darling Anna outside for a little chat. I wouldn't get any little ideas of trying to escape. If you do, you'll never see your children again. And I can't say what might happen to Anna."

He leers down at me for a moment, and the next, I feel myself being dragged toward the door, my mind blank with panic. Nate pushes me into the corridor and shuts the door with a slam.

The small space of the dark hallway feels like it's pressing in on me, and it's all I can do to keep breathing. I feel like I'm trapped in a coffin.

I suppose, in some ways, I will be soon. If I can't think fast and get us all out of this situation. Because I know it's my fault. All my fault that Nate is here. And that he now has Sofia and Matilda.

He is so close that I can feel his hot breath on the side of my cheek. A caress that I once knew so well and now makes me want to run.

He looks down at me. In the murky light, his face appears almost in shadow.

"My Anna. At last. It's time for you to listen to me, and I'm going to prove the truth to you. All of them"—he flicks the gun in the direction of Charles, Freddie, and Jacqueline through the door—"have been lying."

"Nate, please," I say, my voice cracking in desperation. "Just let us all go. I'll do whatever you want. Don't hurt them."

"Shhh now," he says, leaning to press one cold finger against my lips. I try not to flinch away. I know it will only anger him more. I remember. "I don't *want* to hurt anyone. I only took this little gun of yours because I didn't trust that anyone would do what I asked them to do without it."

My stomach twists at Nate's logic. But it doesn't surprise me. Control is Nate's number one driver in life. It was what he did to me for all those years.

Now, he doesn't seem that different. Only older and potentially even more unpredictable.

He bears ever closer, pressing his forehead against mine as he whispers. "It was so easy to jump over the fence and sneak into your house that day—you left your door unlocked. It was like you wanted me to break in," he says. "And so simple to guess your predictable code to the safe: the same one you've always used. I was so happy to find those photos of me in there. Really, it made me even more confident in my plan. You've been harboring hope of me finding you, too."

I don't correct his madness as he tilts his head back to watch my expression. It takes everything in me to remain calm. In turn, I study his face more closely. The years have been kind to him. He still has his looks. The looks that trick everyone into thinking that he is a good guy, including myself.

There is an echo of desperation in his green eyes now, though. And also a slight hint of madness...

When I don't speak, he goes on, his voice low, like he really is my long-lost love. "Did you really mean it? What you did to me? You see, it left a mark, my angel." I cringe at the use of his old nickname for me. As he pulls up his shirt, I see the angry scar across his torso. The mark that I left when I thought I'd escaped. I can't help a gasp escape my throat.

"That's right," he says in a careful caress. "It's horrible, isn't it? And since then, every day has been a struggle for me. I've had barely two cents to rub together for the last twelve years—every spare penny went into trying to find you. That, and my medical bills. You have no idea how long it took me to recuperate. I lost my clients and my reputation. Every day that I lay in that hospital bed, I would imagine your face and what I would do to you when I saw you again. I have to be honest, at first, it wasn't very pretty. But, you know, now I'm prepared to forgive you. If you do as I say."

I blink and, at last, find my voice. "Nate, I'll do anything to save the children. Please, don't hurt them." It comes out in a rasp. It's so hard to listen to his words when all I can think about is whether Sofia and Matilda are really safe. How can I get out of here?

"Is that really all you can think to say? No, 'I'm sorry for what I did to you'?" He chortles, and I shiver, even though I'm not cold. He cocks his head to the side. "You always have been a stubborn one, my Anna. But no, I'm going to give you the benefit of the doubt and assume that all your betrayals began because you thought that I'd organized the death of that precious long-lost sister of yours. So at last, I'm going to give you the truth about that. And then I'm going to tell you what I want you to do for me. Really, I'm being incredibly generous after everything you've done to *me*." As he smiles, my stomach turns over.

Images flash back into my mind of all the ways he hurt me... All the ways he tried to control me over the years.

I can't help but close my eyes for a moment and think back to how he was in high school when I thought I loved him. We were in the same music and drama class and became closer during school band—Nate played guitar, and I sang. We started dating in our final year of high school, and he became my rock. My only escape from my terrible home situation and a mother and stepfather who'd resented my very existence.

I realize now that he'd used that situation to his advantage. He'd used my desperation for love, and I'd latched onto him. What I came to realize later was that he only loved control.

I know that everything in my whole life could have been so different if one terrible thing hadn't happened, which meant Nate would be able to control me for the rest of my life.

When I was eighteen, I killed my stepfather.

And Nate never let me forget it.

# Chapter Thirty-Eight

## Anna

It had been in self-defense. My mother was away for the night with some friends. Not that she would have probably done anything about it—we weren't close.

I was up late, trying to study for my final tests, at the dining room table when the door flew open. My stepfather Mike was standing there, back from the bar. And as per usual, he was drunk and angry. I tried to gather up all my books and escape as I always did because he liked to taunt me. In the last year, he'd seemed to enjoy it more and more.

But there was no getting out of there this time.

He'd borne down on me and started leering, questioning why I was even studying in the first place. Did I think it would make me any better when I was my mother's trash daughter?

I tried to block it out and ignore him. I knew he just wanted a rise. Mike had been on a one-man mission to pull apart my mother's and my already-fractured relationship, and he'd been succeeding. I didn't understand why he wouldn't leave me alone—soon, I'd be leaving home, hopefully getting a place at college.

But then he'd grabbed me by the shoulders, pushing me hard against the back of the table. In the commotion, all my books tumbled to the ground in a clattering crash.

"You want a lesson," he'd hissed into my ear. "I'll give you a lesson." I'd felt his right hand move down my side as his left hand tried to pin the rest of me still.

*No, no, no.* I'd screamed in my head in shock at the realization of what he was going to try and do. I attempted to get him off me, but he was so big and heavy, like a rock pressing against a grain of sand.

I tried again, and finally, I succeeded in forcing him off balance, thanks to his drunken state, with one last almighty push. I ran as fast as I could to the door, hoping I could get out to safety. But even though he was drunk, he followed. He grabbed me by the waist and tried to pull me backward. "You're going to be a good girl today," he'd leered into my ear.

Panicking, I'd kicked back with my legs. He was blocking the entrance to the front door, so I only had one choice. I sprinted up the stairs in front of me. If I could get to the bathroom, then at least I could lock myself inside. But almost at the top, I felt his clammy hands clasp around my ankle, pulling me down.

I'd spun around and punched him hard with my flailing arms on reflex. It was enough to push him off me. And also enough to throw him off balance. I watched in horror as he propelled backward, flying down the stairs. He fell too fast for me to ever have a chance of stopping him. I heard the thump of his body and the crack of his neck as it impacted awkwardly with the floor.

I'd crumpled onto the staircase, breathing hard, not daring to move in shock at what had just happened.

But then I looked down and noticed he wasn't moving.

I got to my feet on shaky legs and looked down in horror to see his body laid out at an awkward angle, his neck twisted in a way that it shouldn't be. *Oh my god. He couldn't be dead...*

But he wasn't moving. I'd killed him.

I was terrified. Even though I'd acted out of self-defense, I knew my mother wouldn't have my back. Probably *no one* would believe me.

I panicked, and only eighteen years old, I did the only thing I could think of: I called my boyfriend, Nate.

That would end up being the worst mistake of my life.

He came over at once and helped me figure out what to do. He said we only had one option: to stage a scene. My stepfather had last been seen completely drunk—people would be shocked, but no one would be surprised that he could have had such a terrible accident.

Nate said we'd tidy up my school books and pretend like I'd never seen my stepfather. We'd say that I'd been at Nate's house all night.

I couldn't think straight, but Nate appeared so calm, so I followed everything he said. The next day, I "returned" back home and called the police, pretending to have found Mike's body. They believed me, not diving into any sort of proper investigation when the autopsy verified his cause of death and his friends stated that he'd been drunk that night. All the same, I couldn't bear to be near my mother after that. I felt certain she suspected something, though she never said it. We became more distant than we'd ever been after that.

But what I hadn't realized was that by calling Nate and agreeing to his plan, I'd struck a deal with the devil. As soon as we graduated high school, we left Colorado. At the time, I wanted that too. I couldn't stand to be around anything that reminded me of that terrible night. I wanted to start again. Nate and I moved to Pennsylvania to try and find some work in the music industry. He had a few contacts in Philadelphia, and it was cheaper than trying to move to New York City.

That first year or so, things were fine. I was so grateful that he'd helped me and readily agreed to anything he said. But as time passed and Nate grew frustrated with his career progress, his moods became more and more volatile. He was jealous and paranoid if I was out late, and over time, he started to become a little violent. Especially when he began dealing drugs on the side to make extra money.

The first time I threatened to leave, it ended terribly. He taunted me with my secret, saying I could never leave him. And that's when I realized I'd put myself in an impossible situation with no way out...

[SECTION]

I blink my eyes back open to the present moment as he continues in his falsely sweet tone.

"Anna. My Anna. Look at you, so scared. Please, I'm here today to save you. Not hurt you. You don't have to worry. You just have to listen and open your heart to me again. It's all of them that can't be trusted..." He nods toward the closed door behind him. "And to prove it, I'm going to tell you how I got over here in the first place."

When I don't respond, he presses ever closer and takes a stray strand of my hair in his hands. I stay as still as a statue. His voice drops to a menacing level. "Well, you know it's been impossible to find you over the years. I suppose you and that sister of yours planned it like that." He shakes his head as though to get himself back on track. "You know, I really almost gave up hope. But I'm so glad I stuck at it. I knew that you wouldn't disappear for good. No one as beautiful as you could. And it was when I discovered "reverse image search" that at last something came up."

He twirls my hair tighter and smiles down at me. "And wasn't I surprised to find out that not only were you now *Anastasia*—fancy, I like it!" He flashes a smile, but it doesn't meet his eyes. "But you'd also changed your surname entirely. You'd become a *Drummond*. But not just any Drummond—the wife, or I suppose *widow*, to a very wealthy Drummond. How do you think it made me feel to read that?"

I gulp, knowing what's coming.

"I felt completely betrayed. Because, of course, my angel, you know that you're mine. I suppose you thought for all this time that I was dead. But there we go. Well, I got to thinking, and I decided I didn't just want revenge anymore... I wanted you back."

"I'm sure you just decided you wanted my money," I somehow find myself spitting out. He lets go of a strand of my hair as though he's been electrocuted.

"Now, angel, that's not very nice to say. But since you're not saying very nice things to me, I'm going to be honest with you about something not very nice, too. Yes, at first, when I saw that picture, I saw red all over again. My only mission was revenge. Revenge for the life and the daughter you'd taken away from me. And I thought I knew how to get it." He leans back against the door. "Through your 'stepson', Jasper."

Nate rolls his eyes and places air quotes around the ridiculous word to describe a man who's older than me. "I hoped that Daddy's heir might be a little distraught at the rumors going around that you killed his father, and so I got in touch, offering my services. I told him I knew a secret about you... something that might prove that you were capable of killing his father."

My eyes flare wide in horror. Had he told Jasper about what happened to my stepfather?

"Oh, don't look so terrified. I never told him exactly what I knew. I had to see if he would give me what I wanted first. I wasn't going to offer up my biggest bargaining chip on a silver platter."

I grimace. Of course not. I should have known. It's so Nate.

"It took a little while and some persistent contacting, but eventually, I got a nibble. When I finally spoke to him on a call, it appeared that some of what I had to say about you and where you were really from matched up with his digging. He wanted to meet. He flew me over, and he invited me to stay in his big fancy house. I did fully intend on cooperating with him. At first, all I wanted was revenge and money, of course. I thought it was my due. And I thought you deserved to rot in jail. But then I met Freddie."

Through the shadows, I can see his glower. "Freddie filled Jasper and me in on where you had moved to—the house just across from his brother and sister-in-law of all places. Charles and Jacqueline." Nate cocks his head to one side. "The name made me pause. Another Jacqueline—the same name as that sister of yours. I didn't think it could purely be a coincidence that you had moved opposite someone with the same name. Something felt off to me...

"And I was right. I got myself invited over to Charles and Jacqueline's house under the ploy of getting to know them and so Freddie and I could find out if you'd spoken to them much at all. Freddie and Jasper thought it was a great idea, and we cooked up a whole story about how Freddie, Jasper, and I were friends going way back and that I was in Bristol looking to move here with my fake family." He chortles. "Even though I suspected something, I still couldn't quite believe it when I recognized her..."

He presses against me. "And so, that day, I decided to give you one more chance to come to your senses. I would make that woman tell you the truth. And then..." He grabs my chin with his hand and tilts it up even further. "And then, my dear Anna, we could all start again. Me, you, and our Sofia. As a family. Then, I'd have everything that I deserve. At last."

He grins that wild smile, and I know exactly what he means by *start again*. He means he wants me back under his control. He wants my money. He wants my daughter. And that, of course, would be his final revenge. Why take me down publicly? When he could have his revenge day after day instead?

I try not to be sick. Because I know that if I'm going to get us out of this situation, I have to be cleverer than him. I must play into his ego and make him think that I'm on his side. But I can't look like I've been won over too easily, either. Or he'll see right through it.

"Nate," I say in as calm a voice as I can muster. "I'll listen to the truth. But please, don't hurt them."

He smiles once more. And I can see the crazed look in his mesmerizing eyes. "Well, of course, I won't. So long as they behave..."

"I can understand why you're upset with Freddie if he said he was going to double-cross you somehow," I say carefully. "But Charles has done nothing to you. Why don't you let him go?"

I've made a big mistake. Nate's smile is wiped away from his face in an instant, and the next, he's pressing a hand around my throat. "Oh, trying to defend your little boyfriend, are you?"

My eyes go wide in shock. "No, what?" I manage to rasp out as he loosens his grip. He looks down at his hand for a moment as though surprised at himself. It was always the same with him. He'd hurt me and then appear taken aback by his actions.

"Well, that's not what I saw through the window last week, Anna, when you were drinking wine together and hugging each other close." He leans down to whisper in my ear. "I bet your criminal barrister doesn't know how much of a criminal you are. You'll see: when he hears the truth, he won't want anything to do with you. I'm the only one who would have you. I suggest you remember that."

And with those final words, he flings the door behind him wide open.

He grabs me with his other hand and throws me back into the room. I propel headfirst toward my vacated seat as the others leap up in shock. It looks like they haven't moved an inch since I've been trapped on the other side of the door. I guess they didn't want to risk finding out if Nate had been bluffing. Smart. We all need to play by Nate's rules if we're going to protect Sofia and Matilda. Where are they now? Are they somewhere safe, like Nate says, or is that just a lie too?

But then Charles speaks up. "Please, let us go. We'll give you whatever you want."

I watch as Nate cocks his head to one side and sighs. "Honestly, this isn't meant to be some sort of hostage negotiation. All I need is for us to have a chat and clear some things up for me and Anna without any of you getting any dramatic ideas." He waves around the gun, and the others shrink back. "Then, of course, we can all go. The children are perfectly safe and far away, like I said. I want us to all leave in one piece."

Out of the corner of my eye, I see Charles and Jacqueline exchange a hopeful glance. But it's instantly quashed as Nate continues. "But I need the truth first. Then we'll decide if that's enough. Well, *I'll* decide." He laughs. I know how much he loves games. "To make it more fun—I'll give you until nine o'clock." We all glance at the clock. It's now a few minutes past eight. My stomach churns.

"Alright, Nathaniel," Charles cuts in before he has a chance to say another word. "That's enough, you've made your point." His voice is as even as if he'd just made an order at a restaurant. I suppose that's what years as a top barrister have taught him: to stay calm under pressure. I look up to see him staring at me, confusion etched across his face. Then he says to Nate, "Just tell us what all this is about."

Instead of getting angry, as I'd have expected at the interruption, Nate grins once more. Which is even worse.

"Well, you see, my dear Anna over there"—he points the gun at me—

"betrayed me and tried to kill me. I do understand why. She thought that I had killed her sister. Except I didn't. Your wife did." He flips the gun over to point at Jacqueline.

Charles looks like he's just swallowed a stone as his face goes bright red.

"What?" Freddie manages to say through a mouthful of dried blood.

"She is not Jacqueline Kelly," Nate says in a cold, hard voice. "She is not Anna's sister. Jacqueline was killed many years ago—by you." He points the gun straight at her. "So, of course, the question is, why? Because, whoever you are, you're sure as hell not leaving here until you tell us all the truth."

# CHAPTER THIRTY-NINE

## JACQUELINE

*Sister, sister, sister...* The words echo around my head as the confirmation at last falls.

I thought I'd done my background work when I became Jacqueline Kelly. I'd thought the only person left in the real Jacqueline's life who could have exposed me was Louisa, and she was taken care of. But clearly, I'd been so wrong.

On the phone, Nathaniel had told me that if I brought Anna here, Matilda and I would be safe. Well, now look at the trap I'm in.

While Anna and Nate were out of the room, Charles, Freddie, and I tried to whisper some ideas about how we could force our way out. For a moment, it felt like we were all on the same team. But now, I glance around to see that everyone is looking at me with a spectrum of expressions on their faces. Nathaniel is smug. Anna is resigned. Freddie is stunned. And Charles—Charles stares at me with betrayal written across his face.

"Jax?" asks Freddie in a disbelieving voice. "What is he talking about?"

I shake my head as Nathaniel comes to stand behind us. "That's not her name, *mate*. It never has been. Why don't we get her to start talking?"

Nathaniel's sudden movement surprises me as he grabs me by the shoulder and pulls me up. I scream. Freddie and Charles jump up on reflex, but Nathaniel tuts, pointing the gun at them.

"I wouldn't do that if I were you." He throws me down on the other sofa beside Anna. "There we are, much better. Boys and girls evenly split." He smiles down at me. "Now, look across at your husband and brother-in-law and tell us who you really are."

Nathaniel stands on the edge of the sofa beside them, a broad grin on a face I once thought was kind. How wrong I was.

I pull my knees into my chest, unable to speak. I'm in shock. All I can do is stare at Charles and Freddie on the sofa opposite. Anger and confusion in their eyes.

"God dammit, we have to save the children!" Charles shouts, slamming his hand on the coffee table. "Just be honest, for once in your life." He glares at me.

"Come on," Freddie barks back at Charles. "You don't believe the guy, do you? He's mental."

Nathaniel laughs down at them. "What do you reckon, Charles? Am I mental?" he says, emphasizing the word in a mockery of Freddie's British accent.

Charles shakes his head. But I know his movements so well. I know he's not shaking his head in denial, but as though he's agreeing with him. Of course, we've been in a rocky place recently. But is he really so quick to believe the worst in me?

"Seriously," Freddie goes on, knocking him in the arm. "This is your wife." He points across at me. "Aren't you going to defend her? Or are you going to stay silent like you did last time?"

Charles refuses to speak again, and a light in me goes dimmer and dimmer. It's all my worst nightmares at once. I'm being found out. I've amounted to nothing. Just like my mother always said I would.

"Hey," Freddie yells once more, hitting his brother even harder on the shoulder. His defense of me causes something in my heart to break.

I do not deserve it.

And my husband seems to know it.

"STOP IT!" Charles yells, losing his temper and pushing his brother away across the couch.

Freddie leaps up as though to attack him back.

Next to me, Anna gets to her feet, too. "WE'RE WASTING TIME!" she screams.

The brothers pause in their tracks, looking up at the clock to see that it's now a quarter past the hour. And as though on cue, the clock chimes.

Nathaniel laughs once more. He's stepped back to lean against the wall. "This is *so* entertaining. But," he sighs dramatically, "I'm getting bored."

And the next second, the gun is cocked straight back at me. That bastard. He said on the phone that if I cooperated, then my secret would be safe. And now, here he is, holding me up at gunpoint to spill my past.

"You lied to me," I manage to say to him through gritted teeth.

Nathaniel steps back in surprise, then cackles like a hyena. "Oh, you think I lied, really?! That's a good one." He slaps the gun against his leg, and we all flinch at the sound.

Then he trains it back on me, and I see the wild edge in his emerald eyes. Anna's right. We should listen to what he says. Because there's no knowing how far a madman might take this. And whatever else, I want to get out of here with my life. And Matilda's.

"Now listen to me—I'm only going to say this once. You tell the truth. You tell Anna exactly what you did to Jacqueline. Because..." and he lets his gaze fall from mine to travel over to Anna—frozen still next to me. "Because, dear Anna, you have to understand I never killed your sister. You left me because of a misunderstanding. And that's one of the reasons that we're all here today." He flicks his dangerous stare back at me. "You are going to be honest. Because whatever you did to the real Jacqueline, it ruined my life."

I bury my face in my hands. How did he find me out?

Then again, I suppose, if I'm being honest, a part of me always knew that this day might come. And I don't regret any of it. Not for a second.

So, as I remove my fingers to look out at four sets of judgmental eyes, I realize that, at last, there's nowhere left for me to hide.

As I stare down the barrel of that gun, I know that if I don't satisfy his demands, then I'm not getting out of this alive. And no matter what, I want to live.

So I dig down... dig all the way down to the depths of my soul to find the name, the person, that I'd discarded so many years before.

Clearing my throat, I say in a firm voice, "I used to be Ruby... Ruby O'Connor."

# Chapter Forty

## Ruby

The name feels like sandpaper on my tongue, and in the back of my mind, I can hear my mother's derisive cackle. Her constant taunts. *Ruby, why do you have no friends? Ruby, why are you such a disappointment? Ruby, you will never amount to anything...*

I try to block it out and continue.

"Let's just say I didn't have the best childhood. I was from a next-to-nothing town in Ohio. My dad left when I was a baby, and my mom raised me, or whatever you would call it, on her own. We weren't close."

I stare at my hands rather than the room of betrayed faces. Maybe they'll all feel sorry for me by the end. I can only hope...

I glance back up quickly to see Nathaniel still pointing the gun at my chest. I hurry to continue my long-lost tale.

"I was counting down the days until I could escape to college, and I did everything possible to secure a scholarship. We weren't from a rich part of town." As opposed to the brothers in front of me. I glance at them to gauge their expressions but instantly regret it. Nathaniel smiles and mouths the words, *Tick tock.*

"And so I did. I managed to get a scholarship to a liberal arts college in Pennsylvania. It was supposed to be my ticket out of my past, away from my terrible mother. I cut ties with her the day I left. We never spoke again. And at college, that was where I met Jacqueline." I look up again at the shocked faces of my husband and brother-in-law.

But now that I'm forced to tell my tale, I am not going to shy away. At last, I am going to tell them my story. About why I did what I did, what I *had* to do to survive.

The words slip off my tongue like a dam unleashed after years of drought. As I think back to that very first day I saw her... Jacqueline.

It was a hot late August day when I arrived fresh-faced and full of hope for my first semester at college. I'd come alone with two duffel bags to my name. I supposed as I looked up at the tall oak trees surrounding the modern buildings, that I should have thanked my mother when I left. In some ways, it was because of her that I'd made it this far—having channeled every awful thing she'd ever said to me into proving her wrong. But I'd left her behind, and it was finally time for a new start. Somewhere where no one knew who I was.

I deliberately avoided looking at all the tear-stained cheeks of parents saying goodbye to their darling children as I navigated my way to the freshman block. It was a simple new build—nothing fancy—but anything was better than the tiny, dank apartment I'd grown up in. It had fresh white paint and proper curtains on the walls. There was even a not-unpleasant smell of lemon disinfectant in the air. It made me feel reassured—cleaning was my happy place, after all.

There wasn't an elevator, and so I started hauling my bag up the wide staircase. Until I heard a deep, "Oh, let me help you." I turned around to see a guy around my age with shaggy blonde hair. He smiled up at me with a crooked grin, and instantly, I felt my stomach do that strange butterfly flip. No one had ever looked at me like that before. Back at high school, the other kids had labeled me from an early age as the loner geek with the "easy mom". But this guy obviously hadn't got the memo. I smiled back shyly; my fresh start was already working.

He leaped up the steps two at a time.

"I'm Adam," he said. "And you are?"

"Ruby," I said quietly, getting lost in his chocolate-brown eyes.

"Ruby," he repeated. On his lips, it sounded like a happy name. All it had ever sounded like to me before then was a sharp bark. I was so distracted that I barely heard his question: "What floor are you on?"

"Oh," I said, shaking my head. "The third. I'm room 301."

"Great," he said, grabbing my two bags easily. "I'll help you up."

We chatted as we walked. He told me that he'd arrived a few weeks earlier from Denver—he'd had to start early because of his soccer scholarship. He explained he was on the floor above and started filling me in on any other useful things about the campus. I listened, riveted.

Too soon, we arrived outside my room. And to my surprise, the door was already wide open. Music blasting. I would have preferred things to be quieter and ordered after my chaotic childhood, but I tried not to let it show.

Adam laughed. "Sounds like your roommate has great music taste."

The next second, a woman appeared in the doorway. The first thing I noticed was her striking, wavy hair. It danced all the way down to her curvy waist. The second was how, when she smiled, it felt like the whole room brightened. And the third was how she seemed to be everything

I wasn't. When I looked at her, I instantly saw a version of myself that I *could* be. We were of similar height, build, and coloring. My hair was wavy, too, and a similar color; if I grew it long like hers, it wouldn't look that different. In that single second, it felt like I was staring at a lighter, more vibrant version of me. Someone that I could have been—if I hadn't had my life.

Adam obviously sensed that too because while he'd seemed a little interested in me before, he now dropped my bags unceremoniously outside the door as he said to the better version of me, "Hey, Jackie, I didn't realize this was your room. Just helping your new roommate…"

She flashed that perfect smile once more in my direction as she gave me a brief hello before walking a few steps toward Adam and twirling her long hair around one finger. "You going to that party tonight?" she asked. And I knew that any interest I'd once held in Adam's eyes had been usurped by my prettier, brighter roommate.

I grabbed my bags and shuffled them into the room. "Thanks for your help," I managed to say through gritted teeth.

"Sure," he said vaguely as he and *Jackie* continued their conversation.

It gave me a moment to take in the medium-sized room around me. A clean strip of a desk and a bed with white walls along one side—obviously my side of the room—with a window directly opposite the doorway in which I stood. I could see the tops of some hazy trees through the glass. Then, my gaze traveled to the other side, and I shook my head in surprise at the multi-colored explosion. Jackie had already started decorating her walls with posters of all her favorite bands. Underneath that, she had a patchwork quilt of colorful scraps and symbols.

And then I heard her voice behind me. "Hey, sorry about that. I'm Jackie—welcome to our room!"

I turned around to see her grinning at me, a hand outstretched. How could she be so happy to see me? We'd only just met.

But she kept looking at me expectantly until I remembered to speak.

"Oh, I'm Ruby." I forced myself to stick out a hand to shake hers. I wasn't really used to physical contact, so I was even more surprised when she pulled me into a hug.

"We're going to be the best of friends," she said, her voice full of infectious excitement. It made me a little nervous. I'd never had a best friend before. In fact, I'd been pretty much friendless my whole life. In my experience, people you care about only ever let you down. It was better not to let anyone get too close.

But it turned out she was right. If my natural way of looking at things veered toward the negative, Jackie was unfailingly positive. She got the guys—Adam included. She got invited to all the parties. She was someone who everyone wanted to be around. And yes, that meant she could be a little selfish. She was beautiful and fun, and that's all she wanted from life.

At first, it grated on me. I quietly seethed at her ability to swan into any situation. But I quickly realized that as much as I could resent her constant buoyant energy, I needed to learn to be more like Jackie—if I was ever going to make it.

As I got to know her, it turned out we weren't that different in some ways—she'd had a difficult childhood, too. Her mother had left her when she was five. She'd run away with a new man and had forgotten about Jackie entirely. But at least Jackie had her dad. I'd never known mine. At the time, she never mentioned a sister. I only learned about Louisa later...

Back in college, all I knew was that Jackie and her dad weren't necessarily that close. She confided in me once that she thought he blamed her for her mom leaving. But it didn't sound like they had *quite* as terrible a relationship as me and my mother. And besides, he still sent her a check every month.

But in spite of her less-than-rosy childhood, instead of being like me and seeing the world as something to be fearful of, Jackie grabbed it with two hands and treated it like her own personal playground. She always said that she was here for a good time, not a long time. And there was something about that attitude that everyone around her found infectious.

As her roommate, I was with her constantly, and I started to convince myself that being like Jackie was my way forward into the me that I wanted to be at college. To my surprise, I even found myself caring what she thought. Was that the first sign of close friendship? Possibly. I'd never experienced anything like it before.

All of a sudden, I found that being in Jackie's orbit meant I was liked by default. She was there for me, too. She gave me CDs just because she "thought I'd like them" and brought me soup when I was sick. I'd never had anyone remotely take care of me before. It was a strange sensation. But I knew I didn't want to lose it now I had it.

The more time I spent with Jackie—becoming more buoyant, confident, and happy—the more people commented on how alike we looked. I grew out my hair, and I guess the regular college meals helped fill in my curves. People started to tease that we were morphing into each other. We could be twins. We would both look at each other and laugh. It was fun having a best friend like Jackie.

I was still jealous of her sometimes because, of course, no matter what, I still wasn't her. I was still nobody Ruby O'Connor without a cent to my name. The other problem was being like Jackie started to affect my grades. She didn't really care about college—she'd only come because her dad wanted her to—so it didn't matter if she partied until late and missed class. But I had to keep my grades up, or I'd lose my scholarship, which was hard enough with having to work a part-time job to make ends meet, even without being dragged along to parties as well. It was exhausting.

It was Jackie who suggested I found an easier side hustle. Something that would even mean that a party could create business for me. She said it would help her out, too, to know someone so well-connected, and of course, I wanted to do anything to make my one and only friend happy. So I agreed, and she put me in touch with the right people to start on my new job of dealing out "party favors" to fellow college students.

I knew it was technically wrong—illegal, in fact. But I told myself that selling drugs to students who wanted them anyway wasn't hurting anybody, and it was definitely helping me. Suddenly, everyone wanted to be my best friend—not just Jackie. Though, she was always my constant. My business started to spread, and I was able to quit my stupid part-time job. Now, I had enough time to party *and* keep up my grades. It was ideal.

Until I got caught. In my final year, I was busted in style. It was like they'd been keeping tabs on me this whole time—waiting for the most impactful moment to strike. The police did a raid on one of my biggest parties of the year. It seemed that Pennsylvania took the sale of illegal drugs very seriously. My mother being mixed up in that world didn't help my case either. I was arrested, and the college expelled me for good measure. After that, I was charged and spent five years in prison.

Everything I'd worked so hard for—gone in an instant.

My so-called friends turned their backs on me. My college degree evaporated into dust, and a permanent criminal record to my name. Every night that I spent in prison, I thought back on the last few years, trying to piece together where I had gone so wrong. It all came back to one person: Jackie.

Maybe I should have been grateful to her. She was the only person in my life who stayed in touch during that time, sending me postcards from different US states. But in prison, you have a lot of time to think and plenty of time to realize that none of it was fair. All of this had been Jackie's idea. Maybe I couldn't blame her entirely, but in a lot of ways, it felt like I'd ruined my life because of her. She owed me. And I think, deep down, she knew that too.

Because when I finally got out five years later, she offered me a place to stay that summer. It was a starting point. I was twenty-seven by then, having been locked away at twenty-two. Plenty of time to start again, she told me. But I quietly resented the years of freedom she'd had. Especially because she'd wasted them.

Jackie had graduated but had barely done anything with her life in the years since. It seemed the fun-loving, party-all-the-time, and do-no-work attitude didn't translate that effectively into the real world.

While I'd been in prison, she'd gone traveling around the country—hopping from place to place and never staying too long. For a time, she tried to model in Los Angeles but ended up partying too much to show up for any photoshoots. She'd only returned to Philadelphia earlier that year when her dad cut her off at last—telling her to get a real job. He'd helped her secure a place to live, and she'd started working part-time in reception at a real estate agency.

All the same, it was still better than my job. When I got out, the only employer that would take me on a semi-regular basis was a cleaning agency. While I was good at that, I didn't want cleaning to be the rest of my life. Every new application I sent off was getting rejected. I didn't know how to start again as myself.

Jackie was grating on me, too. She'd changed—or maybe I had? Because now the behavior that had seemed fun and spontaneous in college just appeared reckless and impulsive. She had lost touch with all our college friends over her years of traveling and living in Los Angeles. She had fewer people worshipping the ground she walked on. She still wanted the world to be her personal playground, though, and she resented that it wasn't.

I'm not sure how things might have turned out if two things hadn't occurred within a few weeks of each other: Jackie's dad dying and me bumping into Adam.

Because what Adam told me changed everything.

# Chapter Forty-One

## Ruby

It was the week before Christmas. All the lights were twinkling, but I wasn't really in the festive spirit. I'd been at a late-night cleaning job in Philly's Center when I bumped into Adam. I was waiting at a quiet bus stop—the brightly lit thoroughfare reassuring me that even at the late hour, I was safe. I had my headphones in. Jacqueline had given me her old iPod. After five years in prison, I was starting to get to grips with all the technological advancements.

She'd been off work for the last week, lying in her bed and refusing to get up. Her dad had just died last week, and after the small funeral, she'd returned more distraught than ever. I think, in some ways, she blamed herself for disappointing him all these years. She didn't have anyone left, she said—except me.

I was thinking about her when I noticed a man waving at me from across the road. I squinted in the glare of the streetlamps as he looked both ways and dashed across the road. I pressed pause.

"Jackie?"

My stomach squirmed as I recognized him. He was a few years older, but it was undeniably Adam. I thought back to the last time I'd seen him, at that fateful party that had ruined everything. After four years of me crushing on him, we'd finally kissed. I'd been so happy in that moment before everything went so wrong. He hadn't bothered to check on me in prison, either.

But all the same, here I was, standing in front of the only real crush I'd ever had. And I was covered in grime. Great.

As he came to a stop next to me, he suddenly realized his mistake.

"Wait, no, Ruby—right?" I registered the horror on his face as he probably remembered our kiss and what had happened to me after. The college had wanted to make an example of me, so I'd experienced a very public expulsion. And the State had wanted to make an example of me, too, so I'd received a serious sentence. I'm sure he must have known about that, too.

I sighed, taking my headphones out and tangling them around the iPod before shoving them into my pocket.

"That's right," I confirmed, dully.

"Oh, wow," he said, his eyes wide like he'd just been stunned. "Really great to see you."

I was sure he did not mean that as I watched him fidget with his backpack. He'd always tended to speak too much when he was nervous, and he carried on. "So, I'm working around the corner. Finally, I finished college and started living the lawyer life. It means late nights trying to prove myself right now—but I'm sure it'll get better soon. How about you?"

I cocked my head to the side.

"Well, Adam, I've just got out of prison. So not doing a huge amount yet."

"Right, right," he said awkwardly, his face falling. "I was sorry to hear about that," he added, with seemingly genuine emotion.

"Thanks, me too," I concede, crossing my arms across my chest. "Hoping I can get back on my feet soon. I'm staying with Jacqueline now. You thought I was her—do you see her much?" I asked curiously. Since we'd been living together, she hadn't mentioned any of our old college friends. In fact, it seemed that she'd lost touch with everybody. I suppose we had that in common, at least.

"Ah, no. I haven't seen her in forever." He said with a shake of his head. "That's why I was shocked. But I'm surprised to hear you're living with her. After everything..."

"What do you mean?" I ask, my ears pricking up at his words.

"Oh," he laughed. But it sounded hollow. "Never mind—there I go, over-explaining. My therapist says I do that when I'm nervous." He shuffled his feet.

"Right," I said, refusing to let it go. "But what do you mean?"

He must have seen the intense expression on my face. One I had honed well over time. He knew he wasn't getting away without answering my question.

"Well," he conceded, "I guess I thought you must have had a huge fight. Because she was the one that called the cops on you that night..."

My heart started to hammer in my chest. *What the hell?* I thought back to that night. What had happened to make her do that to me?

"I honestly don't think she ever thought you'd go to prison for it," Adam said. "But I dunno—well, she and I had a fight. She'd seen us kissing... and I think she was drunk, angry, and high. And well, she called them. I'm so sorry," he added. "I thought you knew?"

But I'd stopped listening to him at this point. On my worst days in prison, I had blamed Jacqueline for doing this to me, but in an *accidental* way. It had seemed that if I'd never met her or been so desperate to be like her, then I wouldn't have found myself locked away. I'd known deep down I couldn't blame her entirely, though.

Now, it seemed that she really had been directly responsible for what had happened to me. Because she'd called the cops and must have exposed my entire past to them, too. It was *all* her fault.

Adam coughed. "Umm, so nice to see you, Ruby. But I better get going—my train is coming."

I barely nodded as he walked away. He hadn't asked to keep in touch. Why would he?

But I didn't care. I couldn't stop thinking about what he'd said.

Jacqueline had betrayed me. It was classic her—doing whatever she wanted without thinking of the consequences. She'd ruined my life.

The bus came and went. I just sat there in shock. What was I going to do? I couldn't rewind the past, and she was the only one giving me a place to stay right now. What would happen if we fell out? But I also knew that I couldn't let her get away with it.

Eventually, I hopped on the bus and journeyed back to our small apartment. Should I confront her then and there? Or wait for later?

I still hadn't decided what to do when I opened the door. There was Jackie on the sofa, in floods of tears about her father.

"I have no one left except you," she wailed. I tried to dredge up some sympathy for her. But it was hollow now. I was still so angry at what she'd done to me. "I have nothing to live for." She cried harder. "And now I have to sort out all this paperwork about my dad. I can't do it. I don't think I can ever face going through everything. Please, Ruby, can you help me?" She'd looked up at me with her tear-stained face. "I can't *think* straight."

I soothed her, letting her words wash over me without really hearing them. Because a little seed of an idea started to take form in my mind. Maybe there was a way to make what she'd done to me right. I just had to be brave enough to take it. And, well, hadn't I always been brave enough to do something once I'd set my mind to it?

So, of course, I offered my help. I offered to help her with all those bits of admin that came with death. And as I helped her over the next month, it helped me. I steadily gained access to all her email accounts, to the important paperwork, to her bank accounts. It was easy enough to go to the Department of Motor Vehicles and change the photograph on her driver's license to a new one of me. All the while, she had no idea. Lost in her grief, she never thought to question whether giving me access to everything was a good idea. She seemed to trust me completely.

And it all seemed like a good idea to me. I had been locked up for five years because of her, and what had she done? Absolutely nothing. Jackie didn't want to live anymore. Not really. She'd said it herself.

So I became certain: someone else should have her life. Someone who wouldn't waste it. Someone like me.

# Chapter Forty-Two

## Ruby

I look at the faces in front of me. Their mouths skewed open in shock. But I stand by it. I was right to do what I did. Jackie ruined my life, and she was set on destroying hers. Someone better deserved to have it instead.

I haven't told everyone the whole story, only the parts that I *have* to, the things that could be easily checked. I will do what I have to in order to protect Matilda and get out of this alive.

So, I told them about my time in prison. But I didn't tell them about running into Adam and what he told me about Jackie's betrayal. I didn't tell them how much I actually wanted revenge when I found that out.

I only say that when Jackie and I lived together, and her dad died, she was incapable of doing anything. I tell them that she asked me to help her, which sets me up perfectly for what I will share next.

I clear my throat as the clock chimes half past. It's enough to jolt Charles and Freddie out of their stupor at my words.

"Come on, *Ruby,* don't stop now," Nathaniel says with a sneer. The gun is still pointed steadily at my chest. I am seething on the inside, and

I promise myself one thing: I will find a way to keep being Jacqueline once I know I am safe.

All my lies don't have to be ruined by this terrible man.

I will kill them all if I must to ensure that my secret never leaves this room. I can take Matilda and run. I've worked so hard for this life. I'm not going to let it all be ruined in one night.

But right now, I must keep talking to save my skin.

"I would argue that I didn't kill her," I say in a calm voice. "But I suppose I inadvertently helped... Jackie was begging me to take away her pain. She had been smoking a lot, but she asked me to help her get some of the strongest junk I could find." When I see the shock on Charles and Freddie's faces, I amend quickly, "I know that might sound unorthodox, I can see that now. But I was young, and at the time, my best friend was so upset that I wanted to do what she asked. I just wanted to help her."

"Bullshit," Anna whispers under her breath. I turn to look at her and see that she's seething. Of course, she's right. I wasn't really planning on helping her. But I have to go on; Nathaniel is watching. I must finish my performance.

"I promise; I really didn't think it would end up like it did. I got home one night after a shift..." My throat constricts as I force myself to remember the scene. I don't like thinking about what I had to do. I like to pretend as though I've only ever been Jacqueline Kelly.

"She was lying there on the couch," I murmur. "At first, I thought she was sleeping. But when she didn't respond, I went over to shake her awake. That was when I realized she was cold. She was dead."

I bury my head in my hands to help with my show.

Glancing up, I see that Charles and Freddie continue to stare at me in horror. I can't bring myself to look at Anna's expression. Nor do I want to look at Nathaniel.

I run a hand through my curly hair. "I didn't know what to do. Of course, my first panicked thought was to call the police. It was clear that she'd had an overdose; there were pills scattered everywhere."

I close my eyes as the awful memory flits across my vision.

I didn't *like* taking her life—but it had been my only option. She didn't deserve to live anymore, not really. So, I'd given her the drugs that killed her. I might have told her that they were weaker than they were, and I might have suggested that she could take a few more than she needed. Ultimately, they were too much for her to handle. So I guess, whichever way you look at it, I'm guilty of her death. But I don't *have* to admit that to all of them. I do have to admit some things, though.

I clear my throat and roll my shoulders back to sit up straighter as I continue.

"I was beside myself. I'd just lost the only person that I was close to. And she'd had so much to live for. She had a college degree, money, and an apartment. She could have done anything she wanted with that. And instead, here she was, dead at twenty-seven."

I clasp my hands in front of me. Surely, Nathaniel will be happy with that.

But then he scoffs. "Finish the story, *Ruby*. Tell us how you took her identity."

The gun remains trained on me. I fidget with the ends of my coat as I avoid the gazes of Charles and Freddie in front of me. Must I really admit to the rest out loud?

"Fine," I say, forcing my voice not to shake. Because even if they can't understand it, two privileged men who have never known what it's like to have a door slammed in their face, I still understand why I did it.

"Well, I thought it was an absolute waste. Like I said, Jacqueline had so much. And I had so little. That's when I realized what I could do. Her death didn't have to be in vain. Because over those last couple of months, in so many ways I had become her. I had access to all her accounts and her driver's license. I knew she'd never bothered getting a passport yet because she'd never left the US. Jacqueline didn't have any other family. Well, none that she'd spoken about. Her father had died, and her mother left when she was a little girl. It would be so easy. So easy to just become her. As for Ruby O'Connor... Who cared if she died? She had even less. She didn't have anything or anyone either—except a criminal record."

I hold my chin up high. "So that's what I told the police. I called them and told them I'd come home to my roommate Ruby dead on the couch."

It had been easy to pull off, really. While Jackie had begun taking the drugs that night, I'd swiped her phone out of her notice. I used my phone to text hers, saying that *I couldn't do this anymore.* So, when the police came, it was further proof of "Ruby's" overdose. I made sure I was beside myself that I hadn't been able to help my poor, messed-up roommate. And as I'd hoped, they treated it as a suicide. It wasn't surprising to them. The shock of leaving prison and coming back to the real world must have been too much for "Ruby". So, with "Ruby's" family non-existent, I verified the body, and no one batted an eyelid after that—just as I'd known would happen. No one ever really thinks twice about a messed-up kid like that. All they want is to sweep them under the carpet like they never existed.

I throw my shoulders back as I finish my tale. "As they wheeled her body away, I realized it was done. There was no undoing it. I was now Jacqueline. And I lived the life that she should have had. I've never looked back. Until today."

# Chapter Forty-Three

## Anna

I can't believe the words coming out of Jacqueline's—I mean *Ruby's*—mouth.

Ruby has made a show of making it seem like she didn't directly kill Jackie. She says what happened was my sister's own actions and that she'd simply taken advantage of a terrible situation. But that was easy for this woman to say when Jackie was dead and unable to speak for herself.

I have to try and decipher the truth. I think back to the last time I'd seen my sister, on that early December morning when she'd given me my way out at last. She had seemed distracted. Her dad was in the hospital after his heart attack, due to have an operation later that week to hopefully help save his life. She was about to drive over to Ohio to see him.

I texted her a few times after that and even tried to call, but I didn't hear from her for over a month. I felt like I couldn't leave until I saw her again. I had to make sure she was okay. It was finally in the New Year when I heard from her. She told me that her dad had died before Christmas. I kept calling her, hoping she'd pick up and I could arrange to see her. I had everything arranged now; I couldn't keep putting off leaving for much longer. Every day felt like a potential risk of Nate finding out. Every day, I feared how quickly he could turn violent.

Just when I'd almost given up hope, Jackie told me her address, and I made plans to see her one last time before I left Philadelphia for good. I wanted to give her—and only her—one way of keeping in touch with me.

But I never saw her alive again...

Now, after Ruby's story, I have to wonder, had Jackie really been so far lost in her grief that it could be true? That she'd overdosed herself? I just wasn't sure.

Either way, I'd never known about Ruby. I'd never really known much about my sister's world if I was being honest. We'd only connected in the last few months of her life when she'd tracked me down. It was all through emails at first during that summer, and then we realized we didn't live too far from each other.

We'd only met a few times in a ramshackle diner on the outskirts of Philadelphia. We kept our meetings secret and infrequent. I didn't want there to be any way for Nate to find out, and Jackie respected that. Especially when we came up with our plan.

I picture the first time we met: that sunny late August morning, the branches of the trees behind the diner heavy with an assortment of colorful leaves. I'd crept out of the house. I hadn't wanted to wake Nate up. I hoped that he would think I'd gone for a run before work, purposefully leaving a note to that effect.

The forgotten diner had been empty, except for one woman framed in the corner of the last window, her curls tied in a jumbled ponytail above her head. She'd grinned and waved, instantly recognizing me. I'd done a double take—thinking it was my mother. I'd purposefully lost contact with her after I left Colorado. She was a horrible reminder of everything with my stepfather.

My heart raced, but as I got closer and Jacqueline's features came into focus, I knew it wasn't her. My sister's eyes were a warm brown, the opposite of our mother's—which were frosty blue. The eyes I had inherited.

Jacqueline had been as bright as the sunshine outside, coaxing me out of my shell as we started to catch up on all the time we had lost. Over the years, and especially in these last few months, I've reflected on how much she brought out of me and how little I'd found out about her.

But perhaps it was because she'd already uncovered a lot about me. She told me that she'd spent months trying to find me after her dad had told her that he thought she might have a half-sibling.

Jackie explained how our mother had cheated on her husband, Jackie's dad, and then got pregnant, deciding to leave her existing family to start a new one. I don't know all the details of that, whether our mother completely abandoned her previous family without a backward glance or if Jackie's dad kicked her out and told her never to come back. I suppose we'd never entirely know. But my early childhood was happy enough, moving from Ohio to Colorado to expand my dad's car business. Things weren't perfect, but I idolized my father, even if I could tell my mother was sometimes jealous of the attention he gave me. Things were fine, but then my father died when I was eight. My mother was completely distraught, and I don't think she ever fully recovered from my father's death. I realized that even the sight of me became too much as I reminded her of his loss.

Without my dad tying our little family unit together, my mother and I drifted even further apart as I entered my pre-teen years. Throughout that time, she was a shadow of herself... Until she found a new man to bring into our lives. Mike.

School had been my respite from my now uninterested mother and increasingly cruel stepfather. School, where I had met Nate. My only escape, soon to be my curse.

I remember when Jackie gently asked me about the small bruise on my arm. The translucent muddy green shade like a mottled patch of grass. I tried to brush it off, as I always did, as an accident. I was "so clumsy," and I'd "bumped" my arm.

Her eyes narrowed at me, and it was the first time I saw something cold in her otherwise warm eyes. "I know you're lying. You get the same expression on your face as I do," she said sadly.

I opened my mouth to deny it. But then I thought, what's the use? I'm speaking to my sister—my *sister*. If I couldn't tell her—who could I tell?

I admitted the truth to Jackie. Not everything: I didn't tell her exactly what Nate had over me, but I said that he knew a terrible secret about me, and he would never let me forget it for as long as I lived. If I ever left him, he'd expose me.

"Well," she said with a small shrug. "You'll just have to disappear, then."

Her words hit home. I know she was right. It had been something I'd been thinking about for a long time. And now, I had to try. Not just for myself—but also for my unborn baby. I patted my still flat stomach. I was only a few weeks pregnant. I had some time, but not a lot of it, to get out of this nightmare situation I was in. I knew that if I had this baby with Nate, it would never be safe. I was going to be a better mother to my child than my mother had been to me. I had to be brave and leave at last.

Over those fall months, Jackie helped me secretly apply for my first American passport and said that she'd get proof of our mother's Irish ancestry. That way, I'd be able to escape to Ireland or the UK and claim citizenship. Nate would never be able to find us there. He didn't know my mother's maiden name, so I prayed that once I left, under my new name and passport, he'd never be able to find me or my baby again. I'd change my name *again* if I had to. I'd go so far away that he wouldn't be able to catch up. Besides, he didn't have enough money to follow me across the world.

Jackie told me that she'd bring me money when she had my passport, and then I'd be able to disappear.

I'd questioned why she was being so kind to me at our final meeting when she handed everything over. She'd looked sad at the question. She'd said that even though our mom had ended up being a selfish waste of space, it didn't mean that we had to be like that to each other. That we could look after each other like sisters were supposed to. It was only at that last meeting that I realized she was also doing it for another reason: to make up for the mistakes that had happened between her and our other sister, Louisa.

The sister who had left her behind. She'd told me then how she had an older sister. But Jackie ruined everything between them in her final year of high school.

"Louisa was four years older than me. I'd idolized her—after Mom left, I guess she took over a bit as my mom. Our father never really recovered from the breakdown of their marriage—he looked after us financially, but he struggled to show his emotions. Anyway, I guess after Louisa left for college when I was fourteen, with no one looking out for me, I started to blame Louisa for leaving me, too. Just like our Mom had done..."

She'd run a shaking hand through her curly hair as she continued. "And I guess that's why, one night, I did something very stupid. Louisa had a long-term boyfriend, Jack. They'd been high-school sweethearts—but he'd stayed at home for community college while Louisa had gone to college in upstate New York. When she was away, he kept an eye on me. We'd grown close over the years, and I had a crush on him. I knew it was wrong, but in the final few months of high school, there were a lot of parties. I suppose now it's strange that he came along to them with me, but back then, I thought it was amazing. One night, we got very drunk... and, well, we ended up sleeping together. We secretly kept seeing each other for the next few months. Jack convinced me to keep it a secret from my sister until after she'd finished her college exams. He said we'd tell her then. I went along with it. I thought I was in love, after all, and I was also angry at Louisa for leaving me. I was so young and foolish. I don't know how I was expecting it to all turn out. But it was much worse than I ever expected.

"I was at Jack's house, *in* his bed, on his birthday, when the door flew open. And there was my sister... with an overnight bag in one hand. She was halfway through saying 'surprise' when her gaze landed on the two of us together. She'd come home for the weekend, even though she was partway through her final exams, as a birthday present. Instead, she found her little sister in her boyfriend's bed." Jackie shook her head sadly as tears glistened in her eyes at the memory.

"After that, everything fell apart. We had a huge fight, Louisa calling me terrible things. She said she never wanted to speak to me again. She broke up with Jack, too, on the spot. Then, she left us all behind. I thought in time, she might cool off, but all throughout that summer, I kept trying to talk to her, and all she did was block my calls. Later, she even changed her number. Jack and I disintegrated soon after that. I could hardly look myself in the mirror, thinking about how much hurt I'd caused her. When I went to college, I didn't tell anyone that I even had a sister. I was embarrassed; I didn't want to tell the story. And I wanted to start again. Throughout college, I didn't even try to get in touch with her. I heard about what she was up to through my father—but her communications with him became even more infrequent. It really did seem like she wanted nothing more to do with us. For good."

She'd paused for a moment, her voice thick with emotion. Before clearing her throat, she'd continued, "But now... with Dad in hospital, I'll try and get in touch. If this doesn't change anything between us, I'm not sure what will."

Jackie had grabbed my hand over the table, her eyes pleading. "But that's why I've done all of this for you. I don't want to mess everything up with another sister. I want to try and make amends for what I did to her."

As I'd left the diner on that cold winter's day, even though I was worried about the anguish etched in Jackie's eyes, I'd hoped that maybe she would find a way back to her other sister after all this time. And I hoped that her father would recover, too.

But everything went wrong. All because of me.

# CHAPTER FORTY-FOUR

## ANNA

That awful night will forever be etched in my memory. I close my eyes, and I see it now.

I was going to swing past my sister's house, now that I knew where she lived, to make sure she was okay. I'd felt like I couldn't leave until I'd seen her again. But also, over these last few weeks, I'd had to prepare my escape, and now, finally, I'd booked my flight out of here. After seeing Jackie, I'd go to mine and Nate's apartment for the final time while he was out on his nightly prowl of dealing. I'd grab the essentials pack that I'd carefully bundled together and kept hidden. Then, I'd leave for good.

But when I arrived at the apartment block where Jackie lived, I wasn't expecting to see flashing blue lights. At first, all I felt was confusion. I pressed close to the other people watching the scene, and I overheard whispers from some nosy neighbors—saying that they weren't surprised. That wild girl in flat fifteen was always doing too many drugs, and now she'd had an overdose.

My pulse started to race. Flat fifteen. That was Jackie's flat. I pushed my way through to the front of the cordoned-off area. It's like time stopped as I saw a body being wheeled out from the front of the building. I prayed it wasn't my sister. But as it passed, beneath the covering, I spied a lock of familiar wavy hazelnut hair. *No. No. No.*

I put a hand over my mouth to stop a scream from escaping.

I couldn't believe what was in front of my eyes. But that was Jackie's hair, and flat fifteen was *her* flat. It had to be her. She was dead.

I stumbled back, suddenly feeling like I was suffocating. I pushed through the hovering people and ran down the road as fast as I could. I retched onto the sidewalk, unable to process what I'd just seen. I collapsed onto the curb, placing my head in between my knees to get a grip.

My mind whirled at what I'd just witnessed and at what I'd just heard the neighbors say—a drug overdose. As I calmed my beating heart, I could only come to one terrifying conclusion: Nate had found Jackie somehow. Nate had done this to her. It was all my fault that she was dead.

***

I ran through our neighborhood. I wasn't sure what I was going to do yet. I wanted to kill him for what he'd done to my sister—but he was so much bigger and stronger than me. How could I take him on? All I knew was that I had to grab my pack. I had to get out of here before he hurt me and my unborn baby, too. I had to save this child, and then I'd figure everything out.

I unlocked the front door to our two-bed walk-up apartment and sprinted up the stairs. We were on the very top floor—and as usual, it was silent. Our neighbors all often worked nightshifts. When I unlocked our scratched metal door, the apartment was dark and empty.

I made a beeline for the kitchen. I'd hidden my small bag where I knew Nate would never check: the very back of the kitchen sink where we kept all the cleaning supplies. It was under a pile of cloths and bottled products.

I didn't bother flicking the switch on as I sped toward it. But as I crouched down to open the cupboard, the sudden appearance of the overhead lights stopped my heart. I jumped up, turning around to see Nate leaning against the door frame.

"Hello, angel," he said casually, one arm behind his back. "Looking for this?" he asked with a smirk as he removed his arm and lifted it to display my small backpack. The one that I thought I'd kept so well hidden.

I couldn't help it as I let out a strangled sob. I was frozen in fear. He'd taken my sister, and now he was going to destroy my only way out, too.

As he walked toward me, he kept speaking, cocking his head to one side and flashing that smile. The one that had made me fall for him in high school and now made me petrified. "Don't bother trying to deny anything. God, I've been following you for months, seeing you meet up with someone in secret. I figured out that it was your long-lost *sister*, of all people. And then those recent texts I saw on your phone confirmed everything. You want to leave me tonight, in fact. Well, I can't have that, can I?"

Mute, I stared up at him in horror, his words confirming his guilt. He was only steps away from me now. "And the thing is, my angel, your sister has ruined everything between us, putting all these crazy ideas into your head. You see why I can't let that go on. You have to remember, I *love* you. I'm the only one who can love you after what you did. So, you are never going to leave me. You are mine. And this child of ours will be mine, too."

He'd guessed the pregnancy a couple of months ago. But it hadn't changed anything in my mind—I'd still kept planning my escape, patiently waiting for Jackie. Jackie—who I was sure he'd just killed to get her out of my life by giving her some bad drugs. What other explanation could there be?

Close up, I could see that the red mist had descended over his eyes. He dropped my backpack to the floor with a thump. I knew what was going to come next. He was going to hurt me. He was going to try and control me. Like he'd always done.

But for once, I couldn't let that happen. I had cowered away from him for so long, but now I had to fight back.

"Get away from me. You killed her." I yelled, backing away from him. "I'm leaving. You will never touch me again."

He just laughed, further proving his guilt in my mind.

"Like I said, you are *never* leaving me." He reached out to grab my wrist tight. And I could see the fury in his eyes and the hard blow that was about to come if I didn't get away now. I knew that if I didn't fight back now, I might never escape again.

So, I reacted on instinct. As I had before, with another angry man.

I whirled and grabbed the first thing I could. The kitchen knife by the sink.

The next thing I knew, I was slashing the knife across his torso and into his stomach as I screamed.

He cried out in pain, and as he fell, he knocked his head on the edge of the kitchen table. He slumped to the floor, unmoving.

My stomach rolled over at the sight as blood pooled everywhere.

Oh god. He was dead.

But I couldn't pause to register what I'd just done. I'd already prepared for my escape, thanks to my beautiful sister. My sister, who I'd barely had a chance to know. I'd start my long-planned journey to Ireland. Maybe I would have to run even further now. To London, perhaps—disappear into a giant city. But I'd cross that bridge when I got there.

All I knew in that moment was that this had bought me some time, and I had to get out of there. I grabbed the bag up from the floor and swore I would never come back. I would get out of the city, the state, the *country*. Before anyone found him. Because Nate was connected, and if they realized I'd killed him, people would be after me. And beyond that, if the police got involved, I refused to be arrested for his death. I had acted in self-defense once more—for me and my unborn baby.

I realized that this was my final chance to run. I had to take it. After everything Jackie had sacrificed, I wouldn't let her death be in vain.

Nate had killed my sister. He deserved to die.

***

Now, I turn to face the woman who has pretended to be Jackie for all these years. The woman who says that my sister was a loose cannon, not caring enough to even look after herself. But that wasn't the woman I knew.

The Jacqueline I knew, albeit briefly, had done everything in her power to help me prepare for my escape. She'd been trying to make up for what she'd done to her other sister, Louisa. I can't marry these two versions of her together.

I look up at Nate in this brightly lit sitting room. I never imagined all my lies would bring me back to him. I'd hoped that he was dead.

He smiles that twisted grin at me once more. "So now you see, my angel, I never killed your sister." He glares across at Ruby. "Of course, when I gave her the drugs that day, I knew she was your sister's roo mmate... But you didn't know who I was, did you?" he grins at Ruby, and she scowls. Then he looks back at me, "As you know, whenever I was doing a deal, I covered my face. But hers became seared into my memory after what you accused me of.

"I knew who the drugs were for. I'd been keeping close tabs on the area since I'd discovered you were planning something with her, and so I knew that this girl lived with your sister. But I wouldn't ever have killed Jackie—or probably not. Not if you'd promised to stay away from her. If you hadn't jumped to conclusions and stabbed me, maybe I could have explained that to you. But you never even gave me a chance. After you ran, once I was back on my feet enough, I started trying to puzzle out what had happened that night to cause you to act so crazy. That's when my guys told me that they'd heard about an OD. The idiots couldn't tell me *which* girl had died, though. But I put two and two together. I remembered you screaming 'you killed her' before stabbing me, so I guessed it was your sister and that you'd decided to blame me for it."

He sighs heavily as though in despair at the whole situation. "Can you see now why I was so *angry* with you? You tried to kill me for something I didn't even do. I couldn't believe it when I came all this way to England and ran into this one again," he nods at Ruby, "pretending to be 'Jacqueline'." He watches me closely as he adds, "I realized that she must have taken your sister's identity somehow, that she might have even forced her to OD to take it. Whatever she'd done, I blamed her for everything that she'd done to destroy us. But I knew I had to be smart: if I could force her to tell the truth about what had happened, then you would see how wrong you'd been to hurt me so terribly, and I could destroy her life for what she'd done to us. Then, you would come back to me at last. So you see," he says, spreading his palms wide to encompass the whole scene around us, "All I've ever done was love and protect you. Now, you just have to do the same for me."

I try not to flinch at his words. Nate might not have killed my sister. But I still don't regret what I'd done that night. Stabbing him and running was my only choice. Nate is violent and unpredictable, obsessed with control. He'd just said it himself. He "probably" wouldn't have killed my sister, but only if I'd done exactly what I'd said. Jackie, and then Sofia, would have been just another tool to control me with if I'd stayed. I might have done many bad things in my life, but everything I'd ever done had been out of love: for Jackie and Sofia. I don't regret anything.

Nate had done many bad things, too, but only for one person: himself. I'd run that day for a reason, and it's clear that he hasn't changed. If anything, as I look up at him now and this scene of chaos he's created, he's become even more delusional.

Right now, though, I have to be smart. I must make Nate think that I not only believe him but that I *forgive* him. Because I have to get out of here and save Sofia and Matilda. Who knows what they might be going through right now...

I whirl to face the deceptive woman next to me, ready to give the performance of my life.

"I don't believe what you say about Jackie's overdose," I tell her in a commanding voice. "I think you killed her on *purpose*. And what the hell happened to my other sister? What happened to Louisa?"

Her nostrils flare. She'd clearly thought she'd put on such a good show that no one would ask her about that.

Across from me, Freddie stares at me in shock. "What? *Louisa* was your sister, too?"

Charles's face drops in devastation as he looks across at his wife. "Louisa?" he says, in a voice that cracks in two. "You knew Louisa?"

The brothers look like their entire world has shattered around them. Again. I suppose it has.

Next to me, Ruby shakes her head and stays silent, refusing to answer. Nate points the gun at her once more—watching me intently all the while with a smile. He must think it's going his way. I have to keep it like that.

"Do as she says," he says, every word laced with threat.

And at last, Ruby opens her mouth to speak again.

# CHAPTER FORTY-FIVE

## RUBY

With Nate's gun pointing at me again, I know that I must give them another answer.

Though honestly, I know as much about Louisa's death as they do.

I twist my hands in my lap. "After I became Jacqueline that January, I left Philadelphia. I wanted to start again somewhere new, but I wasn't sure where. I was on a road trip, searching for the right city to settle down in. In February, I received an email, or Jacqueline did, from her sister Louisa. To say I was surprised was an understatement. I had no idea that she even had a sister. I thought I'd done my research and that Jacqueline had no living relatives left. Or at least, no close ones that she was in touch with."

I sigh. This next part of the story I'm not proud of. All I'd wanted was Jacqueline's life. After that, I didn't want to cause anyone else any harm. I'd wanted to become a *better* version of who Jacqueline had been—not waste the life.

"But it seemed that Jacqueline had tried to get in touch with this missing sister after her father died, sending her a letter. Louisa was finally emailing her back, saying that after all this time, she'd like to see if they could start again. She'd apparently forgiven her for something she did as a teenager. Anyway, Louisa had shared that she was in trouble. She... didn't sound like she was in a good place. She wasn't coping with her new child. She realized she needed family support. And"—I look up at Charles apologetically—"she was having second thoughts about marrying you. She said that she had also gotten herself into a messy situation. She didn't say what. But she thought it might be easier if she wasn't around anymore..."

"You're lying," Charles spits at me. The anger on his face shocks me. I *knew* that he'd be upset if he ever knew the truth, but I suppose I always hoped that maybe there would be a part of him that might understand. Because in spite of all the reasons why I should never have ended up with him, I love him and I've risked *everything* to be with him and look after Matilda. Can't he see that now I'm finally telling him everything?

I lean forward, trying to catch his eye. "I'm not. I've told you the truth about everything else. Why would I lie about this? Anyway, I'm not proud of this, but I ignored her cries for help. In fact, I emailed back, telling her to never contact me again. I didn't want to have anything else to do with her. I couldn't ever meet her, of course—not that she could know why.

"But then I heard about her death in the newspaper." I shake my head. "And I could have ignored it entirely. But for some reason, I felt a tug of responsibility to her, to you, and to the child. I felt... so guilty." It was true. Even though they'd ruled her death a tragic accident, after what she'd emailed me, I'd always wondered if she might have done it on purpose.

I lean toward Charles, but he refuses to look at me still. I sigh and carry on.

"I wanted to check on you and the baby. It felt like something this new Jacqueline would do—and like I said before, I wanted to become a *better* version of her. So I moved to San Francisco and, at long last, found a job in real estate thanks to Jacqueline's previous experience. I was good at it straight away and surprised myself by loving the work. And then, Charles, I reached out to you because I thought that if I helped you and Louisa's child get a new home, then at least I'd have helped you get back on your feet... Or maybe part of me just wanted to see if you were doing okay."

Tears well up, but I wipe them away. "I never expected to fall for you. That was never my plan. But I did." I stare at Charles with pleading eyes as he refuses to look my way. "Charles, please. I know all of this is a shock to you. And I'm so sorry. But you have to believe me—everything that happened between us was real. I came along right when you needed someone. I risked *everything* to be with you."

It was true—yes, I'd orchestrated that meeting with Charles, but our instant connection was real. I wanted to help him. I'd never felt anything like it before. I think it must have been the freedom of no longer being Ruby O'Connor. When I became Jacqueline Kelly, I felt strong, beautiful, smart and powerful. Everything that Ruby O'Connor hadn't been, with her terrible childhood and years in jail.

Then, when I met beautiful, tiny Matilda, it really did feel like it was meant to be. I convinced myself that it would be fine. I did my extra research, and I quizzed Charles as much as I could, sensitively, and it seemed like there really were no other family members that I didn't already know about. When Charles said that we should all move back to the UK, it seemed even more perfect. *This* was the moment I'd been waiting for—this was the way for me to get far away and start again.

I believed that this strange circumstance of receiving that email from Louisa after Jacqueline's death had been the universe's way of making it happen. Because otherwise, I would never have been in San Francisco, I would never have met Charles and Matilda. I realized I was destined to live a good life as Jacqueline. I was destined to be a wife, a mother, and successful. And I wasn't going to say no when it was all brought to me at last on a silver platter...

"Stop lying!" Charles screams at me. I flinch back.

Nathaniel tuts at him. "Oh, Charles, you can't accuse her of that. Not when you're lying to all of us, too?"

"Excuse me?" Charles manages, spluttering.

"Well, you really should be more careful about how you show your affections. You never know who's watching." And then he stares directly down at Anna, a look of thunder on his face. "I know he tried to kiss you..."

Anna stiffens beside me and shakes her head. "No, Nate, I..."

"Spare me," Nate retorts, "I saw your embrace through the window the other night."

Even though I shouldn't be feeling anything at this point, Nathaniel's declaration still sends a wave of despair through me. Of course, Charles and Anna kissed. I was right to be worried about that all along!

"Nothing happened," Charles protests, looking Nathaniel straight in the eyes. "It was just a hug. We're friends."

Nathaniel shrugs, his eyes still locked on Anna. "Well, that's not what it looked like to me. You looked *very* cozy." Then he turns to me, "Does that surprise you?" His tone is almost conversational, except for the wicked glint in his eye.

I wish I could say no, but my heart sinks at the same time as it starts to race in anger. Charles is angry at me for lying to him. But he is also a liar. Lying about his affair last year and now his feelings for Anna.

I never confronted him after Jasper's party. Not after discovering that Anna might be on to my secret. I didn't want to rock the boat of our relationship right when I might need him on my side more than ever. But now? What does it matter? He's heard the truth, my desperate explanation of why I had to take Jacqueline's identity and start again—but that I still love him. He clearly doesn't care.

And now, if what Nate says is true, Charles and Anna have been getting even closer than I thought behind my back. I wonder if he denied her similarities to Louisa all this time because he didn't want to admit his attraction to her.

"No," I say at last, "it doesn't surprise me. Because, Charles, I might not have been entirely honest with you, but you haven't been entirely honest with me. Not about your affair last year and not about your feelings for Anna."

I watch as his cheeks blush, and he opens his mouth to say something—deny it, probably. "Spare me the denials," I jump back in. If my whole world is crumbling down around me now, I might as well do it in style. "I overheard some women at Jasper's party. It's all over the rumor mill that you were getting with your assistant behind my back.

I'm sure you've done just the same with *her.*" I turn to face Anna, my words flying out like poison.

Beside me, Anna is frozen to the spot, seemingly shocked by these revelations. Or she's just unable to utter a single word under Nathaniel's ferocious gaze.

Charles goes bright red and splutters at my accusations. "I can't believe you're accusing me of this now. Amelia and I are work colleagues, nothing more. That's the only reason why we've spent a lot of time together. So, not that it matters, but it's absolutely not true. Not about last year—like I told you at the time—and not about Anna!"

"Yeah, right," Nate scoffs. I'm about to retort, too, when the clock chimes. All our heads whip to it. Eight forty-five.

We have fifteen minutes left to save our children.

Charles starts again, whirling to face Nate in a fury. "Listen up, you need to—"

But he doesn't get to finish his sentence as Freddie jumps up, interrupting him.

"WE NEED TO SAVE THE KIDS!" he screams at his brother. "Stop trying to antagonize him!"

Charles puffs his chest out, the muscles that he's honed over the years from rowing tensing. "I know that," he spits. "But remember, this is your mess."

"How do you figure that?" Freddie spits back at him.

"Whatever this deal is that you coordinated between him and Jasper. It's *your* fault that we're even in this situation. You and Jasper brought him over here in the first place! You needed money, that's what it is, isn't it? You lost it all, and Jasper promised you cash if you helped him dig up dirt on Anna?"

Freddie is silent. I watch as Charles takes that as confirmation. I do, too—I'm not surprised. I've suspected that Freddie's been in a tricky place with money this last year, but I didn't think it would come to something like this.

"That's what I thought. Classic you, always creating the problems, and then I'll have to fix it." Charles adds scathingly.

"Oh, you're blaming me for this," Freddie retorts. "That's rich. You always think you're so morally superior. The big criminal barrister. Where have you been for these last fifteen minutes? Did you not just hear your crazy *wife* admit to stealing someone else's life? And not just anyone's, but Louisa's sister's?!"

Charles shakes his head. "I didn't... I didn't know."

"Of course you didn't," Freddie scoffs. "You never know. You never *see* anything."

"What's that supposed to mean?"

I can't believe the two of them are starting to have one of their never-ending arguments right now. I'm about to jump in and say something, even though I know they'll probably pounce on me after everything I've just revealed, when Freddie laughs. "You acted all heartbroken when she died, but the truth is I don't think you really loved Louisa, not really. There was a reason why you moved on so quickly. I bet you were even *relieved* when it happened."

My mouth drops open in shock at his words. Beside me, Anna stiffens. Nate cocks his head, intrigued, and Charles shakes his in total disbelief. "Shut up, Freddie," he manages weakly.

But Freddie continues, on a roll, "You married her because of the baby, sure, because you are a 'good guy.' Always doing the right thing. But she was struggling, and you didn't help her."

"Freddie," Charles interrupts, pain etched across his features. "Please, that's not true. I tried to help her, I did... But we were both struggling with the sudden arrival..."

"No, Charles. I'm sick of you pretending like you're all virtuous. When you know what, I was the only one who really *cared* for Louisa." His voice breaks, and then his eyes widen. As though he might have said too much.

*Oh my god.* Had Freddie been talking about *Louisa* when he'd said to me at lunch, *"I don't want you to get hurt. I've stood by before..."*? He'd clammed up from speaking any further. At the time, I'd been too distracted by the weird moment between us after that. But had that been a hint, too? Had Freddie tried to become close to me over the years because he'd been constantly trying to make up for whatever he'd "stood by" for before?

I don't know what to think. My mind is whirring when Charles laughs bitterly. "Oh, don't stop now! I've suspected it for ages—why do you think I've struggled to trust you over these last twelve years? It wasn't all to do with work—it was really because of Louisa. I always thought there was something between you two. But I tried to move on from my suspicions because you really seemed to care about getting to know Matilda and being there for me and my family again. And I didn't want to lose anyone else in my life. But here we are, the truth comes out at last. My brother and my wife. How predictable."

I jolt in surprise. I didn't realize that Charles had always *suspected* this. All he'd ever told me was that they'd fallen out around work and that Freddie had abandoned him in his hour of need after Louisa.

Freddie's face is flushed in anger. "I *loved* her," he says fiercely. Then his words tumble out thick and fast, suddenly jubilant at getting the declaration off his chest, "There, I said it. Are you happy? I loved her. We started having an affair that summer just before she realized she was so late into her pregnancy. She knew that the child was yours—so she agreed to marry you. But after Matilda and with our secret affair, her head was all over the place. She felt like she couldn't talk to you anymore—of course she couldn't. I tried to help her, but then she started to avoid my calls."

I can't believe the words coming out of Freddie's mouth. Charles can't seem to believe them either as he listens slack-jawed. Freddie can't seem to stop talking now. "She wouldn't talk to me, and clearly, you didn't support her enough. I bet you were so happy for her to get away on that weekend trip—but really, you sent her to her death. You might as well have pushed her off that cliff yourself!" Freddie screams at Charles.

I flinch—I'm furious at Charles, but I don't think it's entirely fair for Freddie to accuse him of that. It sounds like Louisa was struggling to talk to *anyone,* including Freddie.

"Wait, what?" Charles says, confused at his brother's words. Freddie's eyes widen as though realizing what he's admitted to. "No one knows what happened to her exactly... Were you... Were you there?"

Freddie shakes his head furiously, trying to backtrack. "No, of course not. The police suggested she might have fallen—that's all." But his face is an even brighter red. I can't help but think that's a tell-tale sign of guilt...

Charles lunges forward, grabbing his brother through his T-shirt. He shakes him, his voice breaking. "Tell the truth. Please, Freddie, tell me the truth."

As though hearing the crack in Charles's voice, Freddie's shoulders sink in defeat, and he whispers, "I... I wanted to check on her. I was so worried after she refused to talk to me. I'd been watching her from afar, and so I decided to follow her to the retreat. I was staying nearby. I thought I'd keep a distant eye on her since you didn't seem to care enough to stop her going. I knew she wasn't well...

"No one knew I was there. I followed her early one morning from a sensible distance when she went out on a solo walk. Until she stopped at the top of a giant waterfall. I thought she was just admiring it. But then she turned around and spoke to me directly. It's like she'd known I was there the whole time. Tears were streaming down her face as she said, 'I'm sorry, Freddie. I can't do this anymore. Look after Matilda for me.' And then she stepped over the cliff. I screamed, sprinting, but I was too late. I leaned over the waterfall as much as I could, but she'd disappeared into the rapids below."

Next to me, Anna gasps at Freddie's words. The confirmation of what really happened to the sister she'd never known. I watch as Charles clutches Freddie's shirt. Tears slip down both their cheeks.

Freddie takes a shaky breath as he continues, "I didn't know what to do. I was beside myself. And... and I knew it was too late. No one could have survived that fall. So I ran away. And I kept my mouth shut all this time. It was one of the reasons why I couldn't talk to you after she died.

I couldn't cope with what I was keeping from you. But it was also why, when I'd finally processed things myself, I agreed to what you wanted and kept Matilda's birth mother a secret until she was old enough. I'd have agreed to anything to be a part of Matilda's life and keep an eye on Louisa's daughter. It was the only thing I could still do for her. She'd asked me after all, and I'd failed her in everything else."

Charles lets him go, deflating like a balloon. Freddie adds in a sad voice, "I'm sorry, Charles... I'm sorry for what I just said before about her death being all your fault. That was unfair."

Nathaniel, Anna, and I all watch on in shock, lost for a moment in Freddie's terrible tale. The truth about what happened to Louisa comes out at last.

Freddie continues quietly. "And I'm sorry I wasn't brave enough to stop her or tell the truth then. But now, I'm going to be brave. I'm going to save her child."

Then he punches Charles in the face, and the room erupts into chaos.

# CHAPTER FORTY-SIX

## RUBY

One second, Charles is flying backward, and the rest of us are jumping up in shock. It must have been Freddie's idea of a distraction because the next second, he's hurtling across the room and tackling Nathaniel to the ground.

Nathaniel lands with a heavy thump, the gun flying out of his grasp.

Next to me, Anna is on her feet, sprinting to the door, taking the opportunity to escape.

The movement causes Freddie to look up in surprise. He punches Nathaniel hard once more and then leaps up, racing toward the door.

He's inches away from Anna, whose hand is outstretched, trying to reach the handle. In the chaos, they collide, sending Anna flying to the floor. Freddie grabs the handle. He's about to pull it open wide—when two shots ring out.

At first, I don't register what's happened as Freddie's trajectory continues to hurtle toward the door. But then I realize that instead of stopping to pull it open, he's collapsing. He crumples to the floor, and red starts to rush out of him, almost imperceptible on the dark wooden floor.

I'm frozen at the sight as Charles jumps up, sprinting to his brother. "Oh my god, Freddie, Freddie!'

But I can tell he's too late. Freddie's not moved one inch from where he's fallen.

"I told you not to run. I told you not to disobey me," Nate screams at them both, his face distorted in rage. He picks Anna up like a ragdoll and yells into her ear, pointing at Freddie's body. "This is your fault. This is all your fault."

Then the clock strikes nine.

# CHAPTER FORTY-SEVEN

## ANNA

I can't believe the sight in front of me. Freddie's dead. *Dead.*

I'm in a chokehold as Nate presses his massive biceps into my windpipe. But I had to take that small chance when I saw it. I had to try and escape—to save Sofia and Matilda. I didn't think it would end in Freddie's death instead.

"It didn't have to be like this, angel," he shouts in my ear. "Did it? This is all your fault. I told you that no one had to get hurt. But now? How am I going to explain this?!"

Charles looks up from beside his brother, devastation written across his face.

Nate presses harder against my throat as he screams at me. "I tried to give you a chance to win me back and save your life. But the first opportunity you got, you tried to run. Didn't you realize this was all a test? And now I know I'm never going to be able to trust you. God... and now this." He gestures at the body on the ground. "What am I going to do? I'm certainly not going to take the blame for it. So perhaps it will have to be you. I mean, you're good at killing and covering your tracks, aren't you?" He laughs manically. I struggle against his grip, watching as Charles and Ruby stare at me in horror, unable to move.

"In fact, maybe you'll have to kill them all..." He points at Charles and Ruby. "You have a history of killing, after all; it makes sense that you went crazy. Besides, this *is* your gun. Yes," he muses, his words tumbling out thick and fast as he thinks out loud. "We could pin it all on you... And now, since I can't trust you, my dear Anna, perhaps it's time for you to die, too. Then I could say you killed *yourself* in despair... I'm sure the police would believe me when I tell them about your past."

But there's a wildness to his voice, and I can feel his heart beating fast in his chest. He has no idea what to do right now. He's trying to put on a show of bravado and coming up with ideas, but this clearly wasn't part of his plan. He must have truly hoped that I would go off with him into the sunset once I'd heard Ruby's tale and he'd finished having his fun taunting Charles and Freddie.

I try to squirm, but it just makes it even harder for me to breathe. I'm starting to feel light-headed as the oxygen seeps out of my system.

Ruby, crouched by Freddie's body, gets to her feet.

"Nathaniel," she says in a clear, calm voice. "There's another option you haven't considered."

"And what's that?" Nate sneers at her.

"You really ought to have someone that you can trust to back you up," Ruby says, a cold smile on her face. "*He* won't do it." She looks across at her husband with disdain. "But I will. If you cut me into the deal, I'll cover for you. I'll back up the story that it was *Anna* who killed Freddie and Charles when she found out they were building evidence against her to prove she killed Sir David Drummond. But we stopped her, and unfortunately, she died in the process."

I squirm slightly to see Nate cock his head, listening intently. He's always acted more with his heart than his mind. And Ruby has made him consider something he hasn't thought about before. "Why would you cover for me? I've just made you reveal your little secret to everyone here."

Ruby flashes an icy smile back at him. "Well, that's exactly it, isn't it? I don't want my secret getting out. I want to continue to be Jacqueline. And well, if all the rest of them die, then my secret will be safe. You can let me live. You will certainly need someone to verify your story. And you said it yourself. You can't trust *her*." She looks at me with disgust written across every feature, "You have to admit there's really no point in her life anymore. Not after what she's done to you. Betraying you again and again. You don't need her alive to get her money, either. If she dies, all her money will go to Sofia—and you will be in charge of that, as her father. There's absolutely no need for Anna to live. But you do need someone alive, *me*, to verify this tragic tale."

I try to scream out, but with Nate pressing against my windpipe, it's impossible. My chest tightens in panic—because she's right. Nate *doesn't* need me alive. Not really, not if he decides he doesn't care if I live or die, and all he wants is my fortune...

Charles looks across at his wife in horror as he rises to his feet on shaky legs. "No... no, Jacqueline—I mean, *Ruby*. You can't be serious!"

"Oh, Charles," she says, stepping toward him. "I am deathly serious. I need to save myself somehow—and this is the only way. Besides, this way, you'll get to die alongside the woman that you obviously much prefer to me," Ruby practically spits down at him.

"*No*," Charles groans. "No! What about the children?"

"We'll look after them, won't we?" Ruby says to Nate with a grin.

Barely able to breathe, never mind speak or move, I am as powerless as I am horrified when I feel Nate's body start to shake with laughter.

"Exactly!" he says, his voice loud in my ear. "You have yourself a deal."

# Chapter Forty-Eight

## Anna

I try to scream, but it comes out in a bubbled rasp. Charles's face reflects the shock I feel. He remains frozen, still crouched beside his brother's unmoving body, as Ruby walks toward me and Nate.

I realize that there's no way that they're letting Charles and me leave alive.

"Now, now," Nate says down at me as I squirm. "No need to struggle." And with that, he throws me down hard across the floor, where I hurtle to a stop in front of Charles.

I gasp, trying to catch my breath, as he tries to pull me upright into a sitting position.

Charles whispers against my ear, "Anna, I'm sorry for the part I've caused in angering him. You don't deserve this."

His hurried words make me choke back a sob. Charles is being so kind. But I *do* deserve this – it's all my fault that we're here in the first place. All because of Nate's obsession with me.

"It really didn't have to be this way, my Anna," Nate continues, walking closer to us. "I gave you a choice. You should have chosen more wisely. But now, I can see that you'll never be *my* Anna again. Look how cozy the two of you are—Charles whispering sweet nothings in your ear. Instead, I'll just take my daughter. And through that, your money. There's no need for you in our lives anymore..."

"Please," I say, my voice coming out raspy. "I'll do anything. Please."

"The problem is," he says, as he flashes that terrible smile down at me, "I don't believe you. And now, it's quite appropriate for you to die alongside the man that you're obviously falling for."

I watch in horror as Ruby steps toward Nate—her arm outstretched. As though to take... the gun.

But he holds on to it tight, seemingly questioning whether he can really trust her. "Now, I think this is something we should do together, don't you?" he says. "I don't want to hand over the gun and for you to get any crazy ideas."

"Of course," she says, a determined smile on her face.

Every step she takes closer to him feels like an eternity passing.

I squeeze my eyes shut, frozen in terror. I never thought this would be how I died. I never saw this coming.

My eyes dart to the door, so close but so impossible to reach.

I need a way out—but I can't think, and I wouldn't even know how to find the children even if I did get free. Are they really safe somewhere? Or was that a lie, too?

Silent tears slip down my cheek as I picture Matilda and Sofia locked away somewhere, scared.

Desperately, I speak up in a cracked voice. "Please, please don't kill us." I swallow my pride and address Ruby directly. "Think of our girls—think of my sisters, even—they wouldn't want you to do this. They wouldn't want you to kill us."

For a second, as our eyes lock, I think I've struck a chord, but then she scoffs. "There's no way I'm letting my secret out of this room. And unfortunately, I don't trust you two not to tell anyone. I make a better Jacqueline than the real one ever did, and I'm not going to give it up. So I am saving the children. I will look after them. And they'll be better off without you."

Nate nods in approval as Charles jumps to his feet to protest.

"Shut up and sit down!" she screams at him. Ruby moves into position next to Nate, placing her hands around his on the barrel.

I watch in shock as Charles refuses to do as she says, standing up to block me from view. I remain crouched on the floor. "No," he says, on shaky legs. "I won't let you do this."

"Come on, Charles, do you really want to be first?" Nate laughs.

And it's in that moment, that small moment of distraction, that I catch Ruby's eyes as she mouths, *RUN...*

# CHAPTER FORTY-NINE

## ANNA

It all happens so quickly. One second, Nate and Ruby are about to shoot, and the next, Nate screams. Ruby has turned and slashed the kitchen knife, the one she's had in her pocket the whole time, through his side.

"They must be in the shed!" she shouts across at me, "RU—"

I know I don't have any time to lose, and I hurtle toward the door. A gunshot rings out behind me, but I don't stop.

I sprint down the corridor to the front door. I was so dazed when I arrived here, but I remember seeing a small building down at the very bottom of the garden slope. That must be the shed. Nate said they were "safe" and "far away"—surely Ruby is right, and that is the only place they can be. I hope.

The front door is still wide open, and I take a sharp right. It's pitch black outside, but the small glow from the room we'd all been trapped in sheds some light. In the distance, I can see a building.

I sprint down the hill. I don't want to think about who might have been hit by that last bang. Or Ruby's double cross. Or if Nate is finally, finally dead. I just have to get Sofia and Matilda out.

The grass is soft and slippery, and it takes everything in me to stay upright. But at last, I'm within arm's reach of the shed. In the distance, I think I hear another bang, but I push it out of my mind as I throw open the door.

But inside, I'm greeted by... nothing.

Nothing but an empty shed full of a random assortment of tools and garden junk. I can't help but let out a scream.

Where are the girls?

# CHAPTER FIFTY

## ANNA

I try to calm my racing heart and breathe. Breathe. She said it was a shed—didn't she?

This was the only building I could see...

Unless this is all another trap.

But as I pause, I listen, and I hear a high-pitched squeal and banging.

And that's when I see it. The iron handle sticking out of the floor. A trap door.

Rushing over to it, I grasp the cool metal in my hand and tug with all my might. It doesn't budge. I force myself not to panic as I try again and again. At last, it creaks and starts to pull back.

It drops open to the floor with a crash.

And peering down, I see two terrified little faces staring back at me.

*They're alive, they're alive.*

And as my heart slows, I take in their shocked expressions and begin to register that, in fact, they only appear scared at my sudden appearance. In my fear-induced haze, I'd only seen them and not taken in the rest of their surroundings. But now, my eyes go wide as I notice that they appear to be sitting on a dark blue velvet sofa, popcorn and candy bar packets scattered around them.

"Mama," Sofia calls up at me. "What are you doing here? Isn't this the coolest room ever?!"

My heart feels like it could break in relief.

They thought they were safe. They thought they were safe this whole time. I guess Nate didn't want his own daughter terrified of him. Not yet, anyway. He'd planned the whole thing meticulously. Until Freddie died.

Is it over? Is it over at last?

But then I turn to look back out through the window next to me.

And that's when I see a figure emerge from the house in the distance.

One that I could recognize from anywhere.

It's Nate.

# Chapter Fifty-One

## Anna

He might have lulled the children into a false sense of security whilst he entrapped us—but now that Nate's entire plan has unraveled in front of his eyes, I know he will do anything for revenge.

And I'm not going to take any chances with their lives.

"Get out!" I scream down at them. "Get out, now." I only have a matter of moments before Nate will be down here.

There must be something in my voice that causes them to act without question, as Sofia immediately jumps up and starts directing Matilda up the small ladder.

My sweet, brave girl.

"Run over the fields, and no matter what, don't come back," I tell her as she gets to the top. "As *fast* as you can, okay!"

"What?" she asks in a small, scared voice. "Why?"

I look deep into her rich green eyes. "Please—I'll catch up. Promise. But no matter what, don't trust Nate." It's all the time I have for an explanation as I usher them to the door, looking around desperately for anything that might help me against Nate.

I throw the door open with a bang, turning right—toward the house. Looking over my shoulder for one tiny moment, I watch as their little figures sprint out in the other direction.

"I love you," I whisper out into the cloudless night sky.

Then I turn to face my fate.

Nate's about halfway down the hill. He's clutching his side from the knife wound with one hand, and there is a glint of silver in the other. He must have snatched Ruby's knife. Despite the wound, he's still moving fast. But if I hold him off for long enough, then the girls will get away. I hope. They'll be safe, even if I might not be.

I rush up the hill. Toward the man that has controlled my life since the moment I met him. I know that for certain, one way or the other, I'm either going to be dead or behind bars by the end of tonight.

Because both of us aren't walking out of this.

One of us will die.

As I get closer, I can see that familiar red haze in his eye. The one I came to know so well. Now, I'm ready to be consumed by it once and for all—if it means saving the children. I did the right thing in sending them away—he wouldn't have stopped with just me.

I call out to him, my arms outstretched. "Come on, it's me that you want."

He tries to laugh down at me as we close in on each other. But it comes out more like a strangled cough.

"I *want*," he spits, "to take everything from you like you took everything from me. I gave you a chance, and you threw it away like garbage. It's time you learned a lesson."

He hurtles toward me.

For one small second, his blood-red hand clasps around my wrist like a shackle. He leers over me like a bird catching its prey at last.

But shouldn't he have guessed? Shouldn't he have known from last time?

I will never go down without a fight.

And as he closes in, bringing his other hand up to my exposed throat, I strike.

I swing out with the hammer I'd tucked into my pocket.

And I smash its blunt edge straight into the side of his stupid head.

# CHAPTER FIFTY-TWO

## ANNA

Of *course,* I didn't leave that shed empty-handed. I spotted the best weapon I could find in the mere moments I had. A small iron hammer.

Nate lies unmoving at my feet. My body starts to tremble. Have I killed him at last?

"Anna!" A voice screams.

Charles runs down the hill—the gun in his hand—seemingly ready to help bring Nate down.

But as he gets closer and sees me standing over Nate's unmoving body, the hammer clutched in my hand, he drops the gun in shock.

*"Oh my god."* He comes to a sharp stop at the sight.

"Charles..." I start. "I can exp—"

But then he continues down the hill, closing the distance between us in a matter of strides. He pulls me into a tight hug.

"Oh my god, you're okay, you're okay," he murmurs into the top of my head.

For a moment, I'm frozen. I force my mind to work—and slowly bring my left arm around him, too. My right hand drops the hammer to the ground with a thud. Is it all over? All over at last?

But then, a small voice behind me cries. "Mama!"

I whirl around. Sofia is running back up the hill toward me.

"Sofia!" I scream, sprinting down to her.

We tumble into each other's arms, pulling each other close in a desperate embrace.

"Sofia," I say frantically. "What are you—"

At the same time, she says, "I know you told me to run, but I heard you scream. Matilda's safe, but I came back to help you..." And then she must be looking over my shoulder. Back toward the unmoving body lying on the grass.

She freezes like a statue in my arms. I spin her around, away from the view, and drop to my knees in front of her.

"Sofia, don't be scared. You're safe now." She nods mutely, her eyes brimming with tears. "And I'm safe now, too. Everything is going to be okay."

"That's the man... That's the man who tried to speak to me that day at the aquarium. When we got here tonight, I was scared, but he explained that he was your friend too. And since he was friends with Matilda's family, I thought it was fine. I'm sorry, I'm so sorry..." She bursts into tears.

"Oh, darling," I say, pulling her close. "None of this is your fault. Shh, shh, now."

Heavy footsteps crunch behind us, and Charles appears next to me.

"Sofia, I'm the one that's sorry. I had no idea that he wanted to try and hurt us."

I stand up to face him, clutching Sofia's hand tightly in mine.

"Anna, I'm so sorry," he says, sorrow on his face. "Nate was a friend of Freddie's. We got to know him a bit over the last six weeks, and they said how much the girls would love the cinema room. God, I had no idea it was all a trap." He looks down at my daughter. "Please, please, Sofia—will you tell me where Matilda is?" The way he says it makes my heart break that little bit more at what we've put them through tonight.

She sniffs away her tears. "She climbed a tree all the way back there." She points down to the forest behind the shed. *Smart girl*, I think to myself—very smart.

Charles visibly sags in relief. But then he says urgently, lowering his voice so Sofia can't hear. "Anna, we need to get back to Ruby."

# CHAPTER FIFTY-THREE

## ANNA

Charles had raced back inside to do as much as he could to help make Ruby comfortable while Sofia and I reunited with Matilda. Ruby was in a bad way, and he wasn't sure if she was going to make it.

In the chaos, she'd managed to tackle Nate to the ground, successfully knocking the gun out of his hand as he fired a rogue shot. Charles had flown out of the way but managed to fall and wind himself. He watched with gasping breaths as Nate grabbed the knife out of Ruby's hand and stabbed her badly. Nate had immediately fled the room after that, with the bloody knife still grasped in his hand.

Charles had raced to Ruby as soon as he could get up, but she was struggling. He tried his best to wrap his coat around the wound to stop the bleeding before she demanded that he chase after Nate with the gun, begging him to save Matilda and make sure she was safe.

Now, Charles and the children will wait outside for the emergency services as we swap places. I want to speak with Ruby before they come.

To get there, I must force myself to make my way back down the corridor toward the room that I know will haunt my nightmares for years to come.

*It's over*, I tell myself. Nate is dead. As is Freddie.

And Ruby is alive... barely.

All I know is that one part of my life is over at last. And maybe, just maybe, we can start to move on.

The hallway seems to become narrower and narrower the closer I get to that door. Flashbacks of being pressed against the wall, Nate bearing down on me, threaten to overwhelm me. I can't believe that was only an hour ago. So much has changed.

Clutching the silver knob, I turn the handle and step into the room.

She is resting on the sofa, clutching her side with Charles's coat, now soaked with blood. Her eyes are closed, but I can hear her breathing coming out in ragged gasps. Ruby, Jacqueline... whoever else she might have pretended to be over the years to get by.

There is a part of me that understands what she did. I know what it's like—to take a chance to start again. But I'm not sure if I can ever fully forgive her for what she did to my sisters.

She took away Jackie's identity. She took her life, and she even took her chance for a peaceful death. I don't entirely believe her story that Jackie overdosed all by herself. Even though she was lost in grief at losing her father, my sister had something to live for—me and our other sister, Louisa.

Louisa's death, however... that, I think, will take time to process. The sister I never knew. A sister who needed help desperately from everyone around her—but Charles, Freddie, and Ruby, pretending to be Jackie, had all failed her. I'm sure it wasn't as simple as Charles ignoring her depression, as Freddie seemed to suggest. Freddie even apologized for his harsh accusations moments before he died. But all the same, from what Charles had confided in me even before tonight, I knew that he was still struggling to process his feelings of guilt around my sister's death. It's something we will have to talk through if Charles and I are to remain close friends after all this. And I suppose we will. I want to get to know little Matilda even better—my *niece*. Perhaps one day we will even tell Matilda and Sofia the truth, that they are cousins. But not today.

I continue to watch this woman in front of me, her curls twining down her cheeks. The hazelnut hair that is so similar to my sister's.

I take one step into the room, and her eyelids flutter open. She looks dreadful, all the color drained from her face. I can't help the flashes of sympathy that race through me. Because I have to admit that when it came down to it, she saved us. She saved Charles, me, and our two little girls.

When it came down to it, she proved that whatever she'd done to become Jacqueline Kelly, she loved Matilda and laid down her life to protect her. I think it's going to take me a long time to process the many contradictions of this complicated woman. I suppose, in a lot of ways, maybe we are the same, deep down? We've both had to do what we needed to survive and to save the ones we love most.

"Ruby," I say, walking toward her, carefully stepping around the pools of red that run across the floor. "It's over. The police and ambulance will be here soon."

She manages a weak nod. "I think I'm dying," she says. A statement. Not a question.

I crouch down and look into her hollow eyes. In them, I can see she is right.

"But I want to tell the police what happened," she says desperately.

My eyes open wide with surprise as she continues, "I don't want Matilda's only parent to go to jail if they don't believe your story. I meant what I said. I love her as any mother would. But you have to swear something to me…" she trails off in a weak voice. Of course, there has to be a catch.

"What?" I say carefully. Of course, there's always something with her.

At that moment, I hear the sirens wail and I know that it's the emergency services arriving at last.

She says in a rasp, "I'm grateful for the life I've had taking your sister's place. But now, please look after my family for me."

"I will," I say. "I promise."

# EPILOGUE

## ANNA - THREE MONTHS LATER

I watch out the window as Matilda and Sofia race through the sprinklers on the lawn outside, laughing in the summer sunshine. It's the middle of the school holidays, and we're experiencing a rare British heatwave. I love the heat; it makes me feel alive.

After the last few months, I need that more than most. So do the children. After that terrible night, the night we're all still recovering from.

The feel of Nate's hot breath against my cheek haunts my nightmares. But when I wake up, I remind myself that I'm safe. We all are. Thanks to Ruby.

It's strange to feel grateful toward the woman who, in some ways, took both my sister's identities. But through tricking Nate that day, she saved my daughter's life, my niece's life, and, of course, my life. It's a lot to process.

Ruby was alive just long enough for the police to arrive and for her to corroborate our story. She died on the way to the hospital.

The police inquest is still ongoing, but Nate's fingerprints were all over the gun, so I'm sure it will work out as it should. Besides, I have one of the best criminal barristers around to help us with our case.

Charles and I have been drawn together. I've spent the last few months helping the children cope with what happened to them. I guess after what we've been through, it's only natural for Charles and I to become closer. We want to make sure the children are supported.

I'm not sure if anything will ever happen between me and Charles. I believe that he never had an affair. I think that was all just gossip. But I'm still working through what Freddie suggested about his neglect of Louisa in the run up to her death. I think Charles still is, too. So, for now, I'm happy with us just being friends and concentrating on looking after our two girls. At the moment, it's more than enough.

I take a sip of refreshing lemonade as I watch my daughter happily play through the window. Her dark hair shimmers in the sunshine. She is the one I've done everything for. She is the one who, whatever lies I have to tell, I will always protect. Because even though we might at last be safe from one of the worst secrets in my past, I know that there is going to be so much more to keep protecting her from. Everything isn't over with Jasper Drummond—he will come for us again. And I know that I can't ever let him get too close.

Because I know what Sofia did.

Like mother, like daughter. And I know her darkest secret.

I know that she killed David.

Perhaps not intentionally—but I found his collection of EpiPens hidden in the floorboard under her bed. Her *secret* hiding place. I knew then that I would do anything, that I would tell as many lies as I needed to in order to protect her secret.

She doesn't know that I know, and I want to keep it that way. She's been through enough in her short life. Besides, I already know why she did it. The same reason she ran right back up the hill toward Nate when she heard me scream—she was trying to protect me.

David hadn't been a nice husband in the end. She'd seen the belittling, the raised voices, the little bruises on my arms. And I know she couldn't ever forget the time he'd locked me in my room for the whole day.

I was planning my own way out anyway. But she wasn't to know that, and she got there first. So, I will keep protecting her to my dying breath.

After all, what's wrong with a little white lie to protect those you love most?

# A Big Thank You

Dear reader,

Thank you so much for choosing to read *The Widow's Lie*.

I really hope you loved discovering all of "Jacqueline" and Anna's secrets, and if you did, I would be so grateful if you could share an honest review online, and with your family and friends. I can't wait to hear what you think, and it makes a such a big difference in helping new readers to discover my book too.

I'd also love for us to stay in touch, so if you'd like to stay up to date with all my newest releases, you can sign up to my mailing list on my website, below. You will also receive an exclusive short story, absolutely free! Your email address will never be shared and you can unsubscribe at any time.

Sign up here: www.melaniepricebooks.com

And don't forget to follow me on social media. I respond to all my messages and would absolutely love to hear from you!

# MELANIE PRICE

facebook.com/melaniepricebooks

instagram.com/melaniepricebooks

twitter.com/melanieRprice

Thank you,

Melanie

# Acknowledgements

I can't believe I'm now publishing my third book within one year! Thank you to every single reader and to all my friends and family for cheering me on to get to this point.

This book has been a bit of a rollercoaster! So, I especially want to thank my darling husband, Seb, for putting up with all my writerly wobbles and patiently supporting me through it all.

A HUGE thanks as ever to my amazing editor, Eve Hall—her insights have helped me hone this book into a twisty page-turner that makes sense! And another big editorial thank you to Gabbie Chant for her brilliant copyediting skills to put the icing on the cake!

Thanks always to Lisa Brewster for her epic cover designs and even more incredible patience with my last-minute requests! Also, thank you to Kelly Lacey for all her help in coordinating my review tour.

I also couldn't have made it to the final publishing hurdle without my "Author Group" support—you know who you are. Thank you for helping me see the woods from the trees!

And, especially, thank you to all my American friends whenever I've asked some slightly random questions for context—I didn't really intend for this book to traverse so much of the US—but often, these things aren't always in a writer's control!

Finally, a mega thank you to my mother, Jessica. You have always been my number one supporter, and taught me and my sisters what it is to love fiercely. I am very lucky to be your daughter.

Thank you again to every single reader for picking up a copy of my book. It means the absolute world.

*Melanie Price, December 2024*

# About the Author

Melanie Price is the author of *The Mother-in-Law's Secret, My Perfect Family,* and *The Widow's Lie.* She grew up in Sydney but now lives in London. She loves crafting complicated characters, exploring the intricacies of family secrets, and creating jaw-dropping stories with twists and turns galore.